Lisa~
    Happy reading☺
        God bless~
            Natalie Replogle

A

Rescued

Heart

Natalie
Replogle

Published by White Feather Press.
(www.whitefeatherpress.com)

ISBN 978-1-61808-073-8

Printed in the United States of America

Cover design created by Ron Bell of AdVision Design Group
(www.advisiondesigngroup.com)

White Feather Press

Reaffirming Faith in God, Family, and Country!

DEDICATION

TO MY CHILDREN,
JARRETT, BRAYDEN AND KYLA

MAY YOU ALWAYS DREAM BIG DREAMS AND PURSUE THEM
WITH ALL YOUR HEART.

Acknowledgements

Thank you to my God and Savior, the founder of love and forgiveness. May this novel serve to glorify You and impact Your Kingdom.

Gregory, thank you so much for all your encouragement and support. I am so blessed to have you as my husband and best friend. Thank you for showing me an incredible love that makes writing romance easy.

Jarrett, Brayden and Kyla, I am so honored and blessed to be your mom. I will never forget the dance party we had in the living room the night I found out my book might get published. Thanks for making my life full of sweet memories.

A huge thank you to, Susan Begay. Without you I wouldn't be here today. Your kindness, generosity, advice, editing skills and encouragement have blessed me beyond measure.

To my parents, in-laws, grandparents, and siblings, thank you for giving me the greatest gift—the example of how a marriage is held sacred and full of adventure, fun, teamwork and commitment.

To the best friends a girl could ever ask for, thank you for your countless hours of reading, listening, praying, sharing my frustrations and excitement, and believing in me. For making our time together the highlight of my week (or month, or season...whenever this thing called motherhood doesn't get in our way) and for keeping me laughing until I can't breathe.

Thank you to Michael Culp for answering my unending police questions and scenarios. If there is any wrong information, the fault is all mine.

Thank you to Darcy Holsopple of Darcy Holsopple Photography for taking my author's picture ... and for your gifted skills in Photoshop.

To my White Feather Press family, Skip and Sara Coryell, thank you for taking a chance on this newbie, believing in my story and your willingness to be a huge part in making my dream come true.

chapter one

The mixture of multiple footsteps that paced outside Ava Williams' dressing room door kept her on high alert. Voices mumbled just quiet enough to keep her from the details, but still she knew. With every beat of her breaking heart and every sinking breath that filled her lungs, the realization crept into her knotted stomach. *He wasn't coming.*

Her sister Lucy sat across from her in silent comfort. Thankfully they spoke no words between them. Ava needed time for her unsettled thoughts. Julia, her best friend since grade school, sat beside Ava with tissues in hand, clearly waiting for her to break down and unleash a flood of tears. Surprisingly this hadn't happened yet, partly because of stubbornness and partly because she desperately hoped she misunderstood the tension that formed outside the door.

How long had she been sitting here in this room, waiting? Minutes or hours, she didn't even know anymore.

Ava scanned the room, assuring herself the walls weren't closing in on her. If she could make a clean escape possible, she'd kick off her three-inch heels and run. But the fear of being seen kept her glued in her chair.

Ava stared down at the flowing white dress that covered her in a massive puff, sighing in disbelief. How could this be happening? He loved her, or so he claimed.

He seemed happy.

Or maybe that's just what she wanted to believe.

As he'd hugged her good-night after the rehearsal, a different look appeared in his eyes. She didn't think much of it, until now. Did he look nervous? Maybe a hint of anxiousness smothered in guilt?

What did he say before he drove away?

"I do love you, Ava. Always remember that." Then he'd kissed her on the forehead.

She placed her hand on her throat as the unknown caused her windpipe to close.

A knock at the door tore her away from the sinking thoughts. Ava glanced up to see her mom walk in perfectly tailored for today's event, from her pink dress and matching nails to her professional hairdo and makeup. She turned and shut the door behind her with a gentle click.

"Ava," her mother proceeded into the room with concern etched across her face. She lowered herself onto the chair beside Ava. Her lips pursed, delaying the inevitable. In almost slow motion, she put an arm around her, her strong-scented rose corsage scraping against Ava's bare skin. The pain in her eyes spoke volumes. Her mom didn't even need to continue.

Ava took a deep breath and fought the impulse to cover her ears and go to a happy place where the news couldn't hurt.

"Tim isn't coming, sweetheart. His family just arrived and informed us that he has cancelled the wedding." She pulled a white envelope from her purse and handed it to Ava. "This is for you."

Ava swallowed, trying to clear the lump that had formed in her throat. The word *AVA* was written in Tim's handwriting on the top of the white envelope. The black ink screamed rejection. Black ... the color that dominated her sight while the room began to spin. She put her head down, covering her eyes with her palm. Sweat drops pooled on her forehead. She swabbed her brow with clammy fingers. "I don't feel well."

Lucy jumped up from her chair. "Ava, it's okay," she said while scrambling to her. "You're going to be fine. Let me get you some water."

They sat her down with her head against the back of the chair and urged her to drink some water. Each sip brought her back to reality.

And reality really stunk.

"Ava, are you all right?" Concern coated her mom's words.

"Yes. Thank you. I feel better, just a little dizzy."

Ava stared down at the letter that held her disappointing fate.

"Would you like some privacy?" Lucy asked.

She made no attempt to leave.

"No, I need you all with me." She held onto the letter so tight that her knuckles turned white. As badly as she wanted—no, *needed*—to know the reason behind his hurtful behavior and decision, she was also terrified to know the truth.

Oh God, she prayed, *Give me the strength to endure these words and the faith to know that You will comfort me in every breath. You are my rock. Help me!*

With a final look at the most important women in her life, her hands still shaky, she opened the envelope and began reading out loud:

> *Ava,*
>
> *First of all, I'm sorry for hurting you and ending our relationship this way. I couldn't trust myself to explain in person for fear I would change my mind once I saw your beautiful face. I know that despite my horrible timing and the gut-wrenching feeling it is to hurt you this way,*

*I am still making the right decision. I can't
marry you, Ava. I do love you, but I can't stand
before God and make you my wife. You are
everything I have ever wanted, but the peace I
need is not there. I do not want to create a life-
long "what if" marriage, so I need to let you
go. I am truly sorry. I pray that you will find
happiness again.*

Good-bye,

Tim

Ava wiped the flood of tears that drenched her face.
Her mom rubbed her other hand while Julia continued
feeding her tissues.

"Why was I not enough for him?" she cried between
hiccups and sobs.

She gasped, struggling to breathe as the pain stabbed
her heart. Ava clawed at her chest trying to remove the
agony. She had no warning, no insight into his thoughts.
Within a day she went from rejoicing in the future laid
out before her to being alone and empty. If she could
have only prepared herself, maybe the blow wouldn't
have hurt so badly.

"What am I going to tell everyone? How can I face all
those people again, knowing they pity me? How could
Tim leave me to handle all of this?" she snapped. "What
a coward!" She covered her face with her hands, allowing the walls to break. Finally, after many rounds of trying to compose herself, a new strength built inside, and
she shed the last tear, for now.

"Ava," her mother waited until she had her attention.
"First of all, you are an amazing woman and you *will*
survive this. Now, your dad and brothers have already

taken care of all the guests, so there is nothing to worry about. You just take care of yourself and tell us what you need us to do."

"Thanks. What I really need is our family. Could you have the guys come in? It would make me feel better to see them," Ava said. She could almost feel their comforting arms.

"Of course, honey." A warm smile lightened her features. "I'm surprised they haven't busted down the door already. You know how protective they are of you."

Her mother stood and walked to the door. Lucy rushed to Ava's side, filling the vacant spot. She wrapped her arm around Ava's shoulder and squeezed. Ava leaned her head against Lucy's shoulder.

In an instant her dad entered the room, wrapping her up into his arms. "Oh Ava, my sweet girl." He pulled her back a bit so he could look her in the eyes. "I would give anything to make your pain my own so you wouldn't have to suffer another moment."

"Thanks, Dad." Not many girls were blessed to have such a strong and affectionate father. He didn't waste many words, but people listened when he spoke. The silver that painted his long ago black hair proved his years of wisdom and Ava appreciated the advice that he gave when asked, not forced.

Her older twin brothers entered with scowls on their faces. Despite her sudden crummy life, she remained very thankful for family. As her dad stepped aside, her brothers sandwiched her into the tightest hug.

"Ava, all you have to do is say the word and we can take care of Tim," Jake snarled. She caught a glimpse of his chest puff up slightly. He was serious.

"I see you're hesitant. We don't actually have to hurt him—maybe just scare him a bit," Josh offered.

Ava almost giggled. Her hesitancy wasn't because she didn't want them to hurt him. She was hesitant because she actually considered it. "Thanks guys, I really appreciate it. But I guess if I'm not worth his time, he shouldn't be worth ours." Her anger surfaced easily.

"Ava, you are priceless. Don't let some guy make you feel otherwise, not even for a second," her dad chimed in behind them. He was always her biggest fan.

His words dripped in kindness and what she needed to hear to fill the hollow ache in her heart, but his words were wasted effort. She could identify the shock setting in. She felt numb and empty regardless of the love that surrounded her. Her self-pity had just won the battle placed before her. She fixed her eyes on the picture hanging on the wall, not seeing it, just giving herself a distraction.

She had no more tears. A stone never sheds tears, and that is what she felt like, a stone. No emotion, no senses—just hard and unmoving.

Her mom spoke first. "Okay men, out you go. We need to get Ava undressed and get her out of here." She waved her hand toward the door to help scoot them along.

The guys filed out as Ava sat down in the chair where she had earlier gotten ready. She looked up at the mirror for one last glance. The dress she had once thought would remind her of the happiest day of her life now turned into weights that she couldn't shed fast enough.

The dress she had dreamed about since meeting Tim ended up a waste. Hopefully she could get a good price for it at the consignment shop downtown.

She twisted her engagement ring around her finger, debating whether to throw it across the room or place it on the table beside her.

She left it on.

Julia stood behind her and they looked at each other through the mirror. They shared no words. None were needed. They had years of speaking to one another through looks and signals.

Without asking, Julia freed her hair from the million bobby pins that the hairdresser thought needed to pierce every square inch of her head. The loose black curls softly bounced down below her shoulders, stopping at the middle of her back.

Ava took a deep breath.

Yes, she would survive, but at what cost? Would she ever let herself love again?

chapter two

<u>2 years later</u>

*T*he hallways buzzed with children's voices and laughter, a sound Ava could never tire of. They had just returned from spring break vacation and even though she missed her kids, the break rejuvenated her. She'd opted not to travel anywhere over break. Instead she chose to stay in her apartment with the sole intent to read books, watch movies and catch up on sleep.

She would claim to others that asked, she enjoyed the downtime and planned to store up her energy for her busy schedule the next couple of months. However a microscope could detect the lack of activities had more to do with her skeptical attitude about life since Tim.

"Miss Williams! Miss Williams!" Ava's name echoed from so many directions she didn't know where to look first. Before she had the chance to see who called, little arms wrapped around her legs. She found her balance and glanced down to see one of her students, Beth, clinging to her while grinning up at her with a huge toothless smile.

"Look what happened over vacation, Miss Williams. I lost my two bottom teeth!" A little spit came out while she talked. Ava could tell she was still getting used to the wind that whistled through her gums.

"Oh my, Beth, I guess you did. Were you scared?"

"No, silly. You haven't seen me for a whole week, so I can see how you could forget that I'm a big girl now."

Ava bent down and chuckled. "You're right. I won't let it happen again."

"Okay, see you in class," the little one turned and skipped down the hallway.

With all the excitement, the children would have a hard time focusing today. To help with the transition, Ava planned something special for them this morning.

Once a month she had someone come in and talk about their profession, explain what it is like to have that job, and give the kids a chance to ask questions. It could be debatable between the kids or her, who had more excitement for these days. Today someone from the police department was coming.

Ava had arrived at school earlier than normal this morning, allowing extra time to head to the office to forewarn the secretary about her class' visitor today. She didn't want her to be nervous when a police officer walked in asking for her. It was a good idea until she tried to make her way back to the classroom. The process moved at a slow pace to the door.

Between listening to students talk about their vacations, dogs, favorite foods – questions abounded. She loved the quirky conversations with her students and stored her favorite ones in the back of her mind, hoping to remember the details to share with someone later. Her favorite random moments began when she asked a question and it was answered with something off the wall like, "Miss Williams, did you know that my brother got sick last night? Some stuff came out of his mouth and nose. It was really gross."

"Okay class," she called after announcements finished, clapping her hands. "Welcome back, everyone. Please find your spot on the rug." The round-up proceeded better than she'd anticipated, with only a couple minor pushes and disagreements about who claimed whose spot.

A kindergarten class could be equivalent to mystery chocolates – the kind where you don't know what the center is filled with until you take a bite.

She hoped for a good chocolate day.

Mid-morning the phone rang on her desk. "Ava, your 'Mr. Tall, Dark and Handsome' is here," the secretary quietly spoke with a hint of amusement. Her words held a muffled tone, as if she had her hand cupped over the receiver.

"Who?"

"Your police officer is here."

"O-Okay, send him down."

Her stomach did a nervous flip all of a sudden. *You are being ridiculous, Ava. Get it together. You do this all the time, nothing to be nervous about.*

By the time she settled herself down, a knock at the door filled the quiet room. She turned around to see the officer standing in the doorway. *Wow, she wasn't kidding.* He reached almost a head taller than her five-feet-five frame, with broad shoulders and muscles that looked chiseled under his close-fitting uniform. He looked like he could have played football in college as a tight end or a very fit linebacker. His dark brown hair, chocolate brown eyes and contagious smile had her forgetting why the man stood at her doorway.

Ava smiled back and headed to the door to greet him, praying that her hands would stop shaking by the time she reached him. She shook his warm hand. "Hi, I'm Ava Williams."

"Sergeant Matthew Thompson. It's nice to meet you." His deep and calming voice soothed her nerves. Her tight shoulder muscles relaxed and her breathing regulated again.

"Thanks for taking the time to come and speak with the

kids. They are very excited to have you here."

"I was happy to come," he replied with a sparkle in his eyes.

They walked toward her desk while he questioned her. "Do you have anything specific that you'd like me to talk about?"

"I usually just have the guest talk about what their job entails and why they like their job. Then I like to give the kids some time to ask questions."

"Sounds great. I'm looking forward it," he said while smiling and showing off his perfectly straight teeth.

"Why don't you stand on the front of the rug over there," she pointed, "and I'll get you a chair while the kids get ready." Having his attention on her softened her stance like butter melting. *Focus Ava, you have to focus.*

⊰⊱⊰⊱

Matt watched her walk away and tried not to stare at the classic beauty. Her hair shimmered like midnight and the green sweater she wore fit her perfectly and made her blue eyes dance. She handled the children with firmness, yet saturated in affection and kindness. They seemed in awe of her, and he could see why. She possessed a special kind of gentleness toward them, and in the simple task of giving directions her words encouraged the kids whenever possible. That simple trait could only be natural, not learned.

He took the moment he had to scan her room and get a feel for what made her tick. The room displayed bright colors and her handwriting emerged neat and precise. She had different learning stations set up that appeared in good condition, but if he got close enough he would probably see the wear and tear of daily use from tiny hands.

It didn't take long for the kids to follow her directions

and sit on the carpet in front of him. He took the chair she offered and sat down while Ava introduced him.

"All right boys and girls, thank you for listening so well. Today we have a very special guest with us. This is Sergeant Matthew Thompson from the Rockford Police Department and he is here to share with us about his job. So, I will need everyone to sit quietly and listen."

She gestured toward the children and walked to her desk.

Ava moved from his direct line of sight which allowed his focus to go where it needed to be. He couldn't deny the draw he had toward her and didn't need the distraction while giving his presentation.

"Hi, I am Sergeant Matthew Thompson, but I would really like it if you called me Matt. I have been a police officer for almost eight years. Being a police officer is a big responsibility. I work to keep you safe. I have a police car that I drive around whenever I am working. I have certain areas that I'm in charge of patrolling. Patrolling means that I drive around making sure people are obeying the rules and staying safe."

While looking around at the children he took note at how well-mannered they were. They sat in silence and no one moved. A good reflection on their teacher, he decided.

"When people drive too fast, I have to pull them over and give them a warning to slow down, but if they were going really fast, I have to give them a ticket. Drivers need to know that they must follow the speed limit. It's there for their safety so they and other drivers don't get hurt.

"When there is an accident, either on the road, at a house, or in the city, I'm called to come and help. If there is a fire, I go and help the firefighters by making sure no one comes close to the danger.

"Sometimes when there is someone doing something naughty, I have to go find them and take them to jail for their punishment. It's kind of like when you disobey your mommy and daddy; you might have to go into timeout for a while." A few of the kids nodded their heads. "Timeout is another way to look at jail. They have to sit there until the judge says they're done.

"Now, I'm sure you have heard this before, but I want you to hear it from me. If there is ever someone hurting you or making you feel uncomfortable, don't be afraid to tell someone, whether it be your parents, Ms. Williams, or you can even tell me. But it's very important for you not to be afraid to say something." It was could-have-heard-a-pin-drop quiet.

"I like my job because I enjoy helping people," Matt continued. "The best thing for you is that you don't have to be a police officer to help someone. Every day you have a chance to be kind to someone. It doesn't matter if it's helping your parents around the house or your teacher at school," he looked over at Ava and smiled, "or just being kind to everyone you meet."

⁂

How well he communicated with the kids impressed Ava. He obviously enjoyed talking to children about his job and easily spoke at their level with uncomplicated words for them to understand. "Well, that's all I have for you today," he announced. "Do you have any questions?"

A dozen hands shot up and his laughter erupted.

"Okay, how about you in the red," he pointed at Nick.

"Can I see your gun?" he asked with eyes wide.

"Well," Matt stood and pointed to the gun in his holster, "I can show it to you this way, but I'm not going to take it out. I always wear it right here." He patted the gun and then sat back down. "How about you?"

"Hi, my name is Kelly. Whenever my mom gets pulled over she always plays with her hair. Do you know why she does that?"

13

"I'm not sure," he answered while suppressing a laugh. He looked over at Ava as she covered her own smile with her hand. "Maybe you should ask your mom."

He kept the questions moving.

"How about you?" He pointed at Mikey.

"Sir, what is your favorite part of your job?"

"I love turning on the lights above my car and driving real fast."

The girls giggled and boys' voices called out, "I want to be a cop."

Once they settled down, he pointed to Alex. Ava slowly closed her eyes, fearful of what words would escape from his mouth. Alex entertained her daily with his loose cannon presence in class and she often wondered what went on in that cute head of his.

"My dad mows our yard. Who mows yours?"

"Oh, well I live in an apartment so I don't have a yard. But if I did, I would mow it."

"How about you?" he asked Carrie who sat holding one arm around her knees with the other slightly in the air, timid.

Carrie looked down shyly and then asked, "Are you married?"

He smiled. "No, but I'd like to be some day."

Ava knew where these questions would continue to go. She stood up quickly, stopping the downward spiral before they embarrassed him. At the same time, she realized she was relieved by his answer. For the past two years, dating became the furthest thing from her mind, so why did she care if he was married or not? She pushed the foreign thoughts aside, not willing to pick at the scab that covered her heart.

"Okay, I'm sure Sergeant Thompson has a busy day, so let's have one last question. How about you, Luke?" His hand flopped around in the air, demanding attention.

"Sergeant Thompson – I mean Matt. Could you stay and

have lunch with us?"

Matt glanced over at her. The question threw her off guard. She smiled and shrugged her shoulders, leaving the decision up to him.

Matt looked back at the kids. "I'd like that. Thank you for asking."

Everyone jumped up excitedly. Ava couldn't hide her unexpected smile that amplified from his decision. She came out from behind her desk and stepped toward the children clapping to catch their attention. "Okay, let's not forget to be polite and thank our guest for coming."

"Thank you!" everyone chimed in unison.

The bell rang for lunch shortly after and the students filed into a line. She decided to join the class and Matt for lunch today. It wouldn't hurt to help the other staff out on cafeteria duty. Being the first day back from break, the kids would still be riding high on adrenaline, which would produce a few glitches in routine.

Today's menu boasted chicken nuggets, fries and peas. *Yay, lots of food that's easy to throw. Here we go.*

Between the handsome guy walking beside her and embracing the job ahead, Ava had the strange urge to bounce up and down on the balls of her feet and punch her fists in the air while humming the *Rocky* theme song.

Entering the cafeteria, she surveyed the battle grounds and headed to the sidelines to get a better view of the entire room. After the students made it through the line she and Matt found a pair of seats amongst the kids. They received a lot of looks, more from the adults than kids, but she chose to ignore them. He asked some questions about the school, but the kids kept asking him more questions – thankfully not too personal – and frequently interrupted them.

Halfway through lunch a little girl started crying because someone had taken one of her nuggets, and shortly after Ava had to talk down two boys trying to see who could make milk come out of their noses first. Overall, lunch time transpired with a lack of tension. She'd had worse.

The kids went to recess after lunch. Ava took her few minutes of freedom and walked with Matt back to the main entrance. They took the time they had away from the earshot of the students to finally laugh together about some of their questions. To tell someone about these moments never measured up to experiencing it with someone.

It felt nice.

She extended her hand to him, "Thanks again for coming. You did a great job and I appreciate you taking the time to help me out."

"You're welcome. It seems like you never have a dull moment."

She shook her head back and forth. "Nope, never."

He started toward the door but stopped short. It looked like he wanted to ask a question, but nothing came out of his mouth except, "It was nice meeting you, Ava."

"You too, Matt."

They waved goodbye and went their separate ways. *Maybe dating isn't such an appalling thought after all. Scary, but not appalling. Too bad I'm never going to see him again.* Ava stopped, her legs paralyzed by the shocking thoughts that trickled in. His presence and smile had just become more than she could handle right now.

She walked away relieved for the distance.

In attempts to stay ahead of schedule before the final bell rang, Ava helped the kids with their jacket zippers and saw to it that all the backpacks were off the hooks and onto little backs. She noticed Alex off by himself and realized that he'd been unusually quiet all day.

The boy held an adorable look that constantly had her

fighting the impulse to pinch his cheeks. He had spiky blond hair, a chubby face, and glasses. He reminded her of the little boy from the movie, *Jerry Maguire*. He stood at the back table making sure he had all his *Cars* pencils in order. She took a moment to talk with him one on one.

"Hey, Alex, do you have all your pencils?"

"Yep, I just counted all five." He pushed his glasses up with his pointer finger and smiled. "Now I am making sure they are all safe in my pencil box."

"That is a very good idea," she agreed. "How was your spring break?"

"Well," he started slowly, "it was really sad because my grandma went to a better place." His frown and elongated sigh displayed how upset he was over the situation.

"Oh no, I am so sorry." She put her arm around him. "When did she pass away?"

Concern for him and frustration at herself filled her. She had not heard and would have talked to him about it earlier had she known.

He looked confused. "What?" Then he grinned. "Oh no, she just moved to Ohio," he said while making a fist with his thumb out and thrusting it over his shoulder, demonstrating that Grandma had hit the road, moved away.

It took everything in her not to laugh out loud. "Oh, well, Ohio is very nice."

He gave her a hug and then ran up to the front of the room to find his spot in line.

On the way back from sending kids home, she decided to stop at her friend Kate's room to catch up. They had both started working at the school the same year and their friendship had blossomed instantly. As she approached Kate's room she couldn't help but giggle at the horrible sound escaping from the room. She stuck her head in the open door to find Kate erasing her board and singing some lovey-dovey song from the eighties. Kate held no distress over the fact her life would start a new season by getting married this weekend. It was cute, a little sickening and off tune, but cute. Ava shook her head and then sang the echo part to let her counterpart know she had company.

Kate laughed before she turned around, "You caught me," she swooned.

"I still can't believe you're getting married this weekend. It feels like just yesterday that Kyle proposed to you," Ava said as she stepped inside and sat on the edge of Kate's desk. "Did you get everything worked out with Principal Hunt about all of your time off?"

"Yes, he has been great. He's even letting me take Friday off to decorate the church and prepare for the rehearsal."

Kate was busting at the seams with delight. Ava had a twinge of jealousy—or was it nausea—for just a split second and then pushed it out of her thoughts.

Kate must have seen something in her face because she kindly brought it to the surface. "I'm sorry if this is hard to talk about. I haven't seen or talked to you in a week. I'm sure there is something else we can discuss."

Ava regretted her selfishness on mentally turning their conversation back on her. "Kate, I love talking about your happiness. I am so glad that you and Kyle found each other. Your wedding is going to be wonderful and I'm looking forward to being a part of your special day," she replied with sincerity.

Kate's smile confirmed her contentment with the answer. "Thank you. So since you are okay, do you want to hear about where we're staying on our honeymoon?"

"Absolutely."

chapter three

After finishing up a few more things at her desk, Ava headed out to her car, a red Honda Accord, clearly dated by the rust that covered the bumper. Nothing fancy, it got her to where she needed to go and that's all that mattered. Ava stayed simple when it came to vehicles. She wanted to look around for something different, but her finances just didn't allow it at this time. Her brothers constantly nagged her to buy something newer and cooler, but so far she'd held firm and ignored their digs.

As she reached her car something caught her eye in the corner of the building. It looked to be one of her students, Tessa Davis. She threw her books into the car, shut the door with a loud slam and jogged over to the small child. Tessa was one of her students that walked home after school and she recalled watching her head home earlier that day.

Tessa was a shy and introverted child. Ava continually questioned her home life. The girl's father left a while ago, but her mother always seemed nice and invested in her daughter's life. During the last few weeks, though, something just didn't seem right.

"Hi Tessa, why are you not at home? Is everything ok?"

"Well, I did go home, but my mom wasn't there and I didn't know what to do."

Concern jumped first into Ava's mind, since this had happened before.

"Ok, let's go see where your mom is together. I'm sure she is very worried about you." Ava directed Tessa into the office to call her home. Ava smiled when Tessa reached for her hand while they walked. These little moments made the long exhausting days a little brighter. Ava asked her a few questions to brighten the mood and had Tessa giggling by the time they reached the office.

Tessa's mother answered, quite upset about the situation and apologized for the mix up. Ava sent the little one home, frustrated that her hands were tied. She decided to mentally keep an eye on Tessa and observe her more carefully, maybe even prod her into answering a few questions that swirled around in her mind.

Ava drove to the store to pick up some groceries needed to make dinner, trying to fight the distraction of Tessa in her mind. Jules would be at her apartment soon for their weekly meal together. Between the two of them, Jules was the better cook, which wasn't saying much. At least her critic didn't have a high scale to judge from. Grilled chicken salads…she couldn't screw that up too badly.

Hectic traffic and a packed grocery store put Ava behind schedule. By the time she got home the clock showed six. She threw the chicken on the George Foreman grill and ran back to her room to change clothes. Sweatpants, a comfy shirt and slippers – her girl's night wardrobe.

As she opened the bag of salad Jules knocked and stuck her head in. "Hi. Sorry I'm late, traffic was horrible."

"I know. I just got in myself. My downfall started when I got caught up talking with Kate after school."

"Is this the weekend she's getting married?" Jules asked as she plopped down at the kitchen table, resting her head on the back of the chair. Her autumn colored hair spilled down onto her shoulders.

"Yep, it's Saturday night."

"You're still planning on going, right?"

Ava rolled her eyes when she recognized the hope in her friend's voice. "Yes. I know my record of attending weddings hasn't been very good the past couple years, but I'm looking forward to this one."

"Good. I'm glad. So... are you planning on taking some-one?"

"Ha ha, very funny, Jules."

"You'd have a great time."

"No."

"I know this guy."

"Quit."

Julia's grin started wide and ended mischievous. She obvi-ously enjoyed herself, a little too much for Ava's patience.

"You're not going to let this go, are you?"

"Come on, Ava," she pouted, "just hear me out."

If Ava didn't have twenty years of history with Julia, she might have been a little annoyed at the badgering. They'd met in early grade school and had been best friends ever since. They'd grown up on the same street, riding bikes to-gether and having sleepovers. Besides family, there wasn't anyone else she trusted more. Julia brought up the matter of her dating again only because of concern for Ava's happiness, but even after two years, the subject stayed one that Ava did not like to discuss. Being left at the altar continued to not only be embarrassing, but deeply scaring.

Dating for her was off the table at this point. It joined the same category as skydiving and bungee jumping...it terrified her.

The thought of Matt popped into her mind, and she became frustrated with herself because this wasn't the first time today the handsome officer had invaded her thoughts.

Ava quickly dismissed the idea of bringing him up to Julia. She didn't want the drama that would ensue.

Ava waited, debating if she could handle this conversation Julia pushed. "Fine," she conceded as she grabbed the plates and joined Jules at the table. "You've got five minutes."

"Really? You're starting to break a bit, Ava. I can feel it."

"Four and a half, you better get to it, time's a ticking." Ava tapped an imaginary watch on her wrist.

"Okay, okay, so much pressure." Julia took a deep breath. "I'm not saying that you need to go out and start a serious relationship. I understand that commitment is still not an option for you. But what's wrong with just going out on a friendly date?"

"It seems pointless. Dating should be the first step in seeing if that someone is marriage material, and I have no desire to look for a husband."

Pleased with her rebuttal, Ava smirked, certain her statement would silence her long-time friend. She wanted to lick her finger and make an imaginary mark in the air. *Round one to Ava.*

She licked too soon.

"I see your point, and it's a good one, but it's not going to change me bugging you until you cave." Jules smiled, determined to win this conversation for once.

"I still don't see what good it would do."

"Listen, your heart was crushed. I've been with you every step of the way and know how devastated you were. I stayed with you all those nights when you cried yourself to sleep. But, Ava it's time. Even if it's only a few dates, just to get your feet wet again. You have to trust God to guard your heart. It doesn't have to be anything serious, just go out and enjoy yourself."

It had been two years and still a part of her remained dead. Burying her emotions created a safe environment, why dig herself out of that shelter now. Ava twirled her fork around in her food, stalling. "I'm scared, Jules," she finally admitted.

"I know, but you're never going to know unless you try."

"Okay, tell you what. I'll think about it." Julia lifted an eyebrow and gave a look of determining if Ava was serious or just trying to get her off her back.

She was both.

"Seriously, I will think about it."

"Good. Thank you."

"You're welcome. Discussion closed."

Ava laid in bed that night wrestling with the promise she'd made to her best friend. Jules' reasons held merit. She needed to at least start thinking about dating again. She rolled over and sighed, letting the tension release out into the empty room.

There, I thought about it, that's good enough for now.

chapter four

The week flew by and before Ava had time to get nervous, Saturday had arrived. This afternoon Kate and Kyle were getting married. She settled on the couch to call her mom before she needed to get ready. Her mom answered on the second ring and their conversation jumped immediately to her week and how the kids did with transitioning after break.

When she brought up professional day her mom's interest was piqued. "Who did you have this month?"

"I had a police officer from the Rockford Police Department." *He was gorgeous, great with the kids and that smile...* Ava stiffened as the thoughts trickled in, hoping her mom would not further question about the police officer. Even over the phone, it would be difficult for Ava to hide all that she was thinking.

Ava's muscles relaxed as her mom let her move on from that subject and replay the rest of the week. Her mom made conversations easy, and it helped to tell someone about the ups and downs in her life. She had her mom laughing for a solid ten minutes about all the silly things her students had said. The quiet apartment, dinners for one and lonely nights in front of the television had become mundane. Talking with her mom lifted her spirits.

So, do you have plans tonight?" her mom asked, without masking her hopeful tone.

"Actually I do. My friend Kate from school is getting married later this afternoon."

"That's right." Ava knew she had remembered. "Do you think you will go and stay this time?"

"Yes." She didn't even try to hide her irritation.

"I'm sorry, Ava. I just know you haven't had the best track record with attending weddings since yours."

Ava sighed in frustration. *Why can't everyone just leave this situation alone?* She shivered, letting herself remember why she had problems going to other weddings. The weddings her mom referred to were the three she had been invited to in the past two years.

The first had been from the daughter of another teacher at school a couple months after hers. She'd replied "no" right away and had wanted to write underneath, *"Are you kidding me?"*

The second was a friend she'd gone to high school with. Jules had to work that day which forced her to go by herself. She made it to the parking lot and then just sat in her car crying until she could settle down enough to drive home.

The third was eight months ago when her cousin got married. She made it inside the church and managed to sit through the entire ceremony but chose not to stay for the reception. Was she the only one who saw the progress being made here? She felt good about today, determined to stay and enjoy herself.

She tuned her mom back in while she gave her speech about how she was such a great catch and that someday the man the Lord made for her would walk into her life. Ava mouthed the words along with her. When she finally finished, Ava put in her two cents' worth.

"Thanks mom, I appreciate that you care so much," and

she meant it. "I should probably get going. I need to start getting ready."

After their goodbyes she clicked the phone off and leaned her head back against the couch. It wasn't entirely the weddings themselves that caused the setbacks. They were more or less her trigger point. The problems started with the memories that resurfaced when the wedding invitations arrived. She felt the flashbacks coming now but did nothing to stop them.

Already in her mind she transported the memories back two years.

The week after *the* wedding was brutal. Ava stayed at her parent's house for a few days, mostly locked in her old room, crying until she ran out of tears. Her family gave her space. She needed time to mourn. School let out for the summer, mercifully she didn't have to face her co-workers right away or try to be upbeat for the kids while she was dying inside.

The one positive came with her opportunity to keep her apartment. The lease ended, but thankfully no one had replied to the ad, so it remained hers. It was nice to have something familiar, something that belonged to her.

She hadn't heard from Tim at all after his no show, but a few weeks into the school year he blind-sided her with an unexpected visit.

It could have happened yesterday by how fresh the memories stayed embedded in her mind.

It was Saturday morning and she had just finished the grueling process of cleaning her apartment when there was a knock at the door. She opened the door to find Tim standing there, head down and hands in his pockets. She wanted to throw up.

"Tim. What are you doing here?"

"Hi Ava, I um...I was hoping I could come in and talk with you." He cleared his throat, never looking her in the eye.

His discomfort characteristics hadn't changed.

"A little late for that, don't you think?" She practically spit the words out.

He looked down at his shoes and she had the strongest urge to slam the door in his face. She forced herself to keep it open for curiosity's sake, despite how his presence initiated her blood pressure to spike. She needed closure.

"Fine, come in."

Ava turned and walked to the kitchen, leaving him to close the door himself. "I'm getting a cold soda, do you want one?" *What? Why am I asking the enemy if he wants a beverage?*

"No, thank you."

It was for his own good. She had already come up with a plan to shake the can before handing it to him.

She grabbed her drink out of the refrigerator, the tab cracking open echoed in the quiet living room while she strolled in, flopping down on the smaller couch. She needed the caffeine.

Ava smoothed back her hair and straightened her sweatshirt, annoyed at her self-consciousness about her appearance. She had spent the day at home which made her lounging attire consist of comfy clothes, no make-up, hair pulled back in a ponytail. Having rehearsed this reunion over and over in her mind, this was not what she'd pictured. She wanted to look stunning and make him drool over what he'd thrown away. She'd imaged herself in the hot pink strapless dress she'd bought for their honeymoon and her hair full of curls and pulled back his favorite way, capped off with diamond earrings and necklace.

This was *not* that look.

He followed her cue and sat across from her on the other couch. She glared at him while waiting for him to begin.

"Ava, I know there is nothing I can say today to make up for all the pain I have caused you. I'm so sorry that I didn't contact you sooner. I was nervous and not sure what to say. It was selfish and inconsiderate."

"Well, at least you're consistent."

He cringed, "I guess I deserve that."

"You guess? Do you have any idea how hurtful your actions were to me? How embarrassing it was sitting in that room waiting for you? No warning! Nothing but a stupid letter." Her words dripped with a bitterness that she'd evidently not dealt with.

"You're right, I deserve much worse than your words."

"Well, that can be arranged." She used the tip of her pinkie finger to dab the outside of her eyes to stave off tears. Determination to not let him see her cry surged.

"You're here for a reason, so what is it? Are you finally going to explain why you left me, because if not, there's the door!" she snapped while jerking her head toward the exit.

Tim had a reason that resonated deeper than his mere words written in that heartless letter. She needed him to be honest now and put her out of this misery.

"I am here to explain." He took a deep breath and looked down at his hands. She wanted to yell, *Look at me, coward,* but she held her tongue.

"When I proposed to you it was the happiest day of my life. We had so much in common and I was confident that we would have an incredible life together. The fall was hard, being away from you, but I treasured our time together on the weekends. But the more time we spent apart, the more I became unsure."

When they had graduated college she had found her job quickly, but he searched all summer and finally had to accept a job over an hour away. Difficulty surrounded the long distance, but they both committed to making the weekend trips and phone calls work until they could get married and find a place to live that split the distance. She remembered that time period and how much she'd missed him.

The plan proceeded well until the winter when she began noticing a slight change in him. One day he seemed fine and the next, distant. When they were together he was warm and endearing, but when they were apart he'd often sounded reserved and impersonal during their phone conversations. No matter how often she tried to dig deeper into why he detached himself, he kept silent and would either change the subject or assure her that everything was okay between them.

"The thing is," he started rubbing his forehead, "I began hanging out with another teacher at school named Cara." He quickly added, "Nothing happened, we were just friends, but I became confused as to why I enjoyed her attention and the time we spent together."

And there it was.

She tried to regulate her breathing and bit her lip to keep the angry thoughts to herself. He began rubbing the back of his neck even more vigorously. If he didn't get out what he'd come to say, he leave with no skin left.

"As the wedding approached, I just assumed it was cold feet, but I kept having this uneasy feeling. I knew I loved you, enjoyed being with you, but I felt like we needed more than just getting along and having a lot in common. Plus, I was starting to have stronger feelings for Cara which were complicating the situation."

She kept silent, so he continued.

"The week of the wedding I was sick with guilt and desperate to feel at peace about marrying you, but it wouldn't come. I knew after the rehearsal I needed to end things. I should have told you then, but couldn't. I wrote the letter in the morning and left it where I knew someone would find it."

He looked up and she couldn't hide the tears spilling off her cheeks. It hurt, but she finally had the truth.

"I am so sorry, Ava," he continued. "I know I handled everything wrong and I should have been honest with you from the beginning. I know I made the right choice, but I messed up by not telling you all of this at the time."

He started to choke up while speaking and the ice encasing her heart melted a little.

"Tim, I would never want to marry someone who wasn't sure if I was the one. If you say the Lord said 'no', how can I disagree? It hurts deeply, but I will get over you...you seem to be doing fine."

The observation hurt.

"It wasn't easy getting over you, Ava. You will always have a place in my heart, but I couldn't dwell on something that wasn't God's desire for me."

Where is he going with this? Could he already be over me?

"There is something else I need to tell you." He started rubbing his chin, delaying the inevitable.

"Just say it, Tim."

"Well, I just wanted you to hear it from me instead of through the grapevine. I thought you deserved that." His hesitation made her sick to her stomach. "I've been dating Cara." He waited a bit to let the salt settle in her wound. "We're getting pretty serious, talking about marriage. I thought you should know."

This last confession knocked the wind out of her. She had no desire to ever get back together with him, but she thought she meant more to him than that. It hadn't been more than three months since he left her and now he was dating someone already – someone he had spent time with while he and Ava were still a couple – someone he planned to marry. She felt betrayed and worthless. Could she ever trust anyone to love her again?

Despite the many emotions swirling around in her heart, her mind went blank. She felt out of words, not sure if she could even speak. She wished her brothers would arrive to eliminate the problem and protect her. Tim would have been lucky to make it out the door without a black eye or broken nose.

"I, um, didn't expect this. Not that you've done anything in the last three months that hasn't been a surprise to me."

"I know I'm a jerk. I just felt like you needed to know."

"Sure."

"I messed up so bad in the past, I wanted to be up front and honest with you now."

He hit a nerve. "Was this really for me or just a way to cleanse your guilty conscience?" She wanted to throw something at him.

"For you, Ava, honestly it was for you."

She didn't believe him and yet felt a little bad about what she'd said, just not bad enough to apologize. She couldn't let the anger and bitterness win, but it did feel good for the time being. She *never* wanted to talk to him again and for that to happen she needed to end this conversation well. She didn't want to live with remorse and then somewhere down the road have to call and apologize.

"Okay, is that all or do you have any more bombshells to throw at me today?"

"No, that's all."

"Then thank you for coming and telling me the truth. I might not have wanted to hear a lot of your confessions, but it's the closure I needed."

She stood and walked to the door. He followed behind as his footsteps dragged across the floor.

"Ava, there is just one more thing." He looked distraught. "Do you think you will ever be able to forgive me?"

The voice in her soul spoke, *forgive as I forgave you.*

She hesitated, struggling to find the words.

"Yes, Tim, I do forgive you. If I don't forgive you, it will do more damage to me than you. I don't want to spend the rest of my life feeling bitterness toward you."

"You are going to find happiness again, Ava. God has a great plan for your life. And thank you for forgiving me. You are a better person than I will ever be." She wanted to agree out loud, but moved to usher him out of her life one final time. She needed to be alone.

That day had hurt her pride and self-confidence, and it took Ava about a week to snap out of her self-pity before she began the slow, agonizing process of moving on. Through time the feelings of love she'd had for Tim diminished, along with the ill feelings toward him. Freedom did follow forgiveness.

The problem that she struggled with, that hung around her neck like a noose, was being terrified of falling in love again. How would she know if her next love truly meant what he said, or what if she was wrong again about whom she thought the Lord made for her? Heading down that road again overwhelmed her enough that she decided not to let her heart even go there.

She willed herself back to the present, grateful that the flashbacks were no longer as painful as they'd once been.

Ava headed to the bathroom to get ready for the wedding. The weatherman had been correct on the beauty of the day. The sun shined with a warm temperature, uncommon for April in northern Illinois. She chose a black strapless dress that fitted tightly and came down to the top of her knees. She put on black stilettos and her makeup on a bit darker than usual. It was fun to dress up. She decided not to put on a necklace. *Less is more* was her motto. She didn't want to look cluttered, just elegant.

She grabbed her shawl, purse and the wedding present and walked out the door, ready to try this wedding business again.

chapter five

Traffic in the city was insanely busy but sported less crazy drivers than usual. Ava only feared for her life once. The city of Rockford was split down the middle by the Rock River, with a west side and an east side. The main downtown area was dotted with businesses, government buildings and restaurants. As the city trickled out, it became more populated with houses than businesses. If you kept going you would eventually run into miles and miles of farmland.

Ava's apartment sat on the east side near downtown. Her school was also on the east side, but out of the city, smooshed among neighborhoods. Rockford didn't have a history as an exciting city or drenched in historic events, but it was home. She enjoyed the river and all the events and activities that took place around it.

At the end of each summer Rockford hosted a music festival called "On the Waterfront". It drew in many tourists and music fans. Ava usually stayed at her parent's house that weekend to avoid the enormous crowd. Sometimes she and her friends would go to the festival and listen to the bands play and walk the streets that were blocked off for the big event. The city took pride in making it an annual success.

Ava arrived at the church right before the ceremony started. Once the wedding party made its way down the aisle, the doors closed after them and the music changed to the wedding march. The doors reopened and there stood Kate. Ava looked over at Kyle. He beamed. Her heart sank. She couldn't help but wonder what it would feel like to walk through those doors and see the love of her life look that excited to see her, to want to make her his wife. She pushed the tears back. This day wasn't about her.

Once pronounced husband and wife, everyone clapped as they headed down the aisle arm in arm. The pastor announced that the couple would greet everyone at the reception and to stay seated until the ushers dismissed them.

Ava walked out to her car, relieved. She had done it. She'd made it through the ceremony without any panic attacks and even looked forward to the reception.

The reception building overlooked the river. The open room had circular tables everywhere. The tables were covered in a purple cloth and seated eight guests each. The front of the room displayed a long table for the wedding party, a dance floor in front, with the DJ off to the side. Along the back of the room, a wall full of windows exposed the river below.

The seating chart assigned Ava to Table 10. She found her name tag and smiled across the table at a couple she didn't know. She sat for a short time observing more of the room and the guests that entered until she grew curious about whom her fellow tablemates would be. The name to her left was a colleague from school. She gasped out loud when she read the name at her right: *Matthew Thompson*.

⚜⚜

*M*att came to a halt in front of Table 10. Someone ran into him from behind because of his sudden stop. He quickly apologized, but still didn't move forward. He enjoyed watching her from a distance. Matt could only see her from the side, but that was the face he'd been unable to get out of his mind all week. Not believing the opportunity that had just fallen into his lap— he approached hopeful.

"Ava."

"Matt."

They both laughed while she pointed to his seat. "This is such a good surprise." He took his seat beside her. "Do you know Kyle or Kate?"

"Kate and I work together. How about you?"

"Kyle. We grew up together at the same church. We attend different churches now, but we still keep in touch."

"So where do you attend church now?"

As he told her about his church, he couldn't believe how quickly this topic came up. It would be the deal breaker as to whether or not he pursued her. He took his faith very serious and this was something he would not waver on, despite his attraction toward her.

When he was younger faith did not rank as high a priority for him. He had a handful of serious relationships, but only a few were worthy to bring home to meet his family. Sadly, he could only think of one that he knew for sure had a relationship with the Lord. He wished he could go back in time and change that part of his past. Now that he was older and pushing thirty, it became a necessity for any potential relationship.

"Are you a believer?" He held his breath.

"Yes. I've attended Crossroads Christian Church since birth. It's much smaller than yours, only a few hundred people. But it's a good church that preaches the truth. Plus, I enjoy the fellowship and it's nice because my entire family still goes there."

He finally released his breath in relief. She was a believer. That was now her best quality out of the handful he already knew about her. He had been wrestling all week about wanting to track her down and ask her out. Being a cop, he had resources at his disposal. Getting back into the school in order to run into her would not have been a problem.

The music started and their attention moved to the front. He looked around. *When did everyone get here*? Ava saw one of her co-workers sitting at the table beside her and turned to speak with her while the DJ started introducing the wedding party.

When the clapping ceased, the food came out and Matt turned back to Ava, itching to talk with her again. "I didn't have a chance to tell you this the other day, but I think you are a great teacher. Your students adore you and you seem to really enjoy it." He took a mouthful of food.

"Thanks. I've always wanted to be a teacher." No hesitation stalled her words or need for her to think about it. "I love giving being their cheerleader, giving them confidence in themselves and making them feel special."

"Well, they are very lucky to have a teacher who cares as much as you do."

Her cheeks blushed a light pink. She laid her fork down and dabbed her mouth with her napkin. He hadn't seen any food on her lips and he would know, since he'd been staring at them. She must be just covering up her embarrassment.

"This is such an important time in their lives and I want my class to be a positive impact on them. Sad but true, most kids see more of me than their parents. This is my opportunity to not only teach them, but also to make them feel loved and accepted."

He sat mesmerized by the way she used her hands when she spoke and her facial expressions that told a story of their own. She had a rare passion. He hoped he could spend more time with her to get a better insight into what made her this incredible.

"It's hard to know some kids have a rough home life because in most situations I can't do anything about it. Unless I can prove abuse or neglect, my hands are tied. That's why my time with them is so precious."

She'd struck a chord inside him, a frustration of his own. Being a cop was his passion, but having to walk into situations where children had become the victims, made the weight of this job heavy.

"I can understand that. There were a few times I've had to go in with a social worker to take a child out of an abusive home. It made me sick."

They continued to share their stories until the time came for the garter and bouquet toss. They took turns getting up for the event. Matt couldn't help but notice that Ava hid behind all the other girls.

ᚦᠻᠻᚦᠻᠻ

*A*va took cover behind the squealing girls eager to grab the bouquet. She chuckled at how ironic everything had turned out. She planned on giving Kate grief for trying to set her up with Matt, but it seemed to be pure coincidence and couldn't believe that their paths had crossed again. Ava secretly glanced back at the table, catching a quick look at Matt while a reserved smile formed across her face.

She returned to her seat – thankfully empty-handed. They hadn't sat long when the happy couple reached their table. Ava rose up to Kate and gave her a big hug.

"You look beautiful, Kate."

"Thank you. I'm so glad you're here." Kate looked over at Matt talking with Kyle. "I see you and Matt are hitting it off."

Ava almost expected her to tap her fingers together in a sinister way. "Actually, we met the other day. He was the police officer who came for my professional day." Kate's mouth dropped open in shock while Ava laughed.

"I can't believe it," she said, shaking her head. "All that work to put you next to one another and here you'd already met." Their laughter attracted the attention of the men.

"What was that about?" Matt asked when they sat back down.

"Oh it was nothing. So now it's your turn to talk about your job. Have you always wanted to be a cop?"

He dismissed her weak answer and responded to the change of subject. He told her that his dad had been a cop for over thirty-five years before he retired. He shared how his dad lived his life as a man of strength and dignity, and ever since he was a little boy he wanted to be just like him. He had great respect for his dad and the job he did as a cop, and then as chief of police, before he retired.

"So, I know your favorite part is the lights and going fast," Ava teased, "but is there a certain part of your job you enjoy the most?"

"Well, I didn't talk about this at your school, but I'm not just a police officer. I'm also on the SWAT team."

Just when she thought she was figuring him out, he peeled back another layer of who he was. "Really...wow...that seems like an intense job." *Duh,* she wanted to smack her forehead, *good job, Captain Obvious.*

The clanging of forks against the glasses in declaration that the newlywed couple needed to kiss briefly interrupted their conversation. It did Ava's heart good to see Kate so happy. It had been almost three years since she had seen a successful wedding. Ava quickly brushed away the thoughts before they leached themselves onto her. She turned her attention back on Matt with a follow-up question.

"Why did you choose to join the team?"

"I like the challenge and even though it's intense, I like

the chance to use my skills to help save and protect those in a horrible situation."

"Does the SWAT team get called out very often?"

"We usually get called out a few times a month. Some have been bomb scares, a few husbands out of control, public suicide attempts, and hostage situations. We also tag along when high profile warrants need to be served and help the narcotics unit with drug enforcements."

Before she could respond, the DJ announced that the bride and groom would dance their first dance and that during the next song the floor was open to everyone. Ava watched as Kyle and Kate floated around the dance floor. Kate had talked Kyle into taking dance lessons. He was a good man.

With the lights turned down, Ava took time to compose herself. She needed to pull back from Matt before it allowed her emotions to get more attached. She enjoyed getting to know him, but it sparked the fear she tried hard to bury.

The next song started playing and Matt turned to her. "Ava, would you like to dance?" he asked, extending his arm out like a gentleman.

Her stomach did a flip, followed by dropping like a ball of lead. On top of the idea of being so close to this man, she was a pathetic dancer. He had been invading her comfort zone all night, emotionally and now physically. Yet she found herself throwing all caution to the wind, and took hold of his arm.

So much for Plan A. "Sure, but I should warn you, I'm not very coordinated. You're likely to get stepped on."

"I'll take my chances."

⊱⊰⊱⊰

*M*att took her hand, noting her hesitancy. He couldn't tell if her resistance sprouted because of him or something deeper. He brought her around to face him and placed his hand on the small of her back while she put her hand on his shoulder. He took her hand in his placing them on his chest, hoping she couldn't feel his heart beating faster because of her closeness.

Her soft fingers trembled enclosed in his. He breathed in her fruity scent and slowly turned them around, enjoying the comfortable silence until her foot stepped on the front of his shoe.

She made a face.

"Sorry. I guess I was getting a little overconfident about my *smooth* dancing."

"Hey, I was warned, I brought this pain on myself," he teased and spun her around with speed. She held on tight and laughed. He'd been waiting for this moment all night. "You look incredible."

Her eyes widen in surprise. He'd caught her off guard, but wasn't sorry. All night she had been a swinging pendulum. One minute she would let him in and the next she would distance herself, almost retreating. Ava came across as a hard woman to figure out, but he welcomed the challenge.

"Oh...um...thanks. You look great yourself."

He wore a black suit with a deep red shirt and black tie, his normal wedding attire. Matt had noticed the looks from some of the other women but only cared what Ava thought. He had been pumping himself up all night, and now the time had come to take the plunge and ask her out. Now was as good a time as any.

"I'm really glad that we ran into each other again. I actually have a little confession to make."

"What's that?"

"I had plans to stop at your school next week to ask you out."

Ava took a deep breath and held it. She kept eye contact

but stayed silent. He couldn't read her face, but if he had to guess it looked like torment or panic. She had never mentioned a boyfriend and had not brought a guest with her to the wedding. He debated between changing the subject and finding something to say to make her laugh. He drew a blank on both, so he chose instead to give her an easy out.

"No pressure, Ava. If you're not interested, don't feel bad about hurting my feelings." She closed her eyes and his heart sank. He prepared himself for rejection.

"Matt, you are so sweet and my hesitancy is not what you think."

She took another deep breath and exhaled this time. "I had a relationship end horrible about two years ago and I carry a lot of baggage from it. Starting to date again is very scary for me and so even though I'm interested in spending more time with you, I'm just not sure if it's a good idea. I'm not emotionally ready right now to handle a relationship."

Her up front honesty refreshed his perspective. She was interested. He could work with this. Two years was a long time. Whatever had happened must have been awful for her. He stayed quiet for a moment longer, realizing the impact his next words would need to make.

"Okay, I'll make you a deal. Give me three dates. Nothing serious, just getting to know each other and having fun. If after those dates you still feel the same and would like to just be friends, I will completely understand."

"Are you sure you want to tackle all this crazy?" She lifted her eyebrows.

"Just give me a chance, Ava."

She took a long look at him and he realized he was being studied, weighed. He hoped he measured up.

"Okay, it's a deal. Three dates."

"You have chosen wisely."

The music turned upbeat and they decided to stop dancing and get some cake and punch. While Matt was talking baseball with Kyle's brother, he caught a glimpse of Ava standing in the back of the room alone. She peered out the wall of windows that overlooked the river. She didn't appear sad, just lost in thought. He had just stirred the pot with her emotions and hoped she wouldn't change her mind about going out with him. He breathed a little deeper when he spotted Kate approach Ava and watched the smile that reached her eyes return.

They met back later at the table. Ava seemed in high spirits and his confidence was restored. He needed to seal the deal. "How about next Saturday night? Are you free for date number one?" He didn't even try to hide his determination.

"Well, I will say you are nothing short of persistent."

"That's right. It's one of the many adorable qualities you will learn about me over the next few weeks."

"Adorable, huh? You seem confident."

"Because I am."

"Well, I guess I'll just have to be the judge of that."

"Judge away."

"I won't be easy."

"You won't be disappointed."

Her laughter caused her shoulders to shake. He enjoyed their friendly banter, joking around with her came easy. She had a good sense of humor and a quick wit.

"Yes, I'm free on Saturday. What do you want to do?"

"Ah, that is a surprise. I'll pick you up at six."

chapter six

<u>Date #1</u>

Matt held the door open for Ava as they made their way outside from her apartment complex. He straightened his jacket hoping to shake off the nerves. He had been on many dates before, but these upcoming dates were imperative. To be honest, he hoped that they would be life-changing.

When Ava spotted his Jeep Wrangler she gave a low, long whistle. "Nice ride."

"Thanks, it's my baby."

"You've got good taste."

He turned to her, letting his eyes trace her soft skin and plump lips that spread out from her smile. Her kindness and strong character illuminated as a beacon of light, drawing him in. Yes, he'd have to agree. He did have good taste.

Matt blinked when she caught him staring. "Um, yeah, my excuse is that it's great for the winter weather." It was a little much for city driving, but it was great in the snow and he had always wanted one. He opened her door and quickly ran around and jumped in. He started up the Jeep, letting it idle, enjoying the purr his engine produced. They headed north into town.

"What, no blindfold to add to the secrecy?" she teased.

"It did cross my mind, but I didn't want people to think I was kidnapping you. It wouldn't go over well at work."

"No, I guess not. So do I get a clue?"

"Well, I'm taking you out to eat at this little Italian restaurant I found downtown. Now I'll warn you, I consider this restaurant a diamond in the rough. I found it one weekend and it wasn't what I expected. On the outside it looks like a dive, but the inside is quaint and the food is excellent."

They pulled up to the curb in front of the eatery and Matt saw Ava's facial expression change as she realized he did not exaggerate. He'd thought the same thing when he and his partner came across it one night after their shift was over. With its deep red brick façade and more than a few of the bricks crumbling or missing altogether, the building looked worn and aged. A faded green awning with the restaurant name etched in gold hung over the door. It didn't look unsanitary, just old. No curb appeal whatsoever.

They walked in and the atmosphere changed. Softly illuminated white lights dangled over the round tables in the middle and booths outlined the perimeter of the mediumsized dining room. The aroma of pasta sauce and breadsticks made his stomach growl. Red tablecloths and flickering candles dressed up the tables and booths. The soft, dim lighting made it a good choice for date nights, especially first dates. Waitresses scurried between tables and Matt could hear the cooks laughing back in the kitchen. It was family owned and he had learned that everyone working here was related.

Matt approached the hostess and silently prayed she wouldn't flirt with him like she had the last time. "Two, please. Do you happen to have the booth in the back corner open?"

"Yes, right this way," she smiled while grabbing menus and leading them to the back corner.

When the waitress left with their orders, Matt leaned his elbows on the table, ready to learn more about this remarkable woman sitting in front of him. "So tell me about your family."

She placed her complimentary bread down. "Okay, my dad's name is Steven and he is an architect. My mom's name is Grace and she writes children's books. They were high school sweethearts and have been married ever since. A couple years after they were married, they had my twin brothers, Jacob and Joshua.

"Are they identical?"

"No, but they are very similar. They both have sandy blond hair, the same height and build, but Jake has brown eyes and Josh has blue."

She went on to explain that Jake was an investigative reporter and Josh was the worship pastor at her church. "It's crazy how they can look so much alike and yet have completely different interests and gifts. Jake has won awards for his research and journalism. Josh is very gifted in music and can play almost any instrument."

He made a mental note about the respect and pride she held for her brothers. "I guess they are the perfect example of how God creates each of us differently in the womb. No one is exactly like anyone else...looks, talents, gifts, character... and yet each of us is His original masterpiece."

He thought a bit more about the billions and billions of people God had created and how each was thoughtfully made and loved by the Creator Himself.

"Wow, handsome and deep." She didn't allow him time to comment on her flirtatious statement. "Anyway, I came along two years later and then they had my sister Lucy. She is one of the chefs at the restaurant Riverside."

She took a sip of her drink. "So now that you know about my family, how about you enlighten me about yours?"

"Fair enough. You know about my dad, Peter. My mom's name is Anna and she's a school nurse. They met after college at a party of a mutual friend and were married three months later. My dad calls it love at first sight and my mom calls it insanity. She also says it's the best choice she ever made."

He went on to tell her about his older brother, Gabe, who was an accountant, married to Shelly, with three children. His sister, Sara, was married to Doug, and they were both lawyers.

Both his siblings lived in Chicago and even though they didn't live very far away, he still missed them. His parents went to visit them frequently, but his schedule made the trip a little harder for him to get away. They came to Rockford to visit him sometimes on the weekends, more often in the summer months. They remained very close and didn't let the distance affect their relationship. They never made him feel like the odd man out because he wasn't married or dating. He was as the baby of the family and milked it for all it was worth. He embraced the role as the cool Uncle Matt and enjoyed getting the kids hyper and then giving them back to his brother. He knew Gabe waited to repay the kindness once he had children.

Their food arrived and the waitress refilled their drinks. Matt prayed for the meal and they started to eat. They talked about where they went to college and the experiences they had there. He couldn't help but observe how tense her posture became as they discussed the subject and how she continually turned the questions back on him. It was obvious she did not want to talk about something related to her college years. Now was not the time to push, but if their relationship did get serious, it would be need to be brought up again.

Matt checked the time and didn't want the night to end and hoped she didn't either. "Would you like to go to the coffeehouse around the corner?"

"Did you know that I'm a coffee addict? I would never turn down an opportunity to have my drug."

※※ ※※

Ava excused herself to go to the bathroom. she needed some time to get her thoughts and feelings in check. She stood in front of the mirror and studied herself, tucked stray strands of hair back in place and reapplied her lipstick. Tonight was going well except for her twenty questions during dinner. Besides wanting to avoid talking about her college experience, she couldn't get enough information about him.

Her stomach tightened as her nerves got the best of her. Was she afraid of heading down the same road of getting to know someone, trusting them with her heart, and then being crushed in the end? Or did it stem from the fact that Matt was different and her attraction to him was something she had never felt before, this early on?

By the time she got back to the table, Matt had already paid, waiting to help put her coat on. His gentleman qualities didn't go unnoticed.

He hesitated when they stepped outside. "Is it okay if we walk to the coffeehouse?"

She wrapped her coat tighter across her midsection. "Walking sounds great. I have a few calories to burn off from dinner and I feel pretty safe with my present company. I would hate to be the villain that met you in a dark alley."

He flexed his muscles in a mock weightlifter's pose, which made her burst into laughter. "Yeah, these guns sure do come in handy sometimes," he joked.

"Sometimes? I would *never* want to be on any opposing team from you. I'm sure you wipe up any competition."

"You sound like a competitive person."

"You would be correct."

"You don't seem sorry about it."

"Nope, it's in my blood. My entire family is competitive...well, at least with each other. You name it, we compete. Sports, cards, board games, which person can get from point A to point B fastest."

She grinned as she thought about the basketball game her family played on Sunday and her relentless determination to win. She had a bruised knee for proof.

"I would've never guessed that about you, Ava. I like that. I'm looking forward to playing a game with you at the coffeehouse. I'm pretty competitive myself."

"Oh, it's too bad that I'll have to beat you at something on our first date. Will your ego be able to handle it?" She pushed her shoulder into his and smirked.

"Don't you worry about my ego. Just worry about getting your game face on because you're going down."

They ordered their coffee and found a table by the window overlooking the street and agreed on a game of checkers. Neither had played in years so it made the playing field equal. Both were too concentrated on their game to say much. It stayed close for awhile, but at the end Matt got lucky and won.

"Best out of three?" she asked when he leaned back against his chair looking pleased with himself.

"You must like torture."

"No, I just don't give up easily."

"Neither do I."

She caught his underlying meaning and blushed.

Ava won the next game, but not by much. They took a break and got refills. She burnt her tongue on the first sip and pushed aside her drink until it cooled off. The noise level started to dwindle as the night wore on. The background music became noticeable over voices now.

Matt won the third game by a landslide. As he gloated over his win, she noticed his attention become fixed on the back of the coffeehouse. His large frame became rigid as he fought over where to hold his focus. Ava turned in her seat and followed his gaze to a middle-aged couple in the far corner. The woman looked concerned as she spoke inches apart from the man's face, her eyebrows drawn together while rubbing her hand over his shoulder. The man looked to be growing paler by the second.

Turning back toward Matt his senses looked to be on alert. "Do you think something is wrong?" she asked, observing how Matt's cop side jumped into high gear.

"Not sure, but it wouldn't hurt to go ask." He stood. "I'll be right back."

Ava watched Matt stride across the floor with confidence that radiated with each step. Matt had only made it to a few tables away from the couple when the man tried to stand, but clutched his chest and rolled over the top of the table and fell to the ground with a loud thud that echoed throughout the room.

Panic shot through her veins as the scene play out before her. Matt lunged toward the man while the woman started frantically screaming. Turning the man over, Matt put his fingers to his neck, a frown depressing upon his features.

Matt's eyes reached hers. Ava jumped to her feet before Matt finished calling her name for help. Her body felt in slow motion as she rushed to his side, falling to her knees beside him.

Matt stripped off his jacket and hollered above the panic filled room. "Someone call 911." He turned his attention to Ava. "I think he is in cardiac arrest. I can perform CPR, but I need your help to keep the lady back and calm."

"Okay."

Matt seemed confident and self-assured in his actions as

he tipped the man's head back to open his airways and found the spot on his chest to begin compressions. His triceps bulged with the rhythmic movement, while her legs turned to jelly as she struggled to stand.

The woman's face digressed to a distraught chalky white. Silent tears plowed their way down her face as she looked down at her husband.

"Hi. I'm Ava. Why don't you come and sit with me?"

"Mary...I...my husband...was fine...and then..." her quiet words trailed off to a stop. The shock transformed into a veil that slowly descended over her eyes. The woman fell into step with Ava. She encircled her arm around the woman and directed her to at an adjacent table. Close enough that if Matt needed her she was near, but far enough the man's chalky face didn't come into view.

"Mary is it?" Ava crouched down in the front of the woman and took hold of her hands that trembled in her lap. "Your husband is in excellent hands and help is on its way." The woman nodded, but stayed quiet, starring down at their gathered hands.

Ava looked back over her shoulder, catching a glimpse of Matt between the tables continuing CPR. Sweat beads had bubbled upon his forehead as he worked on the man. He stopped compressions for a moment to check the man's pulse. His grim face showed his findings as he continued.

"Mary, what's your husband's name?"

"Dale..." she whispered so softly Ava could barely hear her.

"Dale looks like he's a fighter."

"Stubborn too."

The woman still had spunk. The crowd stayed gathered around them as she heard a man giving updates to the dispatch. Trying to keep Mary's mind off the crisis surrounding them, Ava continued to question her, asking for any insight that might help with Dale's condition. Mary's answers were short and sporadic, but she seemed to be gradually gaining strength and determination. Time seemed to stand still until finally the sound of approaching sirens squealed outside.

As the EMTs rushed in, Ava stole another glance at Matt as he stepped out of the way to let the men do their job. He lifted his arm and swiped it across his wet forehead. "I believe he has a pulse, but it is very weak."

The medics nodded and immediately got to work on Dale. They had him strapped and in the ambulance in no time. Ava helped Mary outside, giving her a hug as she left for the hospital.

The ambulance pulled away, lights flashing, sirens noiseless. Ava took a deep breath, decompressing from the overwhelming overload of the last twenty minutes. She scanned the crowd in search for Matt and found him near the entrance of the coffeehouse watching her.

He looked unfazed, as if he hadn't just saved a man's life. Cocking his head to the side, he appeared to be assessing her. Probably making sure she wasn't going to fall apart. Matt popped his head back as a silent "*come here.*"

Without even thinking she walked right into his open arms, her head resting on his firm chest as his arms encircled her. "You okay?" he asked as he spoke into her hair.

"Yeah." She was fine, in his arms. How did everything in the world seem right and made sense as he held her? Could beginning a relationship with Matt not end with a crash and burn like it did with Tim? But the facts were still there. She had never suspected Tim would rip her heart out. Why wouldn't Matt do the same thing? When reality caught up to her foolish impulse, she stiffened and stepped out of his embrace.

Matt took her cue and stepped back, crossing his arms to give her space. "You did great. You kept the wife calm and distracted like a pro."

"Thanks, but you were the hero. You totally saved that guy."

He rolled her compliment off his shoulder. "Let's call it a group effort. Come on, let's get you home."

Matt offered to walk Ava to the door. She wanted to pat herself on the back. She had made it through a date. The years of doom and gloom lifted, slightly.

"Are we still on for date number two?"

"I thought I didn't have a choice?" She laughed at his faux hurt expression. "Yes, I'd like a second date. However, are all your dates going to end with this much excitement?"

His laughter filled the hallway. "Well, I was expecting excitement, just not this kind."

"Will the next one be a secret, too?"

"Of course. Are you free next Saturday afternoon? I have to work Saturday night."

"You're really going to keep me in suspense?"

"That's right. I want you thinking about me all week."

As if that would be a problem for her. He had already taken hold of her thoughts without the secrecy.

chapter seven

Ava sat at her desk after the kids had left for the day, twirling her pen between her fingers in a rhythmic motion while resting her head on the back of her chair, gazing out the window. The day shined it's beauty, not a cloud in the sky, and all she wanted to do was go home, pull out her lawn chair, a good book, and soak up the sun.

It was only Wednesday and she already suffered from emotional and mental exhaustion. The kids were having a bad week and pushing her patience. With extreme caution she let herself look forward to her date with Matt on Saturday, which only made the week drag on unbearably.

Tonight she had Bible Study and was glad for the distraction. At least it wouldn't be another night sitting at home alone. Usually it didn't bother her to be alone, but in the last few weeks it depressed her. She had tried to fill her time with church activities, but they only served as scotch tape over an open wound of loneliness.

Two months ago she had joined the leadership team for the church's support group for abused women and children. The group coordinator had asked her to participate because of her experience with children in hopes that Ava would be able to provide comfort for the kids who needed help in the community.

She would have normally never pursued this outreach for the mere fact her lack of experience regarding this subject left her inadequate, but on the few occasions that she might be able to help a frightened child cope with pain and fear, made it worth it. Another meeting had been scheduled for this Friday and she had been preparing for her portion of the series they were discussing.

She planned on sharing with the women in attendance the effects felt by abused children. It was a disheartening topic and she wanted to praise them for being strong and taking their children out of a frightful situation. She had been working with the school therapist on what material she should present and was keyed up about the presentation.

Ava looked up at the clock and groaned. It showed a little before four o'clock and she needed to run a couple errands and eat before going to church. With confidence that she had prepared enough lessons for tomorrow, she cleaned off her desk and grabbed her purse and coat.

She closed the door behind her and headed toward the front doors to make her exit. Surprise quickened her steps when she found her student, Tessa, sitting on a bench just beyond the doors, legs swinging back and forth. She clutched her pink and purple backpack to her chest, wiping away tears that had stained her face.

Ava quickly approached and knelt beside her. "Tessa sweetie, what is wrong?" The little one should have left for home two hours ago.

"I...can't...find...my...mom," she said between hiccups.

Ava's heart broke for her. This was the second time in a little over a week this had happened. She gently rubbed Tessa's back, "She wasn't at home when you got there?"

"No, and the doors were locked and I couldn't get inside." She took her arm and wiped the snot from her nose.

"Well, maybe she's home now. Let's go in and call her. I'm

sure she's worried about you." Ava took the child's hand and led her into the office. Everyone had gone home. The empty office gave them privacy. Ava sat at the secretary's desk, found the phone number, and dialed. Her blood bubbled in her veins with each ring.

Tessa's mother Kim answered just as the answering machine went off. She sounded drowsy and confused. Ava explained the situation as nice as she could. She didn't want to place blame until she had all the facts. Kim sounded sorry about what had happened and asked that Ava send Tessa home. Ava hung up and knew she would do more than just send her home. She would deliver Tessa herself. Small group just got crossed off her list for tonight.

Ava reached down and stroked the girl's hair. "Tessa, your mom is home." She bent down, putting them at eye level. "You know what? It's such a nice day outside. Would it be okay if I walked with you?"

Tessa's face lit up and she jumped off the chair. "Really? Then I could show you my favorite flower that I found."

"Ooh, I love flowers."

Ava kept the conversation light while they walked. The distance from her house and the school wasn't a long distance, but for a kindergartner it must feel like a mini-marathon. Especially when having to walk the round trip twice in one day. The walk was dotted with good landmarks to discuss. A park sat half the distance to her house that the city had fixed up early last summer. It had a large playground designed for elementary ages with a separate section for toddlers, plus sandboxes, picnic tables, basketball courts and a pavilion.

They talked about the trees, the birds and a caterpillar they found inching its way across the sidewalk. They stopped and admired the purple tulip that had earlier caught Tessa's attention. Ava loved how something so simple could please a child.

In a classroom setting, Tessa had a quiet temperament, but in this one on one situation with Ava, she blossomed. Ava purposely made their pace slow in hopes that Tessa would reveal something that would explain what was going on at home. It was crunch time to get some information out of her. She shifted the conversation.

"Tessa, do you like being at your house?"

"Yeah."

"Do you and your mommy spend a lot of time together?" Guilt festered about questioning an innocent child, but she needed to get down to the bottom of why her mom had been dropping the ball lately. She held no peace regarding Tessa's home life. Determination kept her on course to get some answers.

"We used to play a lot, but her boyfriend Ray lives with us now so she spends a lot of time with him."

Ava didn't know much about Tessa's life, only that her dad had left without a word a few years back and never returned, leaving Kim, a young mom, to raise her alone. It was a sad situation, but up to this point, no reason existed to make her believe there were problems at home. Tessa hadn't mentioned her mom's boyfriend before, and that new admission caught Ava by surprise.

"Do you like him?"

"Yeah, he's nice to me, but he makes my mommy cry a lot."

"Oh, that's too bad."

"My mommy painted my room with pretty butterflies on the walls so when he is upset I can go to my room. She says it's my special place."

Ava's stomach twisted. She hoped the situation wasn't what she thought it was. They reached Tessa's house, frustrated that their time together had run out. She knocked on the door and scoped out the rundown neighborhood. Tessa's house missed a few shutters and the siding looked worn. The families who lived on the street had low incomes, but did the best they could with what they had.

Ava grew nervous as she knocked again. She and Kim were not close by any means, but they talked often at school functions and conferences. They were on a first name basis, which she didn't have with most of the other parents. Still, she wondered if Kim would be happy to see her at the front door.

The blinds were closed and the house looked dark. Finally locks jingled and the door opened a crack. Ava couldn't see Kim, but she heard her gasp.

"Miss Williams, I wasn't expecting you." Ava noted the switch in formality, but she couldn't read whether Kim was upset or just taken back.

"Hi Kim, may I come in, please?"

"Um, sure, maybe just a few minutes."

Ava took Tessa's hand and led her into the house, mulling over in her head what her next words should be. Kim looked nervous and Ava didn't want to push too hard. Kim shut the door and immediately Ava saw, even in the dim light that her arm lay in a sling and the side of her face held a line of bruises.

"Kim, are you okay? What happened?"

"Oh, um, last night I fell and bruised my arm and face. I went to the doctor this morning and they gave me some medicine for the pain. I must have fallen asleep and didn't hear Tessa come home."

She leaned down and hugged her daughter with her good arm and kissed her head. "I'm so sorry I didn't hear you come home, baby. You must have been so scared. I made some cookies for you earlier today. Why don't you go into the kitchen and have one? I think dessert before supper would be just fine today."

Tessa skipped through the dining room into the kitchen, oblivious to the adults' uncomfortable silence. Ava sensed that Kim wanted her to leave. It was now or never. *Lord give me the words.*

"I'm sorry about your arm and face, Kim. I hope they heal soon."

"Thank you."

"I brought Tessa home today because I hoped we would have a chance to talk. There have been too many instances in the last month where Tessa has been left alone and I'm just checking to see if everything is okay?"

Ava had debated during their walk to Tessa's house if she should bring this issue to the attention of the principal or school counselor. She wanted to get more facts first, but this situation seemed to be quickly slipping away from her expertise. Tomorrow she would share the details that she had. She wanted to go by the books in case legal measures needed to be taken at some point.

"Everything is fine. There is no need to worry about Tessa." Kim looked down at her watch and started biting her nails.

"I feel there is. I don't mean to push, but I can tell Tessa is very concerned about you. She mentioned that you have a new boyfriend and that he is upsetting you."

The statement took Kim by surprise and her eyes widened. She broke eye contact again by looking down toward the kitchen. Despite the sun outside, inside remained dark and dreary. A musty odor hung in the air.

"She told you about Ray?" Her voice barely reached above a whisper.

"Yes. Is there anything you want to talk about? I know you don't know me well, but I'm a pretty good listener."

Kim's eyes welled up with tears and she shook her head back and forth. She ran her trembling fingers through her short blonde hair, lost in thought. A car drove by and she jumped. Ava hadn't been in the church support group for very long, but she could see the signs of abuse etched in Kim's frightened face.

With ease she touched Kim's arm in the sling. "Did Ray do this to you, Kim?"

How would Kim respond to her blunt question? She guessed that Kim would lie, shut down, or kick her out. It would be a stretch for her to open up. There needed to be a foundation of trust before Kim would leak even the tiniest bit of truth. Ava took the first step and hoped she hadn't pushed too far.

"I...um...can't talk about this right now. I appreciate your concern, but I'm fine. Maybe sometime..."

Gravel crunched outside the dining room window. The vehicle that pulled into the driveway cut her words off and panic exploded in Kim's eyes. "Tessa, baby," she called toward the kitchen, "go upstairs and get ready for supper. Hurry, please."

She turned back to Ava while Tessa darted up the stairs. "You need to go, Ava. Please." She practically pushed Ava to the door.

"Okay, but please call me if you need anything..."

The back door opened and slammed shut. Kim jumped. "Kim, why didn't you bring the garbage can in from the street and why isn't dinner on the table? You're about worthless!" A man's voice yelled from the back of the house. It had to be Ray.

Ava wanted to run out the door because of the harshness of his voice. She couldn't imagine how Kim felt with it being directed at her. Ray swore, followed by throwing something into the sink.

Kim cleared her throat. "Ray, we have a visitor." Her voice quivered.

Ray strolled into the room with a smile pressed across his face. Ava expected to see the cut-out mold the movies always portrayed of an abusive man. Beer belly, white tank top, and gruff sneer. Instead the opposite approached her. An attractive man, clean cut, with the confident look of a charmer.

"Ray, this is Tessa's teacher, Miss Williams."

He walked up to her and shook her hand. His closeness made Ava's muscles tense. She wanted to step back but didn't want to make the uneasy situation more awkward than it already was.

"It's nice to finally meet you, Miss Williams. I've heard wonderful things about you. Tessa adores you."

"Thank you. She is a very sweet girl and a joy in my classroom."

"Your visit is unexpected. Is everything okay at school with Tessa?" His smile was deceptive but she was no fool.

Ava tucked her hair behind her ear and swallowed, trying to get the lump out of her throat. She wasn't sure what to say or how to explain why she had come. The last thing she wanted to do was get Kim in more trouble. Ava didn't want to lie, but she needed to sugar-coat the truth. She'd never been good at thinking fast on her feet.

"I, um, haven't talked with Kim much lately and thought I would walk Tessa home after school to see how she was doing."

"Hmm, aren't you a dedicated teacher?" His words, while spoken through the semblance of a smile, dripped with sarcasm.

"I care very much about my students' home lives and their happiness."

He folded tanned, muscular arms across his chest and took a step toward Ava, shedding all pretenses. Shivers surged through her body from the way he studied her, his eyes tracing the full length of her body.

"Tell you what, Miss Williams. Your concern is noted, but not needed. I am in charge of this household now and we are just fine. Kim and Tessa are well taken care of and our home life is honestly none of your business. Thank you for bringing Tessa home. It won't be needed again in the future."

Helpless washed over Ava. She wanted to protect Kim and Tessa but didn't know what to do. She heard and clearly understood Ray's underlying threat. Her continued presence would only cause further distress for Kim. She turned toward Kim, ignoring him. "Kim, it was good to see you again."

"You, too. Goodbye, Miss Williams."

chapter eight

Ava's legs strained to move as if lead had filled her shoes, while she walked back to the school. Her anger stifled her cry, but once she settled down the tears would come. She had no doubt that man was hurting Kim whether she admitted it or not. In the five minutes that Ava was in Ray's presence she could see how controlling and vindictive he was.

In their last meeting for the abuse support group they discussed some of the warning signs of abuse but also covered the topic of why most women take the beatings silently. The few reasons they discussed were sad and heartbreaking. It was upsetting to hear the statistics at first and not fully understand why these women just didn't run or stick up for themselves. People could easily judge their lack of action when they weren't in the circumstance. After being in a home that showed the signs, their entrapment was understandable.

Some women were simply embarrassed. They thought they knew this man they loved but were rudely awakened when their prince charming became a dud. A number of women kept quiet because they felt like they didn't deserve better. Whether their self-esteem was shot or never there to begin with, it was the best they thought they could do. They also didn't want to be alone or felt they couldn't support themselves, so they mistakenly decided to just stay in the relationship. Several women were so in love, the abuse didn't matter. In most cases remorse followed the abuse, so when the apologies started, they replaced their fear with affection and hope that the abuser would change.

Sadly, some women thought the abuse had been their fault. They put the blame on themselves because they didn't do what they were told or because they made him angry and egged him on to the violence. They put the blame solely on themselves. The bottom line was that their actions deserved the beatings.

The last scenario was the hardest to swallow because the majority of women were afraid to leave or tell someone. They were scared for their life or scared they would get caught leaving and endure an even harsher punishment. Some were in fear their children would suffer and be hurt in the backlash of the anger. If they took the beating, it meant that they spared their children. It was a love wrongly misplaced and confused.

Ava reached the park and took a detour from walking back to the school. The playground appeared fairly empty. She sat on the swings and tried to unwind. The light breeze made the sweat on her forehead cool while she leaned her head against the chains. She wanted to talk with someone, get the frustration off her chest. One person came to mind. Without weighing the consequences and what the undercurrent of her actions meant, she took her cell phone out of her back pocket and dialed.

⁂

*M*att drove east out of the city, doing his best to keep at the speed limit while talking himself out of turning on his lights for an excuse to go faster. The call from Ava came as he left the station, which put them on opposite sides of the city. Ava sounded upset but didn't elaborate on why. She had simply asked if he could meet her at the park by her school.

Their first date had gone well besides the drama at the coffeehouse...or so he thought. When he held her in his arms, he never wanted to let her go. But when she stiffened in his embrace, he needed to. Whatever hidden demons clung to her, pushing her wasn't the answer. From the few words they shared on the phone he hoped she wasn't upset about them. At least Ava didn't say the four words every guy dreaded hearing, 'we need to talk'. However, he would feel better once he saw her.

He handled his car with ease as he approached the park and found a parking spot near the front. About thirty yards from the playground, he spotted her sitting on one of the swings, kicking stones around with her shoe. She looked lost in thought and didn't hear him approach.

"Hey," Matt said as he wedged his frame into the swing next to hers.

Ava looked over. The tears glistening on her eyelashes took him off guard.

"Hi."

Seeing her didn't put his mind at ease and he began to second guess himself about why she had called him here.

"Are you okay?"

"Yes...no...I don't know." Her last words were articulated in frustration. She pushed the swing back and forth slowly, her feet never leaving the ground. "I think one of my student's mom is being abused by her live-in boyfriend."

He realized the redness in her face didn't come from the warm weather, but from being upset. Her shoulders slumped forward as if weights had been placed on her. She was obviously involved in the situation emotionally, so he needed to keep a level head.

"Why do you think that?"

Ava stopped the swing and twisted around to look straight at him. "A few problems have occurred in the last couple of weeks that made me concerned about the home life of my student Tessa. I walked her home today to speak with her mom, Kim. Kim's arm was in a sling and one side of her face was covered in bruises. She was nervous and on edge, clearly hiding something."

"Did she admit to being abused?"

Matt had seen this too much in his profession. If a man had to beat a woman, it only showed that he was weak and a coward.

"No, but I could tell she wanted to, only we were interrupted by her boyfriend, Ray. Matt, he made me feel so uncomfortable. I couldn't get out of that house fast enough."

"Did he touch you or say something to upset you?" All levelheadedness left him. If that man even touched a hair on her head...

"No, it was nothing like that. He was just stern in getting his point across that I was to keep my nose out of their business. It was mostly the way he spoke to her."

Matt studied her, trying to see if he could read her emotions and if she was telling the truth. He speculated she was angry and honest. She wore her heart on her sleeve and her thoughts on her face.

He let her words soak in and watched the sun begin to set and coat the sky with splashes of pink and orange. They sat in comfortable silence, neither eager to break the quiet. Matt figured she called him for a reason, so he would wait. Ava had so many other people in her life that she could confide in. He hoped this was a good sign, the first step in her trusting him.

Ava broke the silence first. "Matt, I need you to do me a favor."

"If I can."

"I need you to intervene and check out this Ray guy, or even get Tessa and Kim away from him." The pleading in her eyes crushed him.

Matt figured this would be Ava's request and he hated having to disappoint her. Domestic abuse frustrated him and left a nasty taste in his mouth. He had taken a vow to serve and protect, but his hands were tied concerning this situation.

"Ava, I'm so sorry, but there is nothing I can do."

"What do you mean, there's nothing you can do?"

"Listen, I know you're upset and I wish I could help, but I can't."

"How can you say that? You're a cop, isn't that your job?"

Her words didn't come across as callous, just discouraged. Any type of abuse was a tricky problem where the law was concerned. Even if a wife was being abused by her husband, unless she pressed charges there was nothing the police could do. If they were called to the house because of a domestic disturbance, he could take the husband to jail for a night or two, but in most cases they would make bail quickly – and sadly it was usually paid by the wife.

If it would make a difference he'd knock at Kim's door right now and check out the situation. However, Ava concern came from a hunch, and even if she was right and Kim was being abused, having a policeman show up would only cause Kim more problems. She had mentioned at Kyle and Kate's wedding about being a part of the abuse support group at her church, which meant she knew the signs, but she also knew the way the system worked. If he were a betting man, he'd put his money on the fact that she knew what his answer would be but felt the need to ask anyway.

A few kids who looked to be middle school age walked across the playground as a short cut to the basketball court.

They were oblivious to the intense conversation that was taking place. He hesitated to answer her until they had their privacy.

Matt stood and came around to face her, crouching down to put him at eye level with Ava. He placed his hands on the chains of the swing, pulling her toward him so her knees touched his chest. He was invading her personal space, but he didn't care.

"Ava, you and I both know there is nothing I can do. Unless Kim comes forward and presses charges, my hands are tied." He didn't like it, but it was the bitter truth.

"Or until he beats her to death."

No accusations laced her tone, only sadness. The anger she'd held earlier diminished and was replaced with hopelessness.

He wished he could save the day, but all he could offer was encouragement. "We may not be able to go in and rescue Kim, but we have a God who can. The best thing we can do is pray for her and hope she gains the courage to walk away or seek help."

Ava gave him a tearful smile and nodded her head in quiet agreement.

"Now, is my job the only reason you chose to call me instead of someone else?"

Ava looked down at her hands in obvious hesitation and back up again, slowly letting her eyes reach his.

"No."

He couldn't hide his satisfaction. "I didn't think so." He seized her hands and pulled her off the swing. "Come on, let's go get you something to eat."

chapter nine

Date # 2

" **W**ow, I'm very impressed."

It was Saturday and Matt had taken Ava to a park outside the city. They found a secluded spot on a tiny hill out in the sun. The day had turned cooler, but the warmth of the sun helped to take the chill out of the slight breeze. Matt pulled from the picnic basket a few pieces of Tupperware and put down a blanket for them to sit on. He had brought chicken salad croissants, a plate full of vegetables and fruit, baked chips, and brownies for dessert.

"My mom gave me the recipe for the chicken salad and Betty Crocker did the brownies. Hopefully you'll be as impressed after you eat it."

They watched a group of children playing on the playground across the grassy knoll and laughed while witnessing a father trying to teach his daughter how to ride a bike without training wheels. She had been nervous about seeing Matt again after her lapse in judgment in calling him earlier in the week to come talk. He had been exactly what she needed. And that was the problem. Each time they were together Matt chipped away at the walls that had guarded her heart for so long. Being vulnerable didn't sit well with her.

Matt finished his sandwich and leaned back on his elbows, looking up at her. "So how was the rest of your week?"

"Honestly, not good in the teaching department." She cringed just thinking about her long and trying week. "I had a lot of behavior issues with my kids. I'll give you an example. On Thursday one of the girls got homesick and cried all day. I tried to comfort her but nothing seemed to help. The other kids noticed and made fun of her at first, but then caught on that my attention was divided and used that to their advantage."

"Thoughts of running away?"

"I had my destination picked out on the computer."

"Warm weather?"

"And complete seclusion."

"Running water?"

"Define running water."

"Ouch, it was a bad week."

She chortled and took a bite of her brownie, savoring the chocolate melting in her mouth. "So how was your week?"

"Wish I could say mine was better."

"I guess misery likes company. Spill the beans."

He sat up and put his elbows on his knees, tilting his head toward her, contemplating. "Besides the normal routine, I had to go to two houses this week because of domestic abuse. One of the calls wasn't serious - mostly a lot of yelling that worried the neighbors. The second one was totally out of control, though. By the time we got there the wife's face was so bloody she wasn't identifiable."

Ava sat stunned and finally grasped his hesitation – his caution was for her concern. The subject bothered her and he didn't want to upset her. Deep empathy tore through her heart. She had been so mindless with her words on Wednesday about him not doing anything for Kim. It was wrong of her to put him on the spot and ask him to do something she knew full well was out of his control. He had taken her to dinner afterwards and she thrived in his company. He made her laugh and never seemed bothered by her comments, but that didn't change the fact that she said them.

"I'm sorry, Matt, that must have been horrible." Her bad week suddenly sounded pathetic by comparison.

"Yeah, sometimes I want to deck the guy and say 'how did that feel?' But unfortunately they frown upon that at the department."

Ava twisted a piece of grass in her hands, examining the blade's detail. She wanted to crawl into a hole, but first she needed to apologize.

"Matt, I'm really sorry for my words the other day. You kindly came at my request and I threw it in your face." Bringing her eyes to reach his, she exhaled slowly wondering if she had caused him to think less of her.

"Ava, there's no need for you to apologize. You had every right to ask me to help Kim. I'm just sorry I can't right now. Have you heard from her yet?"

"No."

"Don't lose hope, keep praying, God is good." He stood and stretched. "I brought a Frisbee, do you want to play?"

"Sure, I haven't played in years. Sounds like a great way to embarrass myself."

They casually tossed the Frisbee back and forth for awhile. Once they both loosened up, they stepped it up, lifting their legs and throwing it underneath, whipping it around their sides and chucking it backwards and backhanded. It was as if they were teenagers again. Matt's throws were smoother than hers and his Frisbee arrived at its exact destination every time. Ava's throws usually made him run. After twenty minutes her arm started to get sore. She agreed quickly when he suggested they take the hike he had mentioned earlier.

They followed the wilderness path at an easy pace, enjoying the beautiful scenery. Ava loved the spring. After the long winter it was nice to see color on the trees again and flowers blooming with their scent of new life.

The sun came out from behind the clouds. Ava closed her eyes, enjoying the warmth upon her face. She realized she closed them too long when she tripped on a log and started to fall forward. Matt's quick reaction stopped her before she hit the ground. His arms gathered around her waist, pulling her back against his chest. He held her a few seconds longer than necessary. She didn't protest.

He released her as she giggled nervously. "Thanks," she said as she rubbed the goose bumps that appeared because of his touch. "I guess you could say I'm not very coordinated."

"Good because perfection is overrated," he teased.

They continued up a small hill that led them into the woods. The air became crisp in the shade. Ava put on her sweatshirt, thankful she'd remembered it. Matt had mentioned while they were driving to the park that if she shared some information with him today, she would get some clues about next week's date. Ava was slightly concerned about what information he would be seeking. She wasn't ready to share anything serious yet. He had already invaded her willpower with keeping a distance and if they bonded over her past she would lose all leverage.

Matt led the way to a clearing with a rickety wooden bench overlooking a small creek. Ava sat gently, not sure if it would break under the pressure of their weight. The water rushing over the rocks had a calming effect on her nerves. The birds chirping reminded her of God's instruction in the Bible about worrying.

> *"Look at the birds of the air; they do not sow or reap or store away in barns, and yet your heavenly Father feeds them. Are you not much*

*more valuable than they? Can any one of you
by worrying add a single hour to your life?
Therefore do not worry about tomorrow, for
tomorrow will worry about itself. Each day has
enough trouble of its own."*

Ava loved the moments when God's word spoke to her heart. Reminding her how He had everything under control and loved her.

Matt turned toward her and put one arm on the back of the bench, careful not to touch her. "All right, I'm ready for my information."

"Your wish is my command," she said, messing around while putting her palms together and leaning forward slightly. She enjoyed how spending time with him made her feel light-hearted and silly.

"I just have a few random questions for you."

"Okay, shoot...oh, well, not literally. I forgot who I was talking to."

He laughed. "Let's start with your middle name."

"Well, this isn't painful so far. It's Noel because I was born on Christmas Eve."

"Do you like having your birthday on Christmas Eve?"

"Yes and no. I enjoy the Christmas season, so it's special in that sense. But when I was younger I always wanted my birthday in the summer so I could get presents spread out twice a year." Now that Ava was older she didn't mind her special day surrounded with busyness. Her family always did their best to make sure she felt significant.

He questioned her about who was her best friend and why. Talking about Jules came easy. She was trustworthy, honest, funny and her rock during the hardest time of her life. She couldn't have survived the last two years without her. Her friend was a gift from God. Her family was great and a part of her, but Jules was special because she was chosen.

They talked about Matt's partner at work and what made their friendship click. He and Derek started the academy at the same time but didn't get real close until they were placed together on the SWAT team. He explained how Derek was also a Christian and how nice it was to know they protected each other not only in force, but in prayer.

Matt asked her about what movies and music she liked. She became embarrassed when he asked her about what she did in her free time. Her pathetic list of hobbies included reading, watching sports and movies and taking walks – she didn't realize how dull she had become until she said it out loud.

When she turned the question around to him she had expected him to blow her simple life out of the water, but was pleasantly surprised by his easy lifestyle. In the winter he enjoyed snowmobiling up north and in the summer he enjoyed hiking. The majority of his free time he spent working out, with friends, and at church activities.

Their second date came as a surprise to Ava. She had been afraid her insecurities would show through and force her to be uptight. Quite the opposite had happened. Matt's questions didn't push, they had purpose. He was setting the foundation of a strong friendship. He was in no rush, simply savoring the time to get to know her. Matt's interest in her life became clear, and if she were truly honest with herself, it delighted her.

"What's your favorite color?"

"Orange. It reminds me of the sunset."

"Not the sunrise."

"Um, that would involve the morning."

"Not a morning person?"

"Full out claws the first ten minutes."

"Have you ever committed a crime?" Ava raised an eyebrow at his smirk. "I'm just checking to see if you are paying attention."

"Alert and no, I'm crime free."

"Good, but I did a background check anyway."

"You what?"

"I'm kidding, Ava." He put his hands up with his palms facing her in surrender. "I just wanted to get you all riled up. You're so cute when infuriated."

She playfully punched his arm as her cheeks flushed with warmth. He brought his arms down and stuffed his hands into the front pocket of his sweatshirt. Leaning back against the bench he straightened out his legs, crossing them at his ankles. "So, what's your biggest fear?"

Ava looked away, fighting the urge to flee. Without even meaning to, he had stumbled upon the one subject she cautiously tried to avoid. Should she lie or tell him the truth? Ava had no desire to bring up her past today, but she had to be honest. He deserved that much. She turned back toward him, facing the inevitable.

"I fear rejection and falling in love."

"Is that the baggage you were talking about at the wedding?" Ava noticed how he tip-toed around the sensitive subject carefully.

"Yes. It's a hard subject for me to talk about. The thing is, Matt, I do want to talk to you about it, but not today. I'm not quite ready."

She could barely get the words out. Afraid she would offend him or make him think she was blowing him off. She just wanted to remember the day as it had started, happy and fun. She didn't want it tainted by the resurfacing of her ugly past.

"Ava, there's no pressure. When you're ready to share, I'll be here to listen."

"Thanks for understanding."

"No problem. Do you want to turn back?"

"Sure, but only if my interrogation is over and now I get to ask the questions."

"All right, let me have it."

※※ ※※

*T*hey reached the end of the trail and headed back to his Jeep as the sky became covered with clouds and released its moisture to the ground. Ava couldn't believe how quickly the afternoon had come to an end. Despite their hours together, the time didn't last long enough.

He pulled up in front of her apartment complex and shut off the engine. "So are we still on for a date next weekend?" His relaxed question couldn't hide the hope in his voice.

"Yes, and I kept up my end of the bargain, so cough up some details."

He laughed and nodded his agreement. "Well, I was wondering if you wanted to spend the entire day with me next Saturday? I'd like to take you over to Lake Michigan for a day of walking along the beach and I want to take you to this great seafood restaurant."

Ava wanted to pinch herself to make sure this was real. She couldn't believe how much thought he put into each date. The only person she had ever dated was Tim and they never really went out on dates. They were poor college students, treasuring every penny they owned, so they usually just spent time in each other's room and with friends. Occasionally Tim would take her to the local restaurant and ice cream parlor, but only when they were weary of cafeteria food. Even after graduation and acquiring jobs, he never took her out. That Matt would take time to plan something special for her was unchartered territory.

"Yeah, that sounds great, but Matt, are you sure I'm worth all this time you're taking to spend with me?" Her past permeated her present thoughts relentlessly. She didn't intentionally try to push him away. It was more of a defense mechanism.

"Ava, whether you choose to spend more time with me after next weekend or not, it's been worth every second."

He was smooth. That definitely made the list of his adorable qualities.

"Okay." She wasn't sure what else to say except the truth. "I had a great day."

"Me too."

He unhooked his seat belt, but she put her hand on his arm to stop him. "You don't have to walk me in. I need to run to the store to get groceries. My car is just over there." She took her hand off his arm to point to her car. The absence of his warmth made her year for it again. Without deliberating her actions until it was too late, Ava put her hand on his and he lightly squeezed hers back.

"Thanks again. I'll see you Saturday."

Ava got out and walked to her car. Matt waited until she got in and then drove off waving. She sat in her car trying to rationalize her feelings. She liked Matt and wanted to spend more time with him, but was it worth being vulnerable to her greatest fear? Ava panicked…she only had a week to decide.

chapter ten

<u>Date #3</u>

*B*y Friday Ava had become an emotional mess. It wasn't that she didn't know if she wanted to start dating Matt more seriously - that emotion she was completely sure about. She yearned for it. It was the fear that dredged up from the comprehension that once she allowed herself to fall for him, there would be no turning back. What if down the road he realized that he didn't want her...she wasn't sure she could survive *his* rejection.

Ava wanted to call in sick for school today and it wouldn't be a lie. She was sick in the head. She mustered through her inner turmoil, got her act together, and headed to school.

Fortunately her students behaved much better this week, and that helped to lessen the load she carried. The kids enjoyed the lessons from the week. They discussed oceans, ponds, lakes and rivers. What made each body of water different and which animals lived in each? She was pleased how perfect it timed out for the letter of the week to be W. Ava had planned a lot of projects about water, whales, walruses, and wind.

The morning started well despite the one little accident with one of the water projects. Ava saw the project going so much better in her head, but the execution had some flaws that she hadn't seen coming. She had brought in two large bowls of water - one full of salt water and the other with pure water. First she had the students taste both types of water to see the difference. They all laughed at each other's reactions. A few amused her as well.

Next she brought in a dozen plastic animals and had them take turns putting the animals into the bowl of water they belonged to.

The project progressed smoothly until some kids at the back of the group got impatient because they couldn't see. They started to push and before she could reach them the table got bumped and two kids in front ended up wet from bowls tipping over. Luckily, at the beginning of the year she had asked parents to keep an extra pair of clothes in their backpacks in case of an accident. Ava cleaned the kids up and had them go change their clothes while the rest of the class cleaned up the spillage.

While the kids lined up to go to lunch, the phone on her desk rang.

"Ava, I just received a delivery for you here in the office."

"Um...okay. I'll come down after I take my kids to lunch." What kind of delivery could she have gotten?

The bell rang shortly after and she couldn't get her kids to lunch fast enough. Her mouth gaped open as she walked into the front office. There on the main desk sat an enormous bouquet of orange tulips.

The secretary stood up behind her desk and pushed the vase toward her. "Is there something you haven't told me, Ava?"

Ava giggled nervously. "Oh...well...I'm not sure. I don't even know who they're from." Although she hoped for who the sender was. Ava grabbed the vase and headed out the door. "Thanks."

She hustled back her room. Setting the flowers down on her desk, she took out the card, opening it quickly.

Ava,

I just wanted you to know that I've been thinking about you all week and I enjoyed our date at the park. You said that you liked the color orange because it reminded you of the sunset. I'm looking forward to spending the day with you tomorrow and watching the sunset together.

Matt

A smile flirted across her lips. Seriously, if this guy had a flaw, it was not obvious. Ava was relieved she had made plans with Julia tonight. They had a lot to discuss.

১৭৪-১৭৪

*J*ules lived outside the city in a late seventies house that she rented. Since they were meeting at her house, Jules took care of the food and movie. She had ordered Mexican food and they sat on her couch to eat, curled up in blankets.

"I'm thinking about getting my haircut, what do you think?" Jules asked while sweeping it up off her shoulders to show what the shorter length would look like. Jules had beautiful long auburn hair, the envy of most women. She could be a model, if she wanted.

"You asked me that last month and my answer is still no. It is a shame to cut off those beautiful locks." She leaned over and pulled gently on her hair, feeling the texture and adjusting the length a bit. "Maybe if you put in some more layers and just had a good trim it would be the change you need." If Jules needed a change in her life, her gorgeous hair was not the way to go.

"I like that idea. I'll make an appointment at the salon soon." She threw her hair back in a pony-tail to put the subject to rest. "Enough about my hair, we have much more important topics to discuss." She sat her plate on the coffee table and turned her focus to Ava. "Tomorrow is your third date with Matt, right?" Jules asked with a light tone.

"Yes. He's taking me over to Lake Michigan for the day."

"That sounds like fun. Have you decided what you want after this date?"

It didn't take her long to blurt out the question, but that didn't come as a surprise to Ava. Jules was the type of person who told you what was on her mind whether you liked it or not. She wasn't shy about announcing the elephant in the room, but at least she did it with tact.

"Jules, I know what I want, but I'm scared. I really like Matt and want to see him more, but I fear getting my heart broken again."

It helped to release her anxiety by talking with someone and voicing her concerns.

"Ava, I know it's unsettling for you to care for someone again, but you can't let what happened with Tim control your life. It's not healthy. You're not giving God enough credit on how much He cares for you and you're not giving Matt the benefit of the doubt. God knew what was going to happen with Tim before you even met him and He knows what life you could have with Matt in it. Have you prayed about what God wants in this situation?" Her best friend spoke in a caring voice as wisdom oozed from her words.

"I have been praying, but not like I should," Ava admitted. Tears brimmed at the corners of her eyes. She couldn't remember the last time she sat down and really sought after what the Lord wanted in her relationship with Matt.

"God is not a God of fear or worry. If you're wavering in your decision on pursuing a relationship with him because you are afraid, then trust is not your issue with Matt, it's with God. At some point you have to let go and have faith."

"I know you're right, I can't live the rest of my life with this fear." Jules handed her a tissue to help stop the tears running down her face. "What do I say tomorrow?"

"Have you told him anything about Tim yet?"

"No, not really."

"Okay, then start there. Tell him your story and see where it goes. He might surprise you."

Ava nodded in agreement, but her emotions kept her mute.

"Ava, come here, let me pray with you." Jules push her blanket off and encircled Ava, speaking passionately to the Lord on her behalf. When she finished she gave her a hug and they agreed to watch a movie to take her mind off the situation. Ava would let it go for now, but when she got home tonight she and the Lord had a lot to talk about.

⁂⁂

*M*att woke up saturday morning ready to face the day. He had spent many of his waking hours in bed last night praying for today and what would come of it. This third and final date in their agreement had him on edge. He couldn't tell which way Ava teetered. He could tell she liked him, but she constantly kept him at a safe distance. Matt honestly didn't have a clue which way she would go and it made his stomach tighten to think about the fact that after today he may never see her again.

He rolled out of bed, forcing himself to let the worry go. Matt knew what he wanted. Now it was just up to God and Ava.

Matt picked Ava up at ten and they headed out on their mini road trip. The weather had become uncommonly warm for the end of April thanks to a burst of high pressure that came through earlier in the week. They both dressed in jeans, short sleeve shirts and walking shoes for the beach. He was glad that Ava brought along a sweatshirt. The temperature dropped drastically by the water in the evening because of the breeze.

He planned to take her to the area of Lake Forest. From Rockford there was not a direct road. He headed south toward Chicago and then cut up north. The trip took almost two hours, but the time passed quickly.

They shared about their life while growing up and some of their favorite childhood memories. They talked about their most embarrassing moments, their pet peeves, and their experiences in coming to know the Lord and being saved. Their conversation was random and jumped all over, but Matt enjoyed every minute. He wanted to know everything about her.

They reached Lake Forest around noon and found a charming café for lunch. Afterward they decided to check out the historic downtown and walked up and down the streets, admiring all the different quaint shops. Out at the lake they walked along the beach while Matt shared about a sailing experience he had a few years ago on Lake Michigan with some friends. An unexpected storm had come over the lake and no one was experienced enough to feel comfortable about the large waves. The storm hadn't lasted long, but it was a fear he had never experienced before.

By the end of the afternoon they were each barefoot with their jeans rolled up. With all the walking they had done in the last few hours, they were both getting hungry. They headed back into town for dinner at the restaurant Matt had been raving about. The conversation was light, but not awkward. He knew they needed to talk about where they were going to go from here, but now was not the time. After he paid the bill they headed back to the beach and took residence at the spot they'd found earlier to sit and watch the sunset.

Along the beach a mound of rocks sat high enough that they didn't get wet by the waves crashing against the shore, yet close enough that it felt like they might. The air quickly began to cool down. Matt helped Ava put on her sweatshirt before they sat down.

They didn't rest long when Ava started to stiffen up and began playing with her fingernails. He was already picking up on her nervous habit.

"Matt...I...um...want to say thanks for being so patient with me these last few weeks. I know we need to talk about where we go from here, but first I need to explain to you where I've been."

"I'm here, but don't feel pressured to say anything. If you need more time, I understand." Matt's pulse quicken as she broached the subject. Time had expired. Would he be able to walk away from the woman he loved if that was her desire? *Love? What? I've only known her for a couple weeks. Is that even possible?*

"No. Please don't think that you have pressured me in any way. I want to talk about this."

He shifted to the left giving him a better angle to look at her square on. His eyes searched hers as he waited for her to continue. He braced himself mentally as she began.

Ava took a deep breath. "When I started college I met this guy, Tim, who was also in the education department and from Rockford. We quickly started dating and ended up staying together all through college. When we returned home after graduation I got my teaching job, but Tim couldn't find one and finally had to relocate over an hour away."

The pieces began to fall in place and Matt realized why she had acted so sketchy when she spoke about college on their first date. This guy obviously surrounded every detail of her college experience.

Matt noticed how she tried to keep her emotions in check while she told the story about how Tim had proposed and how they had planned to marry the following year. She said everything had been going well, but as the wedding approached, Tim became more distant.

"The day of the wedding, I was in my room fully dressed and ready to walk down the aisle when the news came that he cancelled the wedding."

Tears slid down her cheeks, chasing each other. He brushed them away before she could. He slid his thumb across her cheek, not wanting to stop touching her soft skin. She looked up at him and smiled.

She had never looked so beautiful.

"He left a note telling me that he was sorry, but he couldn't make me his wife."

It crushed Matt to watch her have to relive the past. He could see the battle that raged within her. "Oh Ava, I am so sorry. It must have been horrible." He wanted to wrap her up in his arms but chose to give her space.

"I was finally getting my life back to normal when he showed up at my door."

Matt had to control his fury while she told him about their conversation. Anger bubbled in his veins when she said that Tim had spent time with another woman during their engagement and started to have feelings for her. The final blow came for Ava when she had found out he married this other woman shortly after. He was grateful, however, that the guy didn't marry Ava when he wasn't truly in love with her. A woman like Ava needed someone who couldn't live without her.

Ava's fear of being in a relationship completely made sense now. She had trusted this man and he broke that trust into a thousand pieces.

"It's been almost two years now and the problem isn't

that I still have feelings for him or wish that we were still together. It's just that his rejection cut so deep and I've lost trust in relationships and love. I feel wounded and I'm petrified to fall in love again."

Ava turned away, trying to hide her face. She didn't cry, but it was there beckoning at the threshold.

"Ava, look at me," he said gently – barley above a whisper, waiting to speak until she turned to look in his eyes. "Do you like me?" It felt like a grade school question, but the simple words held so much impact.

"Yes." Her answer held no hesitation.

"This we can work with. If your only reluctance is because you're scared to care for me, then I can be patient and walk you through this fear. I'm not going anywhere."

A ticking bomb couldn't stress him out more than as he waited for her reply. The sun shifted lower, causing shadows to shift. A few birds crept closer in search of food. The grass clustered in the sand whispered in the breeze. Ava could be a hostage negotiator for the way she could draw out a conversation.

"I do want to give us a chance."

He let out a relieved sigh. "Okay, that's all I need to know. We can just take it one day at a time." He reached over and took her hand in his, lacing their fingers together. He pointed to the west as the sun began to set down over the trees. "I've been waiting for this all day."

The colors were breathtaking. The sky filled with orange, yellow and pink while the clouds stretched out, racing each other. They sat in a comfortable silence, just enjoying the moment of beauty. The waves crashing against the rocks were therapeutic. Ava shivered as the warmth of the sun slowly left them. He untangled their fingers and wrapped his arm around her, bringing her to his side. She laid her head on his shoulder and he breathed in the scent of her shampoo. It pleased him to see how comfortable she was with his touch and that she didn't refuse and ask him to let go.

Matt spoke into her hair, keeping his voice low. "Did you know if you break your leg, when it heals, it's stronger in that area?"

"I heard something like that. Are you an expert in this area too?"

His smile beamed. "No, but I think the same could be true about your heart. When it's broken and you allow the Lord to heal it, I think He makes your heart stronger than it was before."

"Oh, Matt, you deserve someone so much better than me. I've got roller coaster emotions that will drive you crazy."

Ava was her own biggest critic, but hearing her story, he understood. She had been rejected in the worst possible way and it so obvious that underneath it all, she blamed herself. Ava had left that relationship thinking something was wrong with her and that she didn't have worth. It was time for someone to change her mind.

"Ava, I'd rather have a little crazy than to not have you at all. We're going to get through this together."

The moon illuminated her face and even in the twilight he saw a smirk form on her lips. "Okay, so you have me a little hooked with your suave words and stunning looks. So where do we go from here?"

"Stunning, huh?" She jabbed her elbow into his ribs. "Okay, okay, focus Matt. I get it. I was just hoping to see you every weekend, talk to you on the phone, and when you're ready to admit that you're my girlfriend, we'll take it from there."

"A little over-confident, don't you think?"

"Hey, a little confidence never hurt a man. Seeing that I have suave words and stunning looks, you add confidence to that list and hopefully you'll melt in no time."

"You're awful. What am I going to do with you?"

"Hmm...I have a few ideas."

"That's okay, I'll figure it out myself."

"Just here to help."

He brought his arm around her shoulder for a hug. She nestled her cold face into his neck and it burned against his warm skin.

They sat nestled together, enjoying each other's presence in the darkness that surrounded them. The night turned late and the rocks had become uncomfortable. They decided to head home. Two hours of driving still awaited them.

After a drive punctuated by a few laughs and musings but mostly cloaked in relaxed silence, they reached her apartment shortly before midnight. Matt walked her up the flight of stairs to her door.

"Thank you for such a wonderful day and thanks again for the flowers, it was very thoughtful," Ava said softly.

"You're welcome."

Her next move came as a complete surprise. She lunged forward and wrapped her arms around his neck and held him in a tight embrace. Without hesitation he brought his arms around her waist and brought her even closer. A penny couldn't have been wedged between them. Matt wasn't sure how long they stood there holding each other, but when she released, he didn't like the distance.

"Wow, I should get you flowers more often."

"Are you always full of this much wit and charm?"

"I guess you'll have to just stick around and see."

He moved his hand up to her face and tucked some hair behind her ear. "Sleep well, Ava. I'll talk to you soon."

Matt walked down to his Jeep in sweet relief. They had a long road ahead of them, but a road well worth traveling.

chapter eleven

*T*he alarm going off didn't sound right as Ava reached
over to her night stand to shut off the shrill. After hitting the snooze button twice she realized it wasn't her alarm
clock, but the phone. She glanced over at the bright red numbers screaming back at her, announcing that it was ten minutes after three o'clock in the morning. Ava shot up out of
bed and answered the phone in a panic.

A silence hung on the other end. Ava became annoyed
by the prank call. Ready to hang up, she stopped when she
heard a soft voice. "Ava, it's Kim."

"Kim." She cleared the phlegm in her throat. "Are you
okay?"

"I'm sorry to bother you, but I needed someone to talk
to." She was crying and her voice held a low hush, clearly trying to remain invisible to someone at her end.

"I'm glad you called. What's wrong?"

A long silence stretched between them. Ava wasn't sure if
Kim would continue. "You were right. Ray is hitting me. I'm
just so scared, Ava, I don't know what to do."

When Ava had started with the support group she was
required to take a class on counseling the abused. It prepared
each person on the leadership team on how to respond to the
women seeking help. The class gave great information and

made perfect sense then, but when given the opportunity to use what she had learned, her mind went blank. All she wanted to do was scream, "Run, Kim, Run".

"Kim, I know you're scared. You need to get out of your house. It's not safe to be around him."

"I can't. If I leave him he will hurt Tessa."

Tears pricked her eyes just thinking about sweet little Tessa sitting in her butterfly bedroom while her mom cried downstairs in pain after being hit. No child deserved that life.

"Kim, there are people we can talk to that will make sure that never happens. You have to trust me. The best thing for Tessa is to get her away from him."

After no response, Ava couldn't be sure if her words were getting through. Fear kept Kim a prisoner from the truth and fear would keep her paralyzed from running.

"I know you're right. I just need some time to think about it. Please don't call me, I'll call you." Kim paused and then gasped, "I have to go!"

The line went dead.

Ava hung up the phone and sat on her bed with her face buried in her hands, crying out to God for Kim and Tessa.

※※ ※※

*K*im covered her mouth with her hand, trying to suppress her ragged breathing. Maybe she just imagined the footsteps on the second floor above her. When she slipped from the bed to sneak downstairs and call Ava, Ray was sound asleep, snoring even.

It was a moment of pure insanity on her part. She had tossed and turned throughout the night, debating what to do. Finally, pretending to need to use the bathroom, she escaped down the stairs and hid in the darkened room. As she spoke with Ava, she realized she had just opened Pandora's

Box...and nothing but trouble and danger would emerge.

Ava could do nothing to help her. No one could. She was alone, stuck in her own hell. The only thing that made her life worth living was her sweet Tessa.

Her life felt like a double-edged sword. For Tessa's safety, she needed to leave Ray. Get out of Dodge and never look back. But Ray had once told her if she told anyone about the abuse or left him, he would hurt Tessa.

It was a gamble she wasn't willing to attempt.

As long as she stayed quiet, Tessa would be safe. Those words had become a broken record in her mind, reminding her with each hit that she had no other choice. Keeping Tessa safe was what kept her going and kept her from driving into a tree. Her sweet, angelic, little girl.

Calling Ava had been foolish.

Kim's eyes darted around the dark bathroom as the faint sound of footsteps that started in her bedroom made its way into the hallway and down the stairs.

Ray was awake. How did he hear her? She thought she had been slick as silk in her attempt to make contact with Ava. Her heartbeat pounded against her chest.

How had she allowed her life to get to this point? She thought her life had turned perfect when she met Ray at a mutual friend's party. Her first clue should have been that he and Ray were bar buddies, but who was she to judge? She had gotten pregnant at eighteen by an older man she had no business being with. Sure, he stuck around for awhile, but last year he left one day and never came back, leaving her to support Tessa on a secretary's salary in a house she couldn't afford.

It was a breath of fresh air when she and Ray started dating because he vowed to always support and take care of her. And he did, at first. He would wine and dine her, tell her how beautiful she was, important, one of a kind. For a single twenty-three year old mom, her prince had come to rescue her. After only a few weeks of dating she asked him to move in with her and Tessa.

Enter in the worse mistake of her life.

Perfection surrounded their first couple weeks. Ray had been so good to her and really stepped up to the plate and helped with Tessa. The downfall started slowly, but escalated quickly. Ray's job became more stressful and he often took it out on her. Then he became obsessively jealous, always needing to know where she was and who she was with.

The first time he hit her, he had been drunk and mad at her for going out with her co-workers after hours. He apologized for days afterwards and even cried.

If she could have only seen then what her life was like now. The dominos had started to fall and she couldn't stop them. Now he was hitting her at least once a week, with absolute no remorse.

Last night was her breaking point. What pushed her to finally call Ava. As Ray threw her on the bed and raped her as she begged and pleaded for him to stop, Kim knew she needed help.

However, as the footsteps became more distinct as they closed in, trapping her, she realized the horrible mistake she made. Panic surged through her. How would she get Ray out of her life...and before he someday just finally killed her? At this point, he was capable of anything. At least she was smart and updated her will last week to make sure if anything happened to her, her sister Stephanie would get full custody of Tessa.

The footsteps stopped outside the bathroom. She pushed down a scream.

A hard knock invaded the silence, mocking her that she would never be free. "Kim? Are you in there?" Ray's gruff voice made goose bumps rise on her bruised arms.

With a last second decision, she flushed the toilet and threw her cell phone in the trash, covering it with toilet paper. "Yep, just finishing up."

She washed her hands and opened the door to find Ray glaring at her with his arms crossed at his chest.

"Why didn't you use the upstairs bathroom?"

Her voice quivered. "Oh, I didn't want to wake you or Tessa." She tried to maneuver herself around him, but he kept a hard stance on his position guarding the door.

"I heard you talking."

Kim tried to swallow the lump stuck in her closing throat. She had never been quick with her words and she was a pitiful liar. "No I wasn't."

"Don't lie to me Kim. I heard your voice."

Kim tried once more to get past him, but he pushed her back. She was stuck in more than one way. If he knew she had called Ava, he would do more than hit her, he would hurt Tessa. No matter what she said now, would it even matter?

"I'm sorry Ray that I woke you up. I'm so tired. I must have been talking to myself." She rubbed his bicep, trying to press down the nausea that came with touching him. "Come on, let's go back to bed."

She thought she saw him loosen his shoulders, relax. But he refused to move. His eyebrows furrowed together and she had a sinking suspicion that he did not believe her explanation.

"Kim, you know I hate it when you lie to me." His voice rose with each word. His fist met her left cheek bone with force, knocking her back a few inches. She immediately tasted blood from his knuckle that caught her lower lip with his follow-through.

Better her then Tessa.

Kim closed her eyes and waited for the second blow.

chapter twelve

Only three weeks had passed since Matt and Ava took their trip to Lake Michigan, but it felt like months by the amount of time they spent talking on the phone and in each other's company. Ava couldn't believe the depth their relationship held with only knowing each other a handful of weeks.

In the first week after their decision to continue dating she could tell Matt proceeded with caution. He called her once during the week and again on Friday night just before he took her out to eat and to a movie. The night preceding their date was when Kim had called. Ava struggled to keep her focus on Matt when all she wanted to do entailed running over to Kim's house and pulling her and Tessa out of their nightmare. Matt understood her distance and helped by being a good sounding board.

The next week he became bolder and called her more often. About every other night he would call in the evening just to see how her day went. He didn't talk long, just enough to let her know he cared. That Saturday they spent the entire day together again. Matt took her out for a late breakfast followed by canoeing on one of the lakes just outside the city. He packed a lunch so they were able to spend most of the day at the lake. Afterward they grabbed Chinese take-out and spent the evening at his place watching television and playing games.

The third week he threw all caution to the wind. They had spoken every night and she had even called him twice. One night they stayed up until after midnight talking. It reminded Ava of when she was back in middle school again, only talking to a boy, not a girl. Slowly she gained control of her emotions and letting loose of the fear. As long as she didn't think about the 'what ifs,' everything was fine.

Friday night she went to the gym with Matt and worked out. Ava enjoyed spending time with him and sharing his interests. The view of him working out helped lessen the pain that surged through her muscles. She hadn't lifted weights since high school and her legs burned the next day as a bitter reminder.

Saturday night they had Kyle and Kate over to her place for dinner. She freaked out a little after she realized that she needed to make the meal. She cheated a bit and had Lucy come over and help her prepare the food before everyone arrived. She served lasagna, salad and bread sticks, and Lucy made a cheesecake for her to serve for dessert. At some point she needed to break the news to Matt that he was dating a woman who couldn't cook.

The evening had gone well and the food turned out great. Ava gave all the credit to Lucy for the dessert but saved back the information that she'd also held her hand and directed it through making the main course.

Throughout the evening Matt constantly made sure she knew he noticed her, whether by holding her hand at the table or putting his arm around her when they stood in the kitchen talking. He made her feel priceless and adored.

The weeks went so fast because of her newfound relationship that she couldn't believe that today had already come. It was a bittersweet day - the last day of school. Ava arrived early at her classroom to go over some last minute plans with the other kindergarten teachers. The last day of school remained pointless on the education side of things, but easily the best day of the school year for the kids. The school made it a day of celebration for the kids as a reward for all their hard work throughout the year.

In the morning all the classes went outside and had two massive kickball games going on at once. The older grades played on one side of the field while the younger grades played on the other. All the students looked like they were having fun and thankfully no one got injured.

In the afternoon each grade got a turn to play in the gym. While Ava's class waited their turn they had a party of their own with snacks and games in the classroom. They ended their time with her turning on some lively, kid-friendly music and encouraging everyone to dance. They all did, joyously and without abandon.

Once the day was over and every child made it onto their bus or walked home, Ava headed back to her classroom to work on cleaning and organizing the room for the summer. As she closed one of the storage doors she heard a voice behind her. "Hello there, beautiful."

Ava turned around in complete bliss at the sight of Matt leaning against the door frame with his arms crossed. He looked as if he had been standing there observing for a while. She quickly walked up to him and put her arms around him for the hug she didn't realize she needed until she saw him.

"Hi. This is a good surprise. What are you doing here?"

"I was just driving by and had to see you. How did the last day of school go?"

Ava let go of her hold on him, not happy about the release, but settled with his hand sliding into hers. She tugged him into the room while she explained about the day. "The kids did great and all of the activities we had planned went perfectly."

Watching the kids play kickball was hilarious, especially the sight of their little legs rounding the bases and watching them jump and cheer for their team. Ava could hardly keep in the laughter when they went to kick the ball, missed, and landed on the ground. It was her type of humor that others didn't always appreciate.

"I'm glad you had such a good day. You weren't sad after all?" Matt asked while he rubbed her left shoulder.

Her emotions the last day of school coexisted as a balancing act. She had put so much time and dedication into these kids and would miss them, but the other side of the scale tipped with the anticipation of freedom just around the corner. "I thought I would be sad, but we stayed busy enough that I didn't have time to think about not seeing the kids all summer. I guess I'm looking forward to the break more than I thought."

"Well, how about I take you out tonight in celebration of the start of summer? I was thinking about trying out that new steak place downtown." He raised his eyebrows while giving her his smoldering grin that left her defenseless. Not that she would have refused, but that face would not have given her the option otherwise.

She was in the mood to tease. "A good steak does sound nice, and I suppose I could handle spending the evening with you." He didn't need to know that she had caved so quickly.

"I guess I'll just have to step it up tonight. I didn't realize I'd have to compete with a steak even though it should be in a food group by itself. I'm under a lot of pressure here."

Ava loved how they could banter back and forth. She giggled while he brought her back into a hug. A vibration went off on her hip and jumped back.

Matt quickly grabbed his phone and pushed some buttons. "Ava, I'm sorry, but I have to go. It's an SWAT emergency." He started toward the door and looked over his shoulder. "I have to cancel tonight, but I'll call you later."

Before she even had a chance to answer he dashed out the door. Ava pushed forward through the shock and followed, watching as he turned the corner and ran down the hallway. This was the first time he had been called out for the SWAT team since they had started dating. Fear gripped her heart and caused her to stand there frozen, terrified for his safety.

❧❧❧ ❧❧❧

*M*att raced back to the station with his lights flashing and siren blaring. He hated standing Ava up and leaving her like that, but duty called. He pulled into the parking lot at the same time his partner Derek Brown did and they jogged towards the building together.

"What's with the frown?" Derek asked as they reached the doors.

"Am I that obvious?"

"You look like a child whose candy was taken away from him."

"You are closer to the truth then you realize. I had to break a date with Ava."

Derek laughed. "Well, then I will leave you to pout while I go grab our gear."

When the SWAT team got called they often met first at the station, geared up, and were given a report of the situation. It was time consuming, but they needed to arrive at the scene as a team, fully prepared for the crisis. Showing up without all the information would be unsafe and ineffective.

The team loaded up into the armored truck and headed out to the old warehouse a few blocks south of the station. The department had sent in an undercover cop a few months ago to bring down a teenage drug ring. An exchange went sour this afternoon, leaving the cop and a few other guys at gun point.

Matt pushed his earpiece further in and asked Derek to talk so he could check the sound. "Sheppard to Law Sheep, can you hear me? Over."

Matt laughed. The man didn't have a serious bone in his body. "Loud and clear. Over."

The truck stopped and they filed out the back. The lieutenant gave them their instructions and his team headed into the side of the building. Matt and five other men slipped inside while the rest of the SWAT officers inconspicuously surrounded the building. They needed a surprise attack. It was always intense running into a situation, not sure what they were going to find. The only way of knowing what was happening inside the building came from the microphone strapped to the undercover cop, but fifteen minutes ago the signal went dead. They were going in blind.

Once inside the warehouse, a musty scent encircled them. Matt's shirt clung to his back from the stuffy heat that had no escape. It was an old packaging business that went under a few years back and now sat empty except for some birds that had made it a good home.

Shouts sifted from the second floor and the team took the side stairs up. Their movement flowed swift and identical because of the long hours spent training together. Matt took point once they reached the second floor entry. He tapped Rick and Brad on their backs and pointed up to the third floor, and without question they continued up the stairs. Ben and Mark waited for their signal. Matt pointed to the right and then pointed to Derek to go left with him.

Derek flung the door open and Matt entered the room first with his gun drawn. The team followed, running a sweep of the empty offices. Toward the back of the building there was a large conference room where they could hear the shouting coming from. Matt reported back to the lieutenant that the area was contained and they were in position. The lieutenant gave the green light and they prepared for forceful entry.

Frustration laced his anger to think that just beyond these doors held a bunch of kids barely old enough to drive, yet holding guns. Some probably still had braces on their teeth and struggled with zit-covered faces. Their poor choices had led them to this moment and from here on their lives would never be the same.

Preparing the team to enter proved difficult because these kids would be jumpy and nervous. They were dealing with a bunch of wild cards. Matt gave the signal and the door exploded.

⁂ ⁂

Ava had been unsettled the rest of the afternoon while finishing up her classroom. She didn't want to be at the school but it helped to keep her mind off the thoughts consuming her about the situation Matt was in right now.

She returned home around dinner time, found some leftovers in the fridge that Lucy had brought over, and sat on the couch to eat and catch up on the news. She gasped aloud when the news anchor announced the drug exchange that went bad. At this point all the news could report was that some people were held at gunpoint while the SWAT team surrounded the building. Ava automatically moved closer to the television, as if that would cause her to see the situation better.

"Oh, Lord. Please be with Matt and keep him safe. Give him the wisdom to handle the situation and protect him from those who want to do harm to him and others."

Throughout the next hour the news continued between

the reporter and the anchor who tried to get as many details as they could to the viewers. It wasn't enough for her and she wanted to run down there herself. A little before seven the anchor announced that the drug dealers had surrendered and that no one had been hurt. Ava could see the SWAT team members returning to the truck and the drug dealers being escorted to the police cars. Ava couldn't believe how young the boys looked. What had caused their lives to turn away from innocence?

Distracting herself from the tears that threatened she changed into sweatpants and a T-shirt for bed. Sitting back down on the couch, she tried to watch a baseball game, but her view became blinded by her tears. What was wrong with her? Matt was okay. She needed to grow thicker skin if she was going to survive dating a cop. Frustrated with herself she set off to the kitchen to make some tea.

Leaning back against the counter she glanced around her digs. She loved her apartment. It wasn't much to brag about, but it was her refuge.

The kitchen sported a pale yellow with dark brown trim. The appliances were white and fairly new, not that she did a lot of cooking to justify the need for newness. A small dining room opened up on the side of the kitchen, but she used it more like a breakfast nook. A beautiful oak round table and chairs - a fortuitous garage sale discovery last year - looked just right sitting in the middle of the little room.

The living room was spacious and comfortable, perfect for entertaining. Not that she did a lot of it, but it was nice to have the option.

The walls donned a deep orange and showcased two original paintings by Lucy. A modest entertainment center held a flat screen television, the one splurge she'd made courtesy of this year's tax refund. In the back corner placed a bookshelf and comfy reading chair for her hours of literary comfort.

The bathroom didn't have a lot of extra space, but since it was just her, it did its job. Except for the nuisance of her frequently hitting her elbow on the shower when moving around too quickly.

Her metal tour stopped as her phone rang. She hit her knee lunging for it on the counter.

"Matt!" A small cry escaped her throat. "Are you okay?"

"Yes, I'm fine. Are you okay? You sound like you've been crying."

Was she that obvious? "I'm okay. I was just worried about you." She tried to hold the tears at bay, but it was so good to hear his voice. She sniffled and hoped he didn't hear.

"I'm coming over. I'll be there in a few minutes," he declared.

"Matt, you don't need to..."

"Ava, I'm coming. See you soon."

The kettle on the stove whistled, letting her know the water was ready. She shut off the burner and headed to the bathroom to examine the damage the crying had caused. Her eyes were red around the edges and puffy. She splashed cold water on them and touched her face up with a little foundation and eye shadow. Stepping back, trying to see herself in the mirror, she hit her elbow on the shower. *I will never learn*. Walking back to the kitchen she grabbed two mugs from the cabinet.

While she poured the water Matt knocked on the door. As soon as he entered the room she threw her arms around his neck. He enveloped her with his arms, picking her slightly up off the floor.

He finally spoke while setting her down with a gentle ease and putting his hands on both sides of her face. "Ava, sweetheart, I'm fine. I'm sorry you were worried."

"Please don't apologize. I knew this would happen someday, I'm just not handling it the way I should."

Embarrassment heated her cheeks. What was the right way to handle his job and the danger he put himself in every day?

"Even though you knew, it doesn't mean it wouldn't be hard. I didn't help the situation by leaving you the way I did." He brushed away a piece of hair stuck to her eyelash. "I'm flattered that you care so much."

His words were meant to be supportive, but she stepped back, mortified. "I'm so embarrassed by my reaction."

She turned and walked toward the kitchen, but stopped and turned back to face him, babbling nervously. "Even though I know this was a part of your job, I have no claim to you and no right to be affected this way. All I could think about was you being hurt and it frightened me to my core. We are just dating and I know you like me, but I really don't know what you are thinking. I'm acting foolish. I mean you haven't even kissed me yet and here I spent my evening sobbing over your safety." She turned back toward the kitchen, making herself quiet. She couldn't believe she had just blurted out all those things.

She needed a shovel to dig her hole deeper.

Matt didn't let her get far. He caught her arm and pulled her close to him. He looked at her softly, with tenderness, gradually easing his lips to hers. The kiss started with a gentle touch, as if she was delicate and he didn't want to break her. Ava ran her hands up his arms and then hooked them around his neck. He brought one arm around her lower back and the other behind her head. The passion burned between them and even though the kiss stayed tender, the delicateness he'd expressed earlier turned more intense.

He released her slowly and she wanted to object. "Ava, you can have all the claim to me you want. I have wanted to kiss you since the first day I met you. I would've done that a long time ago, but I didn't want to scare you off."

"Oh Matt, I'm sorry that I make you feel like you're walking on egg shells around me. You deserve someone..."

To silence her he brushed his lips against hers. "Ava, I want *you*. Seeing you worry about me like you have today shows me how much you care and that's all that matters. I'm not going anywhere and I hope you're not either."

Ava shook her head. "No, I'm not going anywhere." She put her arms around his waist and laid her head on his chest listening to the rhythm of his heartbeat. "This is where I want to be."

He kissed the top of her head. "You have no idea how happy I am to hear you say that."

She stepped back to examine him. "Are you sure you're really okay?"

He laughed at her disbelief. "Yes, I've never been better. Not a scratch on me." He put his arms out and turned in a full circle. "Do you need to do a further evaluation?" His crooked smile melted her insides. She wouldn't bite at his offer.

"That's okay. I'll take your word for it." Ava headed into the kitchen to finish what she had started. "I was just making some tea before you came, would you like some?"

"Sure. Is it okay if I check out the Cubs game?"

"Go ahead. It should be on the right channel. I was watching it before you came. They were up by two in the fourth inning."

Matt sat at the end of the couch and Ava snuggled in right next to him with her legs bent at the knees and his arm around her shoulder while they watched the rest of the game. He mentioned halfway through about he couldn't watch a baseball while drinking tea. He got up and grabbed a Coke.

Ava rolled her eyes. He was such a guy.

The Cubs ended up winning, despite looking like they were trying to lose. Ava yelled multiple times at the television out of frustration. Matt just laughed in amusement at her. After the game she laid back on the couch giving her a better view of his face. Her head sat up on the arm rest with a pillow placed on her chest, wrapping her arms around it. She could be content to just watch him the rest of the night. An idea came to mind and she didn't give thought to the consequences before asking.

"Do you have plans on Sunday?"

"Nothing besides going to church. What do you have in mind?" he asked curiously, intrigued by her question.

"Well, Sunday is family night at my parent's house and I was wondering if you'd like to come with me?"

The words were out, the damage was done. There was no turning back.

"I'll warn you up front my family is crazy protective and will probably drill you with questions, so if you'd prefer not to go, I'll understand. Please don't feel like you have to. I mean it might be a little quick to meet my family and..." "Ava," he cut her off at mid-sentence. She had been talking so fast. Did he even understand a word that came out of her mouth? When nervous she talked fast and in large amounts. "I'd love to go. I want to meet your family and I'm not intimidated by a few questions and some interrogation."

"Okay, but it's your funeral if you don't pass." She tried to provoke him but couldn't help but snicker.

"Oh, don't you worry, failure is not an option. I didn't work this hard to get you to be mine and then blow it on meeting the family."

"So I'm yours now, huh? Don't I get a say in that?" She expected him to sweat, but of course he stayed calm and smooth as always.

He leaned over and grabbed her hand, pulling her up to meet his face. "Ava, would you please be my girlfriend?" He softly kissed her cheek and her blood pressure spiked.

"Well, when you put it that way, how can I refuse?"

"Good, now that we have that settled, I wanted to talk to you about something." He sat down his drink. "Seeing that we have stepped into a more physical relationship, I think it would be best if we set a few boundaries. I want to make sure that I respect you at all times and don't create a window to allow myself to lose control."

"Wow, you've thought of everything." His thoughtfulness impressed her. Temptation always stands on the forefront, no matter someone's age.

"I've had some time to think about this and I don't want to screw anything up." He rubbed her hand with his thumb.

He gave her the rundown of what he thought would be best. If they were going to be alone in either of their apartments, kissing needed to be minimal while on the couch and absolutely no lying down. Being alone together in each other's bedroom was never an option. They also set a curfew when alone in each other's apartment. No staying past midnight.

Ava could hear her mother's voice, while she was growing up, as she tried her best to push her midnight curfew later. "Ava, nothing good ever happens after midnight." She couldn't believe she agreed with her now.

Ava mischievous leaned over and kissed his cheek. "Just to make it clear, that's okay, right?"

"Hmm, yep."

She kissed him softly on the lips. "And that's okay?" she asked, smiling.

"I see you're going to make this difficult."

"I do have a playful side."

"I'd call it menacing."

"To each his own."

"I didn't say I didn't like it. Anything else you need to okay?

Ava chortled. "Seriously though, I think it's a good idea

to have boundaries and I will do my best not to tempt." She put her hand up as if she was swearing in at court.

"Good, because what we have is too precious to ruin over stupid hormones." He kissed her cheek and stood up, pulling her with him. "It's getting late, I'd better go. I don't want to break a rule already."

She walked him to the door and hugged him before he left. "Thanks for coming over. I'm glad that you're okay. I promise next time I'll only freak out a little."

"I like you freaking out...it gives me an excuse to come and see you. Sweet dreams."

Ava shut the door and sighed. Of course they would be sweet, because he would be in them.

chapter thirteen

Sunday morning started off dreary and cold. It matched Ava's mood. She had slept horrible because of a bad headache that woke her up in the night. By early morning she finally started to have some relief after her second batch of painkillers. When a dim light peeked through her curtains, she quickly opted out on going to church and decided to stay in bed. Early afternoon she rolled out of bed with her stomach growling, warning she had missed lunch.

Ava went to the mirror to assess the damage and groaned. She looked like she had been in a fight. Even though her headache improved, her reflection didn't help the situation. The mirror revealed dark circles under both eyes that enhanced the red that streaked through the whites of her eyes. Her hair was matted on one side and sticking out in every direction on the other. She also had a bright red mark through her left cheek, announcing the place where her head met the side of the pillow for hours at a time.

Wonderful.

Matt was meeting her family tonight and at this point she looked like she had been run over by a bus. The phone rang. She made her way to the side of the bed, confident who would be on the other end.

"Hello." Her groggy voice betrayed that it was the first

she'd spoken all day.

"Ava, it's Lucy. Mom is making me call. Are you okay? We missed you at church today." She had been tricked. Her mom was getting sly in her older age with making Lucy do her dirty work.

"I'm fine. Sorry to worry you. I had a horrible headache last night and it took until a couple hours ago to get some relief."

"Are you still coming tonight...and bringing Matt?" Lucy asked hopeful. If her family asked one more time if she was still bringing him, she might scream or rebel and not come at all.

"Yes on both. No worries, we'll see you tonight."

"Okay. I can't believe I finally get to meet the infamous Matt. I can't wait. See you later."

Later. Why did she dread that?

❦❦ ❦❦

Ava left to pick up Matt around five o'clock, thankful the swelling around her eyes went down and the red streaks had subsided. Her mood had improved as well and once again she looked forward to tonight. Her nerves had triggered her frustration toward her family for badgering her about whether Matt was coming. She was nervous about him meeting her family and whether they would like him or not. But in the last few hours as she prayed and gave herself a big pep-talk, she realized that they would see all the wonderful things she saw in him.

Ava had never brought anyone home to meet her family except for Tim. Would they be overly protective and drill Matt with questions while her face turned red in the process? Would she be awkward with Matt around her family or uncomfortable about displaying affection with them watching? Tim usually clammed up around her family and became reserved and hardly even held her hand. Matt was a whole new ballgame. Anxiousness surrounded her thoughts about how the night would unfold.

She shook off her fears and looked over her outfit once more while driving. Not the smartest idea in evening traffic. She was such a girl, placing fashion over safety. She took a deep breath while approaching Matt's apartment building and pulled into the parking lot.

He was sitting outside on his porch steps, talking on his cell phone. He looked up and smiled while nodding his head. Just seeing him calmed her nerves. She had nothing to worry about. He finished his call, jumped up and walked to the passenger side door. He slid into the seat and leaned over, kissing her on the cheek.

He looked striking in his dark maroon sweater and jeans. "You look great," was all she could muster. Great? What a pathetic adjective for the sight her eyes were beholding.

"I did until I sat next to you."

Ava blushed and then impulsively leaned over and kissed him. It didn't last long, but her pulse quickened as her heart thudded against her chest.

When they pulled apart Matt sighed. "Wow, if that's how you're going to react to compliments, I have a few more I could add."

She put the car in reverse and started backing up. "I think I'll save the rest for later." Two could play at this flirting game.

The drive to her parent's house was full of conversation about their weekend and what they did in each other's absence. Matt had to work Friday and Saturday so they hadn't seen much of each other for a couple days. When they turned onto her parent's street, an unsettling thought popped into her head and she needed to face the inevitable.

"Matt, I can't cook."

"What?" His eyes squinted in confusion.

"I know my brothers and they'll go out of their way to embarrass me. I've been meaning to tell you for a while, so before they can tell you my deep dark secret, I thought I'd better reveal it myself." She barely let up for a breath as she talked fast again. The habit seemed unbreakable.

"First, if that's your deep dark secret, I'm impressed. Second, you made dinner for us that night when Kyle and Kate came over and it was really good." He still looked confused as she pulled into her parent's driveway and parked.

"Matt, I have another confession. Lucy came over that night and helped me make it. I mean I *can* cook, but only if I'm using 'Cooking for Dummies' or the recipe has four ingredients or less. I mean, you are looking at a woman that could burn soup." Heat raised from her neck and gathered in her cheeks. She hoped he didn't notice.

"You don't have to be Her nerves had triggered her frustration toward her family for badgering her about whether Matt was coming embarrassed, Ava," he said while brushing his finger along her cheek. "I don't care that you don't like to cook. I'll be in charge of making meals and we'll just put you on clean-up duty. I loathe washing dishes."

Looking up her smile faded when she noticed her family watching them through the family room window. "It looks like our audience is ready to meet you," she said, pointing at their gawkers. "We better go in before they come out."

By the time they entered the house everyone had scattered. Lucy and her mom's voices trickled in from the kitchen and her brothers sat in the living room watching a basketball playoff game on television. Her dad met them at the door and the introductions started. After shaking Matt's hand he invited her to help the ladies in the kitchen while the guys entertained Matt. Ava would've rather sat down

with them to watch the game but knew she should go help...
or stand around helpless until someone told her what to do.
She waved at the guys.

"Wow, does that shirt come with batteries, Ava?" Jake
teased.

She looked down at her bright green shirt and smiled.
"What? You don't like it?"

"It's giving me a headache."

"You have no eye for fashion."

"And now no sight."

She ran over and jumped on him, faking a wrestling move.
Her family was known for teasing, practical jokes and med-
dling in each other's lives...it was best that Matt saw them for
what they were.

Tonight, instead of ordering pizza as planned, Lucy offered to make it homemade. She made the dough while Ava
and her mom prepared the toppings. While the pizza cooked
they watched the game with the boys. The Chicago Bulls
were ahead by ten points, which made the mood in the room
good. At her mom's request they ate in the dining room.
Lucy served a Mediterranean salad and bread sticks with the
pizza.

"Wow, Lucy, this is really good," Josh complimented.

"Thanks, it's my own creation," she said proudly.

"You should write your own cookbook," their mom
added. "You're always coming up with your own recipes, I'm
sure you have quite a few by now. I know some people who
could help." Because their mom was a children's book author she had connections with some editors and publishing
companies.

"I've actually been thinking about it. I'll let you know
what I decide. It would be a huge project, but I think I'm
ready for something new." Lucy embraced her role as the free
spirit in the family. It didn't surprise anyone that she was

ready for a new challenge in her life.

Ava and Lucy came as opposite as you could get, but their bond held strong. Sharing a room while growing up gave them the chance to grow together instead of apart, despite their differences.

Lucy was always the life of the party and full of energy. She never allowed herself to get bored and poured her talents into cooking and painting. Her short, dark, pixie-styled hair matched her spunky personality. She was carefree and independent, ready to face whatever life threw at her.

Ava's dad spoke up, changing the focus to Matt. "Ava tells us you're on the SWAT team. We saw on the news this week that the team was called out. Are you allowed to talk about it?"

Her dad's question came as a slap in the face. Ava had been so worried about him when he came to her apartment, she didn't even think about asking him what really happened. If she hadn't been so preoccupied with looking for bullet holes she might've thought to ask him what actually happened in the building.

"Yes. I'm sure you saw that there was a drug exchange that went bad. I'm part of the unit that works inside the building and assesses the situation. If the circumstances are a setting that my unit can handle, we go in and take care of the problem. If it's beyond what we can do or if it's too dangerous for our inside unit, we call in backup and penetrate together."

"Oh, my goodness, so what happened?" Her mother asked sweetly. She was a mother above all else, whether it was her child or not. It must be that inner instinct.

Matt reached over and took Ava's hand under the table. Either he wanted the affection or he thought she needed moral support for what he was going to say.

"Well, we felt the problem was more of hothead teenagers riding on power than intending to use their weapons on each other. We burst in and before we got halfway to the group, the guns were on the floor along with themselves." He looked over at Ava. "It was nothing, really."

Nothing. His definition of nothing and her definition of nothing were quite different.

Her family packed in a few more questions about his job and Jake quite strategically moved the conversation to personal questions. His skills as an investigative reporter shined as he threaded his questions throughout Matt's responses to get the answers he was satisfied with. As a whole, their inquiry into Matt's life came across tasteful and Matt held his own but by the time the questions tapered off she was surprised they hadn't asked his shoe size and if he could get his dental records.

Her family seemed happy for her and their excitement showed despite all the questions. She continued to be blessed by her family's supportive streak. Overbearing and in her face at times, but they did it out of love. Their encouragement helped settle her nerves about stepping into the dating world again.

Finally they cleared the table and headed for the kitchen.

"Hey Matt, you want to come out with us men and shoot some hoops?" Josh asked as he placed his dirty dishes into the sink.

Matt glanced over at Ava for the okay. "Sure, I'll do about anything to get out of washing dishes." He looked down at his dress shoes. "I'll either use the shoes as an excuse if I lose or a huge asset when I rub it in your face that I won." The guys all laughed as they headed out back to the court. Without needing words, Ava could tell the votes were in and Matt had passed with flying colors.

After the kitchen had been cleaned up and the boys had finished their macho basketball game they settled in the living room. Lucy walked into the room with spoons in her hands.

"Anyone interested in a game of Spoons?"

Matt passed, claiming this was a sight he needed to see. He sat on the couch with her parents while the four of them got on the floor in a circle. Williams's family night tradition came with dinner and games. "Spoons" had been a childhood favorite. They put the spoons in the middle, pulled out the cards, and the madness began. Everyone held an extremely competitive side, so no one would go out easily.

Lucy was out first and Josh followed her in the next round. Jake and Ava were left for the last round. It was for all the marbles and bragging rights. Their hands flew through the cards. They both grabbed at the last spoon together. Her brother was stronger, but she had more spunk. Before she could stop it they were wrestling on the floor, with everyone laughing and cheering expect for her mom, who was warning them about the table in the corner.

Ava held her own until Jake started playing dirty and tickled her. She was a goner and let go immediately. "Cheater," she shouted while laughing and getting up from the floor.

"All right, let's take a break and get some ice cream," her mom interrupted.

"Did you make that, too, Lucy?" Josh teased.

"Very funny, Josh...and I could if I wanted to." Lucy shot back in a mimicking voice and then punched his shoulder. He grabbed his arm, faking that it hurt.

"Hey, you better be nice, one of these days she's really going to whoop up on you," Ava said, joining the friendly banter.

"Oh Ava, are you feeling left out?" Josh came over and put her in a head lock while taking his knuckles and raking the top of her head with them. She detested when he did that. He knew it and savored the enjoyment of irritating her.

"All right, kids," her mom laughed while herding them into the kitchen, "I guess things will never change."

Change. Ava looked over at Matt and he smiled. He came up behind her and placed his hands on her shoulders. Her life was changing, but would it end up for the good? She could only hope and pray.

chapter fourteen

Ava made her way across town toward Kim's house, still in disbelief that Kim had called and asked to talk. It had been so long since she'd called the first time in the middle of the night and this time her tone didn't seem as hopeless.

The last few weeks had been driving Ava crazy, not knowing how Kim was doing. Tessa always seemed fine at school and would answer her questions, but now that school dismissed for the summer, she was clueless on the situation without her little inside scoop.

She reached for her sunglasses and put them on when the sun came out from behind the clouds. Stopping for a red light, she took a breath to calm her nerves.

A few nights ago she and Matt had been talking about Kim. Ava shared her frustrations about not hearing from her again while Matt voiced his concerns about the situation. He had respectfully asked that Ava stay away from the house. She appreciated his desire to protect her. They didn't know how Ray would react if approached and Matt was afraid of what he would do if he found Ava at his house again.

Remorse clogged her thoughts for not following his suggestion, but Kim had asked her to come and she couldn't chance Kim changing her mind if she asked to meet elsewhere. As she approached Kim's neighborhood she turned on her turn signal and merged into the right lane toward her exit. Taking out her cell phone, she dialed Matt's number, hoping to catch him at a good time. It was Monday afternoon and he was working, but usually he answered unless in the middle of something. His voice mail came on immediately. She left a message telling him where she was headed.

Kim's house had changed since the last time she had been here. The yard had been mowed, the broken shutters fixed, and the porch boasted a new coat of paint. Flowers now bordered the sidewalk and Ava recalled Tessa talking about the new flowers.

Kim ushered Ava into the house quickly, being forewarned that they didn't have much time to talk because Ray would be home for dinner in a couple hours.

"Thanks for coming, Ava." Ava wished she had better prepared herself for the unexpected appearance of Kim. She had lost weight and her eyes were sunken in with black circles underneath. Despite the hot temperature outside, she dressed in pants and a turtleneck. Her left hand was wrapped in gauze and her hair was pulled back, exposing a deep purple bruise on her left cheekbone.

Ava reached in and gave Kim a hug. She could sense Kim's resistance at first, but slowly she relaxed and accepted.

"I'm glad you called me. How about I help you make dinner while we talk?" Ava offered. She didn't want Kim to get in trouble if dinner wasn't on the table when Ray got home.

Kim sat at the breakfast table peeling potatoes while Ava chopped vegetables at the counter. "Ray wasn't always like this, you know," Kim began. "He used to be such a gentleman, but once he moved in everything changed."

"Tell me about it." Ava didn't want to say much. This meeting was for Kim to talk and get things off her chest.

"Once he moved in he became controlling and always

117

needed to know what I was doing and who I was with. At first he started hitting me because of his bad days at work but then later on he also did it because I didn't do something his way or I voiced my opinion. Last week I accidently burnt his eggs so he burnt my hand." Kim lifted her wrapped hand to show Ava. Her eyes spoke of the pain that had been inflicted upon her.

Ava swallowed the lump in her throat. "I'm so sorry, Kim." Her words didn't do justice to the deep sadness she had for Kim.

Silence lingered for a moment. "Did you know I had to quit my job?"

"No."

"Ray made me."

"Why?"

She pulled up the sleeves on her shirt to expose the bruises that covered her arms. "People were starting to notice. I've also had to switch doctors a few times to make sure no one would catch on."

Ava fought against the tears threatening to show. Kim needed her strength, not her pity. In a sad way, it all began to make sense. Without a job, Kim would feel she had no other choice but to stay with Ray. Without an income, she wouldn't be able to provide for Tessa and the fear of losing her probably outweighed the fear of Ray.

She shifted her piles of vegetables and grabbed the carrots and began slicing. "Why didn't you talk to someone earlier?" Her question held no judgment, just seeking understanding.

"I didn't know who to talk to. I have no family here and I've lost all my friendships since I've started dating Ray. My life is so out of control right now, Ava. I don't know what to do!"

Sobs erupted from Kim's chest and filled the room. Ava stopped cutting the carrots, grabbed a tissue from the top of the desk, and placed it in Kim's hand. Kneeling beside her she placed her hand lightly on Kim's arm, making sure not to put too much pressure on the bruises that hid underneath her cotton shirt.

"Kim, I know you're scared and in fear for Tessa's safety, but you have to get Ray out of your life. I can help you, but only if you are willing." It was the hard truth. If Kim didn't jump on board, all her efforts would be meaningless.

"I just feel so alone." She wiped away the new tears that stained her face.

"You're not alone, Kim. I'm here whenever you need me and most importantly, God is with you. He knows your hopes, fears and your insecurities. He made you and knows the number of hairs on your head. With God's help you can do this." She didn't plan on preaching, but couldn't pass up the opportunity to share God's love. Human efforts could only go so far. The only way Kim would truly feel free would be with God's help.

Kim didn't object to her sharing about God. Ava took it as a sign to keep rolling with it and encourage her to attend the support group at her church, but the sound of a vehicle pulling into the driveway cut her off. Kim jumped up on her feet and looked out the window. "Oh no," she panicked. "It's Ray! He's home early!"

Ava peered out the window and gasped when she noticed that he had blocked her car in. Ava's stomach churned wildly. She had no way of escape. If she stayed it might help Kim...or make it worse.

"I can leave, Kim." Thinking the scenario through she realized she could always walk down the block and have someone come pick her up. However, Ray would still know she had been here because of her car. She wasn't sure what would be in the best interest of Kim and there wasn't a lot of time to come up with a well thought-out plan.

"No, it's too late. Go up to Tessa's room, it's the first door on the right. She should be in there looking at books. Hurry Ava. Run! And lock the door behind you!"

Without arguing Ava turned and ran to the stairs. In her haste she tripped on the second step and didn't get her hands out in time to brace her fall. She smacked the right side of her face hard on the stairs. As she scrambled up the rest of the steps she put her fingertips to her nose for pressure to stop the bleeding from the impact. Her right eye throbbed and made her sight blurry.

She entered Tessa's room bubbly in hopes she wouldn't frighten the little girl. "Hi, Tessa!" she exclaimed cheerfully.

Tessa looked up from the book that had been grabbing her attention and her eyes grew big. "Hi, Miss Williams, what happened?"

Ava shut the door behind her and locked it. Looking down at her shirt, she cringed. She had blood stains all over the front of her shirt. She was going to have to step up the bubbly.

"I was coming up to see your beautiful butterfly room and I fell on the steps." She scanned the room, "Wow, your room looks great." She hoped her diversion worked. She found a tissue box, thankful for something other than her hands and shirt to stop the blood.

"Thanks. Wanna see my butterfly book?"

"Absolutely."

It didn't take long for the yelling to start downstairs. Tessa kept right on telling her about each butterfly as if nothing was happening. Ava sat in shock.

This was normal.

Ava couldn't hear what they were saying. The words were muffled, but intense. Finally Ava couldn't tolerate just hiding up in the room any longer. She couldn't bear to leave Kim defenseless downstairs, even if that was her wish, it was time for Ava to do something.

As Ava stood she heard Kim scream, followed by a loud crash and then an eerie silence. Enough was enough. Ava pulled out her cell phone and dialed 911. Tessa started to cry and Ava put her arm around her while she gave the dispatcher the address and information on the situation.

Heavy footsteps stomped up the steps. "Hurry, please," she pleaded into the phone.

The door knob jiggled followed with a fist pounding on the door. "I know you're in there, Miss Williams! It would be better for you to just open the door."

He swore at her. Tessa screamed while cowering behind Ava. Ray pounded on the door again with more force. Ava jumped up and maneuvered Tessa's dresser in front of the door. She tried to move the bed, but it was too heavy. Wiping the sweat from her hands onto her shorts, she was able to grip the bookshelf easier and push it in front of the dresser.

She quickly moved to the window, unlocking it with haste and pushed up the heavy glass, hoping for an easy escape. Her heart sank with disappointment. It looked to be a good fifteen feet drop to the ground below. She could probably make it, but the distance would be too far for Tessa.

She had done the best she could do. Only God could protect them now. Ava picked Tessa up off the floor and carried her into the little alcove of her closet. Tessa shivered. Ava wrapped her arms tighter around her.

Ray continued to hit the door as the wood started to splinter. Her obstacles wouldn't stop him much longer. In the distance she heard the sirens. Rescue was on the way, but would it be soon enough?

ཞུ༈ ཞུ༈

*M*att listened as dispatch gave the location of the call and asked all units in the area to respond. Matt turned his squad car around in the empty parking lot and raced east out of town while radioing back that he was on his way. He wasn't *exactly* in the area, but nothing would stop him from responding to this call. He knew the address by heart. Ever since Ava confided in him at the playground that evening about Kim, whenever he was in the vicinity he would pass by her house just to check on things. He hadn't mentioned it to Ava yet. She didn't need to know about the depth of his concern for Kim. It would have only worried her more.

He flipped on his lights and siren and maneuvered through traffic. Matt had received Ava's voice mail only an hour ago. Did she have enough time to talk to Kim? Had she already left? The pit of his stomach churned with the reality he feared would be true...she was still there.

When he arrived, Kim's house was surrounded with three squad cars and an ambulance. A disgruntled man he assumed to be Ray was being escorted out of the house in handcuffs. Matt parked the car and jogged up to the house. All hope diminished when he spotted Ava's car blocked in the driveway. His heart shot up into his throat at the sight through the open front door of the house. Someone was lying on the floor being prepared for loading onto a gurney. Not sure how he would handle it if that person was Ava, he leapt onto the porch and peered over the EMT's shoulders to see a woman he didn't recognize.

Relief washed over him. *Thank you, God.*

Thankfully Kim appeared coherent and her condition didn't look life-threatening. Matt surveyed the house. The dining room table sat sideways and the chairs were scattered near where she laid. He poked his head into the kitchen. Vegetables sat on the counter and peeled potatoes scattered around the room.

Where was Ava? He headed upstairs when he noticed an officer at the door at the top of the stairs. "This is the Rockford Police Department. You're safe now," he heard the uniformed policeman say to the door.

Matt skipped a few steps and reached the top in seconds. "Who's in there?"

"We don't know for sure and the door is locked. The lady downstairs kept crying out for her daughter, Tessa. We're assuming she's in here," the officer replied. Matt had seen him around the station before but didn't know him well.

"May I?" he asked, not wanting to overstep, but if Ava was in the room she would respond better to his voice than a stranger's. The officer nodded his approval and stepped out of the way.

"Tessa, my name is Sergeant Matt Thompson and I'm here to help you. Can you open the door, please?" He hoped the silence didn't mean that something was wrong.

"Matt." His knotted muscles loosened with the sound of Ava's voice.

"Ava, can you open the door?"

"Yes."

Scuffling noises started inside the room and the sound of her grunting as if furniture was being pushed around. Finally the door jiggled and opened. He rushed in and swept her up in his arms. Matt ignored the dried blood on her face for the time being only because she seemed okay. He held her and stroked her hair while she cried softly. Pulling her back, he caressed her face. "Are you okay?"

"Yes."

"Why is there blood all over you? Did he hit you?" His resentment toward Ray brewed.

"No. My battle wounds are between me and the steps. I tripped while running up the stairs. I'm fine."

"Have you looked in a mirror?"

"Is it that bad?"

"I still think you're beautiful."

"You don't count. Your opinion is biased." She stepped close to him again and wrapped her arms around him. "I'm so glad you're here." Her words were muffled against his chest.

He kissed the top of her head. "Do you want to talk about it?"

"Not yet."

"Okay."

"How's Kim?"

"On her way to the hospital, but that's all I know." Her face tensed from his answer. Together they looked back toward the closet where the other officer was helping Tessa out. Her big brown eyes glistened from the tears. No child should ever have to deal with this kind of fear.

"What happens with Tessa now?"

"She can go to the hospital with us. I don't think Kim's injuries will keep her there more than a night, if that. Tessa can just stay with us there. It would do her good to be with her mom right now." The poor girl just needed the comfort and presence of her mom. They would have to call CPS, but Matt decided to drop that bomb on Ava later. Chances were good that nothing would become of it and Tessa would be able to stay with Kim, but they had to follow protocol.

"Is this the end? Will Ray be out of their lives now?" Ava looked up at him with such hope and he struggled with the lack of response he could give.

"That's up to Kim." Another officer entered the room and interrupted their conversation.

"We're wrapping it up downstairs. We'd like to take your

124

statement now." He looked over at Ava and she frowned.

Matt stepped in, trying to make both sides happy. "Why don't we all head to the hospital now, get Ava checked out and cleaned up, and then we can get her statement?" An hour's delay on her statement wasn't going to affect her memory. It would be etched in her mind for quite awhile.

"Sounds good, I'll meet you over at the hospital," the officer agreed and walked back downstairs.

Matt looked over at Tessa who sat on her bed with her arms crossed over her little chest. "Ava, why don't you help Tessa pack a few things for the hospital? On the way we'll stop at your apartment and get you a change of clothes."

"Okay." She agreed and his heart squeezed when her voice quivered.

"I'll see you downstairs." He turned to walk away but she grabbed hold of his hand. He smiled and squeezed it. "I won't be far."

She smiled back and reluctantly released his hand. He wanted to lean in and kiss her, but it wouldn't be appropriate. While on the job he needed to separate his emotions.

Matt reached the bottom of the stairs and felt like he truly exhaled for the first time since hearing the dispatcher's call for help. He walked around the house again, trying to get a feel for what had happened this afternoon. He found one of the officers outside and asked for a briefing. He wanted to be prepared before Ava gave her statement later. By the sound of things, it was going to be a long night.

chapter fifteen

*T*he summer raced along quicker than Ava had anticipated and she couldn't believe that it had reached mid-July already. She and Matt had been spending more and more time together and their relationship had deepened. She knew where her heart stood...and it simply terrified her.

Over the last couple weeks since Kim had been released from the hospital they had spent many hours helping her to get back on her feet again. Ray was still in jail but would be released soon. Kim remained steadfast on her promise to not let him return to her house, but only time would tell. She had started attending the abuse support group and yesterday marked her first counseling session. Watching Kim make an effort to turn her life around gave Ava hope that this situation could turn out successful.

Ava's bruise had faded quickly and the only sign from the horrible afternoon she experienced came from a pasty yellow tint covering her right cheekbone. Last weekend she joined Matt at the department's annual barbecue cookout for the officers and their families. Ava enjoyed meeting everyone that Matt worked with but couldn't help notice how much they knew about her. He talked about her with his friends... a lot. What did that mean? She spent most of the evening watching Matt and Derek in their prime with their one-liners and common interests. She could see why they were so close.

Earlier in the week she had mentioned to Matt that she wanted to paint her spare room. Yesterday morning he showed up in painting clothes with roller and brushes in hand. They went to the store and picked out a tan color and got to work. It was nice to have his company, and the fact that he could move the heavy furniture without grunting or breaking a sweat was an added bonus. They were able to get the room all done in one day and their exhaustion showed. This morning Lucy came over and helped her rearrange the room to look more organized instead of looking like the room just threw up furniture.

Tonight Matt had planned an entire evening for her and kept her clueless as to what he had in store. He had not staged a surprise date in a while. She was taken off guard when he mentioned it yesterday while painting. Matt said to dress comfortable and to come with an appetite. He left a map with her and said to meet him at the place marked at seven o'clock. Ava dressed in a purple tank top, jean Capri's and flip-flops. She left her hair down because she could tell he liked it best that way.

Matt's directions led her to a fishing lake north of town. Ava had never been to this area before. The lake did not have the popular appeal because the surrounding land was mostly wooded and privately owned. She found the path on the map that he indicated that she should take. As she trudged up a little hill a metal sign hung between rusted chains that connected to wooden posts that read "No Trespassing." Underneath the sign a piece of paper with handwritten marker stated, "Except for Ava."

She laughed.

The directions said to take the path until it curved and there she would see a small clearing on the right. The walk lasted longer than she thought it would be, but enjoyed the peaceful surroundings, despite a few attacks from mosquitoes.

As she picked up her pace she passed a small sand beach to the left that went into the lake. The water sparkled from the sun as the tiny waves lapped against sand. She stopped a moment to appreciate the quaint area, she could picture little kids making sand castles and running into the water.

Looking up the trail the clearing came into view. When she reached the grass knoll, she gazed over and held her breath. Matt stood at the top of the small hill, holding a red rose in his hand. On the ground he had a blanket spread out with a picnic basket in one corner. He had tiki torches lit all around the area and soothing music playing from his iPod.

"Matt..." she quietly gasped.

"Hi." His voice was thick, drenched in emotion. He came toward her and took her hand, leading her back up to the blanket. "Happy half birthday."

"What?" Ava looked down to see a small birthday cake and wrapped presents off to the side.

He helped her sit down. "You said that you liked your birthday on Christmas Eve but sometimes felt overlooked and wished when you were a kid that you could have had it in the summer. So, today we are celebrating your half birthday. And trust me, you will not be overlooked."

"Oh Matt, what did I ever do to deserve you? I don't even know what to say, it's so thoughtful and perfect. Thank you!" She put her arms around his neck and just held him, silently thanking God for him. She instinctively knew that whatever was inside those boxes, they would be the best gifts she would ever be given.

Reluctantly she released him, not sure what more to say. She was relieved when he started first. "So what do you want to do first? We can eat or you could open your gifts," he said while wiping away a tear that had exposed itself down the side of her face.

"Well, I can always eat."

"You're in luck because I had this amazing chef make us dinner tonight." He smiled while opening up the picnic basket.

"Lucy was in on your plan?"

"Yeah, I told her what I had planned and she insisted on making the food. She has become quite the asset when it comes to you."

I've noticed." She grabbed the plates and utensils from him and began to lay them out.

He pulled away, but Ava put her hand behind his head and drew him back. He dropped the Tupperware he held in his hand and brought her up to sit on his lap. The kiss was innocent, but not lacking in desire. She cupped his face with her hands while he had one arm around her waist, stroking her hair with his free hand.

Out of pure force, Ava pulled back. They sat still, their eyes locked on each other and she thought her heart would burst. She'd been burying these feeling for some time and all her security would be blown apart if she shared them with him.

Ava's nerves exploded when she identified her deep feelings reflected back in his eyes. Breaking their stare, she moved back to her spot on the blanket. "So what do we have to eat?"

He looked at her with concern for a split second, but let the abruptness pass. He pulled out a bag that kept the food warm and out came grilled chicken with a salsa mix on top, sliced baked potatoes, asparagus and garlic bread.

While they ate, Matt explained to her about how he had a friend of the family who owned this spot and that is why he was able to have the picnic there. After dinner they had cake and finished off with her opening her gifts.

The first was a CD she wanted. Next she opened the exact purse she had been saving up for. "How did you know I wanted this?" she asked in disbelief. He even had it right down to the color.

"I called Jules last week to ask her if there was something you mentioned that you wanted. She said that when you two were out shopping earlier you showed her this purse. She went to the store and picked it out for me and dropped it off at my apartment the other day."

"You are very sneaky and quite resourceful."

"It comes with the job."

"I guess I should never underestimate you."

"Now you're learning."

He handed her the last gift. A small black velvet box. Her stomach began to bubble up in her throat. She opened the box slowly. The open lid revealed two diamond earrings shining back at her.

"Oh Matt, they're beautiful."

They must have cost him a fortune. Ava put them on, glad she had forgotten to put on any earrings when getting ready and pulled her hair back a bit so he could see them. "How do they look?"

"I can't really concentrate on them next to your face." Matt leaned over and kissed her cheek. He took her hand and kissed the top. His hands held a slight tremor. It was strange for her to see him so obviously unsettled.

He looked toward the lake, watching the sun creep towards the tops of the trees. Looking back at her, he stroked her face with a shaking thumb. "I love you, Ava," he whispered softly.

Those should have been the best three words she'd ever heard, but instead she panicked. It was the bomb she knew was coming, but it still caused damage. Under duress she removed his hand and stood. "I um...I..." Her voice thickened. "I..." She turned and started walking away.

Ava's heart screamed to turn back around and declare her love, but her head shouted louder, yelling "Run!" So she did. She ran, despite her blurred vision from the tears, down to the little beach she'd seen earlier.

What was wrong with her? She loved Matt. Reaching the water's edge, she wrapped her arms around her waist and let the tears of fear flow.

જ્રેણ જ્રેણ

*M*att stayed seated while she ran away. she needed space and he would give it to her. He anticipated it would be hard for her to hear those words, but he had not expected this. He thought for sure she felt the same way, but maybe he assumed wrong.

He cleaned up their dinner and finally made his way down the path where she had headed. He found her standing at the beach, looking out over the water. He paused briefly, not sure he was ready for the answer his question would bring. "Ava, what's wrong?"

She glanced back at him and turned away again, but she didn't ask him to leave. He took that as a good sign and sauntered to her side.

Her words came out in a burst. "I know you think you love me now, but what if that changes? What if you start to have feelings for someone else? What if you realize I'm not who you're supposed to be with? What if ..."

"Ava," he said, interrupting her. "I'm *not* Tim. I know that you had such a horrible experience with him and for that I am truly sorry, but *I am not Tim*. The past is the past and there is nothing we can do to change it."

He had never spoken with such frustration toward her. It made him mad to be compared to another man, and especially to Tim.

He paced back and forth to blow off steam before positioning himself to stand in front of her. "You and me," he took his finger and pointed back and forth between them, "that is what matters. This is now".

"It's easy to say that now, Matt."

"Why?"

"Because our relationship is new and exciting."

"Compared to old and comfortable?"

"Don't make fun."

"I'm not." He ran his fingers through his hair, not sure where to go from here. "I'm not saying that I'll never hurt or disappoint you, because I'm only human. I *will* fail you, Ava. As for the future, I *don't* know what it holds. I know what I want it to be, but for now, I only know that I love you."

She looked down and moved the sand around with her foot. Her silence was killing him. "I'm scared," she finally whispered.

He exhaled, keeping his frustration in check. "I know. If you're upset because you're afraid then you need to hear and understand that I'm not going anywhere. You have to trust that God, not me, will take care of your heart. However, if you're upset because you don't have the same feelings in return, than please just put me out of my misery."

He turned and walked down the beach a few steps, keeping his back to her and rubbing his forehead with his fingers. He needed to breathe and remember that Ava was still weighted down from the bondage of her past, but it didn't take away his feelings of weakness, doubt and potential rejection.

Matt didn't know what else to do but pray. This relationship wasn't going to work on Matt's efforts alone. Ava needed to trust God before she would ever be able to trust him. It would be a process and she would surely stumble along the way, but was she ready? Was he pushing her too soon?

Her arms slid around him from behind as she laid her head on his back. They stood motionless surrounded by a chorus of grasshoppers until she kissed the back of his neck and walked around to face him.

"Matt, I'm sorry I took a beautiful moment and ruined it. Everything you just said to me was true and I'm sorry that I allowed my past to affect what we have right now."

She touched the side of his face. "I panicked because my feelings for you are so real and intense, but you're right, I don't need to be afraid. I know there will be times that I'll struggle and be tempted to let those negative thoughts in, but I'm hoping that you'll still be there right beside me, encouraging me along the way."

She flashed him her puppy dog eyes and he couldn't resist. He pulled her into his arms. "Ava, of course I'll stand alongside you. All I've ever wanted is for you to want me."

"I love you, Matthew."

He closed his eyes in relief and then opened them, smiling. "I've waited so long to hear you say that."

"Can you humor me and say it again to me? I want to really enjoy it this time."

He grabbed her around the waist and lifted her off her feet so they were eye level. "I love you." Then he kissed her like it was the first time their lips had met.

chapter sixteen

Ava walked along the eight foot table, doing a mental check list that every detail had been set for the abuse support group meeting. The aroma of spaghetti and garlic bread made her stomach rumble. The group had their meetings once a month at the church and a few women from the congregation volunteered to bring in dinner for everyone. They all had different gifts. Whether they spoke to the group, watched the kids, counseled, or brought in food, each service held importance.

Tonight's meeting had been sparked by an idea Ava had at the last planning session. As ideas bounced around the room, Ava voiced that it would be useful for the women if they attended a meeting that touched on the side of the law enforcement. Most women in the group had already made steps to hold their abusers responsible for their actions. However, the women had started to invite other women that were caught in ruts and hadn't yet broken free from their abusers. They needed support and encouragement as they teetered on the fence on what to do.

Ava's idea came to a unanimous vote of yes, and she had the resources to make it happen. Tonight Matt and a fellow officer were coming to talk to the group. They wanted to encourage the women that the law was on their side by showing that they cared about their safety and wanted to help. To share what steps were needed to take when pressing charges and how to file for a restraining order.

Her heart melted as she remembered the conversation she and Matt had earlier in the week about which points needed to be highlighted and stressed. He wanted the women that came tonight to be as comfortable as possible.

Matt came up with the suggestion that he should bring a female officer with him, that it might help break the ice. That maybe the women in the group would respond better and feel more comfortable with a fellow woman in the room. He also proposed that he come in civilian clothes and not drive his squad car. It might make some of the woman nervous to see him in uniform and the squad car parked outside the church.

Just one more reason why she loved him. Wow. She loved him. Ava was still trying to get used to that fact. She caught herself smiling at the thought of him. Checking the wall clock, she scolded herself for not staying on course as she noticed that the group would be trickling in soon. Making her way toward the lobby to welcome the women, she met up with Matt and the fellow officer.

Ava wished she could run up to him and hug him like she wanted to, but they both agreed it would be best to keep all public affection at bay. "Ava, this is Officer Linda Caldwell. Linda, this is Ava." The women shook hands.

"Hi Linda. Thank you so much for coming." Ava stood next to Matt while their arms brushed. It would have to make due.

"Once Matt told me about your group and what you wanted to be shared, he couldn't keep me away. I think this is great. These women need all the help and support they can get."

"Yes they do. If you follow me I can show you into the

135

room where the meeting will be held."

"Could you show me to the restroom first?" Linda asked.

"Oh sure." Ava pointed toward the hallway. "Three doors down on your left."

Ava turned back toward Matt, silently praying for the women that would be walking through the doors any minute. Praying that lives would be changed, revelations would be made, and the Lord would be seen. One thing was for sure, all of this put her past and present into perspective. These women were trying to get away from horrible men while Ava had been pushing away the best thing that had ever happened to her.

Matt's voice broke into her thoughts. "What are you thinking about? You look a million miles away."

"Just praying. My heart breaks for these women."

"God can do great things in their lives. He can make beauty come from ashes."

The entrance doors opened exposing the newly arrived guests while Linda returned from the bathroom. Matt motioned for Linda to follow him. "We can head into the room and get set up while you are greeting. Over in the fellowship room, right?"

"Yes. I'll meet you there."

Once Ava felt confident that everyone had arrived she made her way into the fellowship room, shocked to see all the tables full. It was great to see the old and new visitors mixed together. Kim and Tessa shared the table with Matt and Linda. Ava was glad that Kim made good on her promise to come. Plus, it was nice to see Tessa. She had been missing her so much since school had been out.

Ava filled her plate and made her way over to the table and sat down next to Tessa. After dinner Ava corralled all the kids and took them to the room they had set up for them while the meeting took place. This was Ava's department, her way to give to the group. She and a few volunteers watched the kids to allow the mother's the freedom to attend the meeting without any distractions.

She did no counseling with the kids. She would leave that up to the professionals. Her job was merely to spend time and play with the kids. If something came to her attention that needed addressed she would pass it along to the pastor.

She counted fifteen kids total. The age range spread out from toddlers to pre-teen, which made the activities hard to plan for the evening. They set up the room to have one side for the younger kids and the other side for the older. A television had been placed in the corner with a Wii set up and ready to be played. Someone in the church had donated it to the youth group and they kindly offered for the kids to use it during the meeting.

Ava laughed over the excitement the older boys had over it. Most of them would never be able to afford to get one. At least they would have a place to come and play one.

The evening progressed without a glitch until one boy became angry when he didn't get his turn. Ava had been playing with a few toddlers on the floor and didn't make it to over to the boys in time before a wrestling match broke out with fists flying.

Ava rushed over trying to pull the boys apart while dodging any hits that lost their aim in the scuffle. The teenage girls who'd volunteered to help with the kids looked shocked, standing off to the side, mute with wide eyes. Having no other choice but to get help, she turned toward the girls, "Brittany, go get Pastor Rick!" The teenage girl turned and exited out into the hallway while the other girl went to console the younger children that got upset over the fight taking place.

Ava pried the boy on top off first and held him back while the other boy stood up, wiping the blood off the corner of his mouth.

Despite being flustered, Ava was able to keep her voice calm as she said, "Boys, this is not how you handle your anger. Hitting is not acceptable."

The older elementary boy glared at her. "You can't tell me what to do."

"Maybe not, but I can remind you that we have rules here and expect you obey them."

The younger boy that stood behind her crossed his arms. "Hitting is what you do to get people to listen to you."

Ava let out a long sigh, realizing the challenge she stood up against and one she didn't feel confident to handle. These boys had probably seen things she could never fathom. Sadness weighed on her heart to see their home life magnified through what just happened. Just more proof that if there wasn't a stop to it now, the chances grew that they would grow up abusing others around them. The sins of the parents could easily fall from one generation to the next, an evil cycle that held no end in sight.

The pastor walked into the room with Brittany at his heels. "Ava, how can I help?"

"Sorry to bother you, Pastor Rick, we had a situation, but it seems to be under control now."

Pastor Rick looked between the two boys and understood the underlining of her concern between the cut lip on one and the darkening black eye on the other. "I see. Well boys, it looks as if your faces need to be looked at. Why don't you come with me and I'll see if I can get you cleaned up."

Remorse filled the boys' faces as they followed the pastor. Ava was certain the situation would be handled. Pastor Rick had a skill of meeting people where they were and getting to the root of the problem. Ava had a few counseling sessions with him after Tim dumped her. She had firsthand experience of how he cared and wanted to help people.

138

Half an hour after the boys left, the meeting finished and the mothers came to get their children. Not having a lot of time to talk, she took a quick moment to ask what Kim thought of the meeting as she picked up Tessa. Her response came across positive and she said that she would be back next month. The newfound friends hugged before they departed. Ava played with Tessa's pig-tails as she promised Kim she would call her tomorrow.

Once all the kids had been picked up she headed to the fellowship hall to meet up with Matt and Linda to see how the meeting went. Hopefully it went better than her night. Linda sat at a table, deep in discussion with a woman while Matt kept a quiet stance in the corner, trying to stay out of sight, Ava assumed.

She came to stand beside him. "How did it go?"

"Good. I think Linda is making headway to convince this lady to leave her husband and stay with family until he can get the help he needs." He looked down at her as he crossed his legs at the ankles and slid his hands into his pockets. "I'd ask how your night went, but Pastor Rick gave me a quick run-down."

"Yeah, I could use a little detox."

"How about some ice cream instead?"

"Sold."

chapter seventeen

*L*ove is a strange thing. It can make a normal life feel incredible and take someone from their lowest moment to their highest, and then back again, all in the blink of an eye. Love can make someone a better person or create a monster thriving on acceptance. It can make a person feel vulnerable and strong all at the same time. Love is free and yet full of worth. It can cloud judgment or give wisdom beyond years. Love can capture someone's heart or break it into a million pieces.

Love and freedom were luxuries that Ava hadn't experienced in a long time. She had begun to wonder if the road she had traveled had become so broken that she was doomed to a life entangled in lies and fear. But now she felt like a new woman, allowing herself to start breaking the bondage that weighed her down. Her healing may not be complete yet, but she could breathe in that scent of freedom that pushed up through the cracks.

She was in love.

God had taken her crushed heart and gave her the capacity to not only love again, but to live. For two years she had just been walking through the motions, getting through each day. Now she had been given a second chance at love and living a life in His freedom.

Ava still had her times when panic tried to push its way back in, but she could control the dampening thoughts and rise above them with more ease now. Before, she had held back, afraid to give anything for fear of not getting it back or being rejected in the end. Finally she realized that loving someone was worth the chance of failure. Failure in its essence is not pleasant, but the anticipation of success made life worth living.

Ava had decided her turn had come to do something special for Matt. He always put so much thought into everything he did for her. Her excitement bubbled as she put her plan into action. Whether it would turn out to be a blessing or a curse remained unclear, but she decided to make his favorite foods for dinner. It would either go well or they would have to order takeout at the last minute.

She prepared herself for option number two.

Ava was borrowing her neighbor's grill for the occasion. Mr. Smith was a nice older man who lived two doors down. He kept his grill outside on the back patio and often loaned it out to anyone who asked. Ava, of course, had never asked. He seemed a bit surprised by her request, but covered well as he chuckled while mentioning something about leaving the fire extinguisher by the grill. Just because she had brought the fire department out once when her smoke alarm went off from a tiny fire on the stove, and nobody on her floor let her forget about it.

Ava planned on making steak with grilled potatoes and vegetables. She asked Mr. Smith if he could come out and start the grill for her when she was ready to begin. She wasn't stupid. Maybe naive about what she was getting herself into, but not stupid. She told Matt to come to her apartment at five thirty. Checking her watch, she noted that she still had an hour to get physically and mentally prepared.

The steaks had marinated all day in one of Lucy's original recipes and she had just finished chopping the vegetables and potatoes. Earlier in the day she had been trying to think of something creative to do for Matt. A way show him how much she cared and showcase the improvements she'd made over the last couple weeks. Ava came up with a "Top Ten List" of reasons why she loved him. The reasons fairly flew out of her heart and onto the paper.

~ The Top Ten Reasons Why I Love You ~

The sweet ways you show your love for me.

Your connection with my family and how you take the time to develop a relationship with each of them.

Your humor...I will never tire of laughing with you.

Your passion for your job and how you continually put yourself in danger to keep others safe. I may not like it at times, but it makes you who you are, who you were created to be. For that I'm thankful.

Your smile...it makes me melt every time.

The way you make me feel safe and how I fit perfectly into your arms.

Your friendship...I'm blessed to be in love with my best friend...well, you're tied for first with Jules, but she's tough competition. Hang in there.

No matter where we go, you always make me feel like I'm the most important person in the room.

Your character...you are honest, trustworthy, kind, respectful, thoughtful and desire to live a righteous life dedicated to the Lord.

Your persistence…thank you for not giving up on me.

I love you~

Ava

She folded up the paper and put it in an envelope, placing it next to the movie she had rented for the evening. It was a suspense thriller - a "guy" movie. Matt had mentioned last week that he wanted to see it. She stopped by the video store on her way home from the grocery store this morning to pick it up. What she had planned for the night - dinner and a movie - wasn't exciting, but it fit them. They enjoyed the simple pleasures in life. Last night they just sat on his front stoop and talked while they watched the neighbor kids pedal their bikes back and forth.

The oven timer started to beep at her and for a quick second sat confused as to why she had set it. She leapt off the couch remembering it was her warning to start getting dinner around. Putting everything on a big tray, she walked down to Mr. Smith's door and knocked.

He opened the door, reading glasses perched on his nose and a book in his hand. "Good afternoon, Ava. Are you ready for me to start the grill?"

"I am. Thank you for letting me use it." She stepped aside for him to exit through the doorway. They walked together down the back steps to the patio, chatting about the nice weather.

The patio was a small slab of cement, but a nice asset for the apartment building. The tenants didn't use it very often, but everyone tried to be respectful when it was in use. An adequate-sized yard sat in the back with a couple trees lining the property. A wooden picnic table sat to the side of the patio. Nothing flashy, but at least she had a place to take her shoes off and run her toes through the grass.

Mr. Smith had the grill fired up in no time. He showed her how to use each knob and how to shut it off when she was finished. "Good luck," he called over his shoulder, "and come get me if you have any problems."

"Thank you. Matt should be here soon for back up." No pun intended. Ava looked down at her watch. She had about fifteen minutes to get the food started before he would be here. She had texted him earlier about meeting her out back, but hadn't gotten a response yet. That wasn't like him.

The food was close to being done when she heard the beep on her phone, announcing a new text from Matt. *"Sorry. Running late. I'll be there soon. Love you."* Those last two words still gave her butterflies. She glanced at the time. It was past six.

She looked once more at the food, almost praying over it. She thought she had picked a simple menu, but then she hadn't taken into account if the meat would be dry or tough. If the vegetables and potatoes would get cooked enough so they wouldn't crunch. She tried to do a little taste test but burned her tongue.

Cooking was overrated.

She considered eating dinner outside but the mosquitoes were bad tonight and she had already spent her inadequate cooking experience swatting at one every few seconds. Shutting off the grill, she pondered whether to take the food upstairs or wait here for Matt. Just then he appeared around the corner of the building, still wearing his uniform. She didn't see him in it very often and each time the sight was striking.

He looked upset. "Hi, honey. Sorry I'm so late."

"It's fine. Are you okay?" She shortened the distance between them and he wrapped her up in his usual bear hug.

"Yeah, right before I left work this afternoon we got a call about another bank robbery. We didn't get there in time and the thieves got away. I'm just frustrated, that's the second one in less than a month. We are beginning to suspect it's the same guys each robbery."

"I'm sorry. I know you take these situations personally and take pride in low crime rate. I'm sure you did the best you could." She took his hands in hers to comfort him while kissing him on the cheek. "Do you want to talk about it some more?" The food could wait, he was more important. It wasn't often when Matt got upset about something. His even temperament didn't challenge him to get riled up over petty issues.

"Maybe later, I'm hungry. I worked up a good appetite being angry."

"Well, you're in luck. We will either have a mediocre dinner here or a fantastic dinner downtown. Either way, you'll be fed." She turned toward the grill and opened the lid to place the food on the plate.

"What! Ava, you made dinner?" She had been looking forward to his reaction all day.

"Yes. Now wipe off that surprised look and get the door for me," she said, laughing.

He came up behind her and put his arms around her waist, kissing her neck, which was readily available because she had pulled her hair back in a ponytail within moments of cooking over the hot grill.

"Thank you."

"Don't thank me yet, you haven't tasted it, and you won't unless you open the door," she teased.

"Geez, get the woman to cook and she's got a spicy attitude to go with it." He dropped his arms and opened the door, bowing.

"You think this is feisty, you haven't seen anything yet."

"Feisty. I can do feisty."

ఇౕఴఄ ఇౕఴఄ

*D*inner went better than Ava predicted. The steak was a little tough, but Lucy's sauce made up for it. The vegetables and potatoes were satisfactory and she was quite pleased. Maybe this cooking thing wasn't so hard after all. However, she wasn't ready to admit that fact out loud yet.

Ava washed the dishes while Matt went to change his clothes and clean off the grill. When he returned she had just finished up. She snatched the movie, note and a blanket for them to share on her way to meet him on the couch.

She sat beside him, a little anxious to give him the note. Her voice quivered when she began to talk. "I couldn't stop thinking about you today, so I put some of those thoughts down on paper." She handed him the paper.

He took the note without saying anything, but a smile spread across his face. He began reading. Ava sat watching him read, disregarding the awkwardness of her staring, but she couldn't take her eyes off him. By his facial reactions she could guess what number he was reading on the countdown.

He laid the note down and left his mark on her lips. "Thank you. I'm enjoying getting to know the side of you that isn't afraid to tell me how you feel. I'm so proud of you for the steps you've been taking lately." He leaned over and kissed her again. "You're the most remarkable woman I've ever met. I love you."

"Good. Are you ready to love me some more?" She pulled out the movie and flashed it at him. "And that's not all."

She got up off the couch and dashed to the freezer and pulled out two pints of ice cream. One was Cookies 'n Cream, Matt's favorite, and Mint Chip, her favorite. She grabbed two spoons and handed him his pint. "What's a shoot 'em up movie without ice cream?"

She put the movie in and turned down the lights. As she

passed by Matt he took her hand and guided her to sit on his lap. "I'm not sure what I did to deserve you," he whispered lovingly.

Ava rubbed the scruff that started to grow on his face. "I'm exceedingly confidant that I win on the 'not deserving' end of this relationship," she whispered back.

She placed her fingers against his mouth when he tried to protest and then laid her head on his shoulder, snuggling into his warm chest. She could've stayed in his arms all night. She kissed his neck, slowly working her way up to his mouth.

They kissed for a short stretch of time. Disappointment escaped in a sigh when Matt pushed her back with, "Maybe we should start the movie."

"What movie?" She asked, kissing him again.

"Ava," he chuckled while he gently pushed her back again. "Seriously, we better stop. I'm not sure I can resist the temptation of not crossing our boundaries right now. I'm feeling a little weak in that area."

"Oh, I'm sorry. I forgot that physical things are different for guys than girls. I guess I always just look at you as indestructible." She moved off his lap to sit next to him.

"That couldn't be further from the truth at this moment. I feel very human right now."

"Okay, let's start the movie. We don't want our ice cream to melt anyway."

❧❧ ❧❧

Ava didn't realize how tired she was until halfway through the movie when she stretched out on the couch and couldn't keep her eyes open. Despite all the action in the movie her eyelids lost the battle. She awakened to Matt gently rubbing her legs that rested on his lap. Through blurred vision the credits rolled.

"Ava baby, I'm going to head home so you can go to bed," Matt said softly.

She rubbed her eyes, willing herself to wake up. "Sorry I missed the movie. I guess all that cooking wore me out." She sat up and stretched. "Did you like it?"

"Yeah, there was a huge twist at the end that surprised me. I was a little distracted at times, so if you want to watch it again sometime, I'll watch it with you."

"Why were you distracted?" His crooked smile showed his slight embarrassment telling her everything she needed to know. She was the distraction. "Me? I'm sorry, how did I distract you while sleeping?" She pulled her hair tie out and let her hair fall. As she rubbed her temples to ease the headache that had started, her eyes widened suddenly. "Oh no, did I snore? I'm sorry. I usually don't unless I'm really tired."

He pulled her close to him, running his fingers through her hair. That confirmed it for her that he liked it the best when she had it down. "I was in a trance watching you sleep. No worries, no snoring, you actually looked peaceful and I couldn't take my eyes off you." He placed his fingers on her chin and held her face, not allowing her to look away. "You are so beautiful."

Heat flushed her cheeks. "And you are too kind." She continued to work on accepting his compliments without rebuttal. She nestled herself into his chest. "I wish you didn't have to leave. Can't you just stay and hold me like this all night?"

He pulled her tighter into his strong embrace. "Oh Ava, you have no idea how much I wish I could do that. Someday I hope that you'll be mine so I don't ever have to leave again," he murmured while kissing the top of her head.

"I look forward to that future, too," she agreed softly. As her head rested on his chest, his heartbeat quicken. He gently positioned her so they faced each other.

"Really?"

Ava grinned and couldn't hide the beaming that shined through her smile. She also couldn't believe she'd said those words, but she meant them. A future with Matt was what she wanted. "Really."

He took her face in his hands and kissed her with such intensity that Ava could sense that his walls were down. He never allowed himself to kiss her with such passion. The atmosphere changed and the restraint they typically controlled had vanished. Ava's head recognized the danger that drew them in, but her senses screamed in delight louder. Without consideration she grabbed his shirt and pulled him down onto the couch with her and he didn't resist.

The moment began to escalate and boundaries crumbled, setting them up for failure. Without warning Matt jumped off the couch. Breathing heavily, he put his hands up in surrender and then placed them on his head. "I can't be like this with you, Ava. I have to go."

He walked over to his bag, picked it up, and walked out the door. "Matt, don't go..."she called out after him as the door clicked shut. Ava sat in disbelief of how the evening had taken such a bad turn began to cry. Her tears dripped with shame. She knew better.

Matt warned her he struggled to keep his desires in check, but instead of being supportive, she had been weak and made the situation worse. Guilt consumed all her thoughts. Was he as mad at her as she was with herself? Would he call tonight or ignore her the rest of the week?

She stood and went to the bathroom to get a tissue and splash water on her face. What did she do next? Should she call him, or just give him the space he clearly needed? Her questions were answered when she returned to the living room and found Matt leaning against the door. "Matt..." She slowly walked up to him but kept a space between them,

149

afraid to touch him.

"Ava, I'm so sorry. I should've never allowed myself to be so close to you when I knew I was physically vulnerable." He cleared his throat. "And I shouldn't have walked out on you like that. I needed space to clear my head, but I can only imagine how horrible I must have made you feel." He stepped forward and clutched her hands in his. "Forgive me."

She lowered her head in remorse. "I'm the one who needs to seek forgiveness. I tempted you and for that I'm deeply sorry."

"Don't you dare blame this on yourself! I'm accountable for my actions," he said while pointing to his chest. "We're fine, Ava. We know our limitations now. We just need to keep a tight rein on our cutoff point before we have to worry about crossing our boundaries." He stroked the side of her face. "I love you."

"I love you, too."

"Okay, I'd better go. Thanks for tonight." Turning toward the door he looked back over his shoulder. "Hey, the good news is I didn't get food poisoning."

Sarcasm came through rich in her laugh as the tension between them disappeared. "Well, the night isn't over yet. Do you want me to run to the kitchen and whip something up?"

"I think I'll pass, I've already had enough excitement for the night and I don't need an unwanted surprise in an hour."

"Very funny," she said while scrunching up her nose in mockery and pushed him out the door. "You've just cost yourself a night of making me dinner, 'oh great one in the kitchen'." Ava smiled, enjoying the ease between them.

"You just wait, Ava Williams," he whispered through the crack of the door. "I'll soon have you eating out of my hands for the rest of our lives." He winked and disappeared down the hallway.

chapter eighteen

The food court at the mall buzzed with commotion while Ava waited at the table for Julia to return with her food. Ava wanted Chinese while Jules preferred Subway. Splitting up to claim their chosen meal seemed to be the best plan. Earlier they had shopped at a couple stores in hopes to find a few good deals they couldn't live without. Ava needed some new clothes for the upcoming school year and also kept her eyes open for a new outfit to wear on her next date with Matt. The break came at a good time as her stomach growled, pleading for nourishment.

Julia sat her tray down, pulled out her seat and sat down. "I guess I should have gone with you, the line took forever."

"Yeah, but you will be rewarded for your healthy choice. These egg rolls are just going to show themselves off on my thighs." Ava took a huge bite, savoring every calorie.

"So ice cream later is out of the question?"

"When have I ever turned down ice cream?"

"True."

"I guess I'll just have to go and workout with Matt sometime this week. Darn." She swirled her fork in the noodles trying her best not to get such a huge bite in order to avoid having to suck in the stray noodles left outside her mouth.

She took a bite.

Nope. Not possible.

"Thanks again for changing your plans with Matt tonight to hang out with me." Jules opened her fat free pretzels and popped one in.

"No problem. I've missed our quality girl time." Since she began dating Matt her free time wasn't as accessible and along with Julia's sporadic hours at work they just couldn't get their schedules to coincide.

"Matt wasn't upset?"

"Not at all." She had plans to hang out at Matt's apartment tonight, but Jules had called this afternoon with her request. Matt kindly understood and mentioned that he might call Derek to see if he'd want to go down to the shooting range.

"Good."

"So what's up? You don't seem like yourself." Jules wasn't a needy friend by any means. Ava had taken care of that role the last two years. When she seemed off on the phone, Ava knew Jules needed to be her first priority tonight.

"I guess I'm just struggling with feeling discontent, and to be honest, lonely."

The fact that Jules didn't have a husband yet surprised Ava, shocked was more like it. Jules walked with grace and dignity – an all-around beautiful woman, inside and out. She was outgoing, funny and kindness overflowed from her heart. Ava wiped off her lips from the juices that the noodles left while entering her mouth. Next time no Chinese. "What happened with Scott? I thought you guys were starting to move into a more serious relationship?"

Jules was a pediatric nurse at one of the hospitals in the city and for the past year she had been interested in a doctor that she worked alongside. He constantly flirted with her and they spent almost every weekend together. The last she'd heard, he had hinted towards something more permanent.

"He was serious about leading me on. I guess he was taking out one of the nurses from the third floor also." Jules placed her chin in her palm. "I really liked him Ava."

Ava cringed. Her friend was hurting and she didn't know how to encourage her. Their roles had become reversed and she needed to step up to the plate. "Oh Jules, I'm so sorry. When did this happen?"

"A few days ago." Jules caught on to Ava's shock that she just found this out now. "I didn't say anything before because I just needed some time to lick my wounds." Jules pushed away her half eaten sandwich. "I feel like a fool. I can only image the talk that is going on behind my back at work."

Ava understood what drama could unfold at work when people felt the need to gossip. It could be cruel and relentless. She could pick out a few people at her school that could make the day miserable if they so deemed. No one needed an audience while recovering from a broken heart.

She had only met Scott once when he attended Julia's surprise birthday party back in March. He seems like a nice guy.

He now just made her hit list.

"I know you don't want to hear this, but it sounds like you are better off." Ava admitted. Jules would have been honest with her. She was required to do the same. It was in their best friend hand book after all. "However, it doesn't make it hurt any less."

"No, it doesn't."

"Is that why you've been feeling discontent?"

"It started a while ago. I'm just not sure if I want to stay on the pediatrics floor anymore. It's taking an emotional toll on me and I think I just need a break. I love working with the kids, but it just doesn't seem...enough. Now with what has happened with Scott, maybe now is the time to take the change that I need."

Ava sipped on her diet coke while listening. Julia's declaration came as a surprise. All she had ever talked about since High School surrounded becoming a pediatric nurse. She waited for her time to intervene. "I think you can do anything you put your mind to. If you feel the Lord drawing you into a different area of nursing, go for it. As long as you are in God's will, that is where you need to be."

"That's just it. I'm not sure what God's will is for my life. I'm so confused with where I am supposed to be, with my love life and my job. Do I stay with pediatrics or go along the lines of ER or a scrub nurse in the operating room. I think I'm ready for a new challenge or maybe that's just the confusion talking." She laughed at herself. "I guess I sound like Lucy."

Her announcement did sound like Lucy's characteristics. "Yes, but you would have to change jobs about five more times to make those comparisons valid."

"Ugh, why does dating and life have to be so hard sometimes? I just wish I could find someone as perfect for me, as Matt is for you."

He was perfect for her. She needed to be better at proclaiming to him that very fact. Ava reflected on her hard and painful journey to meeting Matt. Sometimes God had to take you through the dessert to reach the springs. As God's children we are not called to live an easy life, only one that loves and honors God. "You will. Just remember that His timing is perfect."

"You're right."

"I just want you to be happy, Jules. You deserve it."

A child the next table over started to scream and broke up their conversation. Depth wasn't as personal when you had to yell at each other to be heard. They smiled at each other. "Ok, enough of me being Debbie Downer. Let's keep shopping. I could use some retail therapy."

chapter nineteen

Ava snuggled up in her oversized plush chair, sipping her herbal tea while engrossed in yet another book that had sucked her in during her summer break. She stayed up late last night reading, unable to put down the mystery novel. She was hooked.

This morning she slept in, did some much-needed cleaning in her apartment, and after lunch rewarded herself for her hard work by spending a few more quiet hours with her nose in the book. Hoping this time she would finally finish the book so her life could go back to normal again and not revolve around "who done it."

Even though it was smoldering outside with a heat wave that hit earlier in the week, she found comfort sitting inside in her air-conditioned apartment, swallowed up in a blanket. She rubbed her hand over the fleece material, wishing Matt sat beside her so she could soak up the warmth from his body heat.

The phone rang and for a brief moment Ava considered not answering, but on the chance it could be important, she tossed the blanket off and retrieved her cell phone from the counter.

The number displayed was Kim's. She answered quickly. "Hey Kim, what's up?"

"Hi Ava, sorry to bother you, but do you have a second to talk?"

Ava frowned, wondering when Kim would ever realize that they were friends...and friends always made time for each other. She was never a bother. A smile spread across her lips, hoping Kim would feel her sincerity.

"Kim, I've got the rest of the day."

Ava heard her breath exhale, relief oozing. "Okay, well, if you are sure..."

"I'm sure. What's going on?"

Kim started slowly, words drawn apart, hesitating. "I just wanted you to know that early this morning I went down to the police station and dropped the charges for Ray. But I did file for a restraining order."

Ava's heart sank at the thought of Ray being free, roaming around the city as he pleased. While working with the abuse support group a few women had done that in the past to hopefully soften up their abuser. To show kindness and hope that it would be reciprocated.

Usually it worked, but in a few cases the women ended up going to a shelter for a while until the guy calmed down or moved on. Ava hoped the best for Kim, but the sick feeling that gnawed in the pit of her stomach didn't spread confidence on how it would play out.

Kim didn't need to know the depth of her doom and gloom over the situation. "That was a good idea about the restraining order. Have you considered getting out of town for a while?"

She didn't like to think about Kim and Tessa leaving, but it was important to be proactive. Kim would be better off to be overly cautious than to have to come up with a last-minute plan that put her on the defense.

Ava massaged her forehead with her fingertips, trying to figure out the best strategy of action. She needed to call

Matt. He'd know what to do.

"I've been thinking about that. My sister and I have just recently mended our relationship, so that's an option. I'm sure Stephanie wouldn't mind some company. Until I finalize my plans, I've sent Tessa to her friend's house for a couple days."

"Great idea." It pleased Ava to hear the steps Kim was willing to take to protect herself and Tessa. She couldn't believe the changes Kim made in the short time that Ray had been in jail, as if she could finally see clearly.

Ava checked the time. "Hey, why don't I come and take you out for dinner? We can discuss this then." It seemed like a better plan to work the options out face to face and most important, away from Kim's house. Plus it would give her time to talk to Matt and get his opinion. He dealt with this on a weekly basis, he would have better insight on how to keep Kim and Tessa safe.

"Okay, that sounds good. I could use a little sunlight in my day."

"Just let me get cleaned up and I'll be over. Look for me in about half an hour."

"Thanks Ava." Kim's voice broke and she cleared her throat. "I don't know what I would do without you."

"Kim that is what friends are for. I'll see you soon."

They exchanged their goodbyes. Ava placed a call to Matt. He didn't answer. She had to settle with leaving him a detailed message about the situation and asked him to call her.

Ava undressed from the pajamas that she'd sported all day and pulled on shorts, a tank top and sandals. To help quicken the process she put her hair back in a ponytail and put on a light layer of make-up.

As she grabbed her purse and keys there was a knock at the door. Detouring, she looked through the peephole. The hallway appeared empty. She smiled at the probability that it was her next door neighbor's kids who were too short for her to see and liked to play hide-and-seek with her often.

She whipped the door open. Her smile faded as Ray pushed her back into her apartment. Anger radiated from his gruff features and if he was a cartoon character, he would probably have steam blowing out from his ears.

Ray slammed the door behind him, blocking her only exit. Her body trembled from the fear that paralyzed her as an evil grin spread across his jaw, clearly enjoying her terror.

A bubble popped in her throat as her shock wore off and a high shrill of a scream escaped. She could only hope her neighbors were home and could hear her shout for help. Ray lunged toward her, placing his hand over her mouth to keep her quiet. She bit the inside of one of his fingers hard. He yelped in pain, taking his hold off her enough that she was able to free herself to run toward her phone on the counter that separated the living room and kitchen.

She snatched the phone up but didn't have enough time to place a call before strong hands gripped her, tearing the phone from her ridged grasp.

Ray threw her phone against the wall. It shattered into pieces. Panic set in as she realized it would have been smarter to have tried to escape the apartment than to waste time grabbing her phone. She took her purse and began hitting him with it while screaming for help again. The battled seemed pointless, but she wouldn't give up without a fight. If the opportunity presented itself again, she would be a blur as she raced out the door.

Without much force Ray grabbed the purse from her in one fluid motion. He pulled out a Swiss army knife and flipped open the blade, pointing it in her direction.

She backed up a few steps and fell silent, afraid of what he would do if she screamed again.

His laugh held no humor. "I thought you'd see things my

way, Miss Williams."

Her voice quivered as she spoke. "What do you want from me?"

"I want you to leave Kim alone." As he talked he moved slowly closer. "You have caused us all these problems. If you had just left us alone like I told you to, we wouldn't be in this mess."

Ava's anger surfaced, her face twisted in disgust. "I don't regret helping Kim! The things you have done to her are pure evil. You deserve to rot in jail."

Not her most shining moment of wisdom, she realized, as his features darkened. She had just provoked the beast.

Ray stepped forward. "No one speaks to me that way."

Ava crossed her arms, grabbing her elbows for balance. She did her best to act calm, unfazed while her insides shivered.

When she didn't answer him, he continued. "I love Kim and I am going to get her back. You hear me! You leave Kim alone if you know what's good for you."

"She will never go back to you." At least Ava prayed she wouldn't. She finally was released from the spell Ray had over her. Kim stood stronger now. She lived more confident and at last gained some much needed self-esteem and self-respect. Would that all change if Ray came groveling and begged her to take him back?

"She will if she wants her precious Tessa kept safe."

Ava stared at the devil himself. She stood up taller. "No, she won't."

Ray unexpectedly sprang toward her. His fist rushed at her face, giving no time to defend herself. The blow connected to her jaw and the force propelled her onto her back as she slid across the floor.

Then everything went black.

chapter twenty

*K*im finished packing her suitcase for her visit to her sister's house, thankful that she and Stephanie had made amends. Piece by piece she was getting her life back together again. She had taken Ava's advice and called Stephanie as soon as they had hung up. When Stephanie heard that Ray had been released from jail, she insisted that she and Tessa move in with her until everything settled. Kim didn't need much convincing to accept her invitation.

She stood facing her closet, debating between her tennis shoes, sandals and flats, and then just threw them all in the suitcase. Kim didn't know how long they would be gone. She might as well be over prepared. The last time she had seen Stephanie was two years ago. At that time they were still the same size. If worse came to worse, she could always borrow clothes from her.

After zipping up the suitcase she lifted it off the bed and made her way toward Tessa's room to pack a few more items for her. She would stay at her friend Kelly's house tonight. In the morning she would pick up Tessa and head straight to Stephanie's.

Kim could breathe easier knowing Tessa was safe and away from the house. She had a restraining order for Ray but had just barely obtained it. Per law, a person can't file a restraining order against someone they live with. She found that pretty messed up, but the law was the law. However, Ray still had his house up for sale, and that worked in her favor. She obtained the protective order because he could live there.

Last week she had come across his keys, boxed up all his stuff and moved it back to his house. Enough was enough.

Kim stopped at the threshold of Tessa's bedroom, soaking up the details of her butterfly decorations. She had painted the walls a pale purple. A border that displayed the fluttery insects at play ran along the top of the wall. The curtains were a solid deep purple, both for fashion and to help block out the sun's morning light. Kim had found seven butterflies made out of mesh to hang from her ceiling. The room gave a calming effect, a peace in the midst of the war that surrounded her.

Tears sprung to her eyes as she imagined the hours her innocent daughter waited up here, listening to her and Ray fight, sounds of her mother crying, pleading for him to stop.

She was going to get her life back in order, she demanded of herself as she wiped the wetness off her cheeks. Tessa deserved more than this.

Kim glanced up at the clock, noticing how late Ava was. It wasn't like her to be five minutes late, let alone the twenty minutes it was creeping to now.

She headed down the stairs to give her a call. At the bottom of the stairs she jerked to a stop.

"Hi Kim. Did you miss me?"

"Ray! What are you doing here?" Kim's heart slammed against her chest. How did he get in here? She had a locksmith come out just this morning to change the locks. Her mind raced throughout the house, trying to figure out where she messed up. She stopped the mental tour when she remembered the kitchen window she opened earlier to get rid of the burnt smell from her lousy attempt at making chocolate chip cookies for Tessa. How could she be so absentminded?

"I live here."

With a strength she had never possessed before, she took a step forward. "Not anymore. I moved all your things back to your house. You know I have a restraining order. You can't be here."

He stood still as his features softened. "Kim, baby, I love you. I know you are upset with me, but things will be different this time. I'll change. I promise."

She mocked a laugh, "Like you know what love is. All you do is hurt people." She took a brave step toward him, determination backing her renewed spirit. "And you are done hurting me."

She made her way around him, surprised by the fact he let her pass without resistance. He followed her into the kitchen where she retrieved her phone, noticing how her hands trembled.

"Please Kim. Just give me another chance."

Kim couldn't be sure, but she thought his lips quivered as he made his pathetic request. He could grovel until his face turned blue, she would never take him back. She was young with a full life ahead of her. She wanted to get her GED, attend college, maybe become a teacher or work in a field that involved children. The possibilities were limitless and that awareness excited her. But not as much as the idea of a life that did not have Ray in it.

"No, Ray. We're over. You need to leave."

"No, you are mine!" he growled.

She ignored his degraded statement of claim, letting it roll off her shoulders as she turned. Grabbing her car keys off the counter, she slowly tried to head toward the back door. "Listen, there is somewhere I need to be. You can go now or have the cops escort you out."

She flashed her phone in front of him, proving the seriousness of her threat.

An evil smile broke across his face. "If you are planning on meeting Miss Williams, you are wasting your time. I don't think she will be showing up."

Kim froze, but her heart quickened with each beat. "What are you saying?"

"I'm saying she and I had a little talk and I don't think she will be getting in between us anymore."

Frustration came out as a ragged sigh. "There is no 'us', Ray." She stepped backward, attempting to keep her anger at bay. "Please tell me you didn't hurt Ava!"

"She got what was coming to her. We would have been fine if she hadn't gotten in the way."

"You are crazy!"

Kim covered her mouth with her shaking hand. Poor Ava. This was all her fault. She had brought Ava into her messed up life and now her friend had also paid for her mistakes.

Adrenaline jolted her as he started to invade her space. She needed to get out of here, first to get away from Ray and second to check on Ava. What had he done? But despite her worry for her, she didn't have time to dwell on that question.

Kim raced for the back door in the kitchen that led outside to the driveway. She held it open for a second until strong arms encircled her waist, dragging her kicking and screaming back into the kitchen. Ray slammed the door shut with his foot.

Through the open window above the sink she could see her neighbor pulling weeds in her flower bed.

Kim's throat burned as she screamed for help. Ray lifted her up even higher and threw her against the butcher block island. Kim gasped in pain as she clutched the left side of her rib cage, certain a rib had cracked.

Ray closed the window and rushed his walk toward her, his eyes burning with fury, nostrils flaring. She'd never seen him so crazed. Kim closed her eyes, praying that there was a God. The one Ava spoke about. The one she loved and served. And that He would save her now.

chapter twenty-one

*M*att parked his cruiser in front of Ava's apartment and broke out into a full sprint toward the entrance. The phone call from Ava's Dad scared him to his core. He had been held up at a deadly car accident and this was the first he could get away.

It made him sick knowing that Ray had been in her apartment, threatening her, touching her. Ray Connors didn't realize who he was messing with.

Rushing through Ava's unlocked door he found her family had already arrived. Her mom perched on the couch holding an ice pack to Ava's jaw. Her dad stood in the kitchen on the phone while Lucy fidgeted with the coffee maker. Her brothers paced the floor, like tigers ready to pounce.

He reached Ava and placed a kiss on the top of her head. Kneeling down in front of her he let himself soak in the damage. Her jaw was swollen and the left side of her face had a bruise the size of a plum. Thankfully nothing looked broken.

His anger boiled over. "I'm going to get this guy, Ava!"

"Matt, don't get him for me. Get him for Kim. I'm so worried about her. I can't get a hold of her. What if Ray has already gotten to her?"

Ava's mom rubbed her shoulder in attempts to keep her calm. Matt couldn't believe how under control she seemed after being attacked. It was just like Ava to put others before herself.

"I can send an officer to her house, but I'm not leaving you."

Tears filled her eyes as he reached up to stroke her cheek with his thumb. Lightly tracing the bruise he swiped a tear that escaped down the outside of her face.

"Please, Matt. Do everything you can to help her. I'm fine, really." A slight grin lightened her eyes in hopes to convince him. "Kim needs you."

Matt stood, stretching his aching muscles from his workout earlier in the day. They were both too stubborn to have this conversation right now. Did she not understand the depth of the danger she had been in?

He figured Ray just wanted to scare her enough to back off. But he could have, without much effort, done so much more damage than a bruise and a sore jaw.

Matt suppressed a humorless chuckle to himself. Ava was a spitfire. Ray probably realized as he jumped in blindly that Ava was a force to be reckoned with. She stood up for what was right, for those she loved. Pity the fool that tried to butt heads with her.

Which brought him back to the conversation at hand. The one he would lose if he didn't think a little faster on his feet.

"I know you think you are fine, babe, but the shock will wear off."

Ava stood and pulled him into the short hallway that split the bedrooms to keep their conversation semi-private ... or so he could save face. She reached up on her tip-toes and wrapped her arms around his neck, placing the good side of her face against his.

"Thank you for loving me so deeply and always wanting to protect me." Her words trickled out, barely above a whisper. She leaned back and he took a moment to savor the love her eyes radiated toward him. "But I am fine. Plus, my family is here and I'm pretty sure my brothers could take on an army right about now."

He was still in disbelief that she was okay. That the drama she experienced didn't rattle her more. Matt was sure her fear for Kim ranked higher than her own. Defeat exhaled out with his sigh while he nodded his agreement. In his heart he wanted to be here with Ava, but it was his job, his duty, to check on Kim.

"Okay. I'll go. But you have to promise to call if you need me."

"Deal." She brushed his lips with hers as she repositioned back into hugging him tightly. "Thank you," her breath tickled his ear as she spoke.

After a quick conversation with her family and his pointed recommendation that someone stay with her until he could return, he left, reassuring them that he would call with an update.

Once inside his squad car he decided to call dispatch and get a cruiser to Kim's house just to be safe since traffic was heavy at this time of day.

His heart sank when dispatch replied that an officer had been called to that address fifteen minutes earlier. He should go back inside and let Ava know, but he didn't want to add anymore unneeded stress to her day. He would go and check out Kim's house first, find out why they had been called, and then let Ava in the loop.

Matt prayed for Kim as he merged into traffic. At this moment it was the best and only thing he could do for her. "Lord, help us not to be too late. Keep Kim safe. Protect her." His prayer bounced around in the empty space of his interior.

Matt pulled into Kim's driveway fifteen minutes later.

An ambulance parked in front of her house along with two other squad cars. As he rushed up to the front door he noticed an officer talking to the next door neighbor. He made a mental note to find out what information she gave in her statement. The front door hung open and Matt rushed in. The EMTs had just loaded Kim onto a gurney and were strapping her down.

Matt turned his head away at the sight of Kim. It wasn't often that a domestic abuse made him nauseous, but the surprise of seeing Kim's battered body made him want to fall to his knees and lose his lunch. At least she wasn't zipped up in a black body bag, but by the looks of things, she wasn't far from it.

Matt caught the attention of the middle-aged EMT woman whose skin turned paler by the minute. "How is she?"

"Critical. Many broken bones, low blood pressure, probably internal bleeding." She secured the last strap and looked up at her partner. "All set. Let's roll."

Matt backed out of their way as they wheeled Kim out to the ambulance. As they closed the doors he made his way outside and walked around to the side to jump in on the neighbor's statement. The elderly woman had a plump figure that reminded him of his belated grandma. The woman wrung her hands together as she spoke.

Matt walked into the conversation during mid-sentence, "... and then I saw him run out the back door and into the street behind our houses and leave in his truck."

"How long ago did that happen?" the officer asked.

"Right about the time I heard the sirens."

"What color was the attacker's truck?"

"A rusty red color, I believe. It was too far away for me to give you a make or license plate number."

"That's okay. Can you tell us what he was wearing?"

She paused, taking a moment to remember. "I think he had on jeans and a gray T-shirt, with a navy blue or black baseball hat on. I'm sorry, it all just happened so fast."

Matt looked down at the officer's tablet, cheating by taking a peek at her name. "Mrs. Marron, I'm Sergeant Thompson." He stuck out his hand for her to shake. "You are doing a great job and we appreciate any information you can give us. Can you tell me if the man you saw running away from here was the same guy who'd been currently living here, or was it someone different?"

"I...um...can't say for sure. I didn't get a good look at his face because of the hat. But the truck looked like the man's that lived here. I never met him. Only saw him from a distance." Tears pooled in her eyes. "I knew that poor girl was in trouble, I should have called for help sooner than today. I didn't want to be a nosy neighbor."

Matt wondered how many other situations could have been stopped if someone had stood up and said something. How many lives would be changed right now if someone had the courage to speak up? Domestic abuse usually stayed a hidden lifestyle. Many people could cover the secret with finesse while neighbors, family members and friends were left in the dark. Some may have an idea, but not enough to approach. It was a fine line that many people never crossed.

The other officer spoke up, "Mrs. Marron, you have done great. You probably saved Miss Davis's life by calling the police when you heard her screaming. Today you were her hero."

Matt excused himself to take a walk around the outskirts of Kim's property. After rounding the house twice to look for anything out of place and also to blow off some steam, he ventured back into the house to see how things progressed inside. The technicians had started their search for fingerprints and any fibers that would testify as to who was here.

Their prime suspect would be Ray, but in case Kim didn't make it or was unable to tell them her attacker, they needed evidence to insure he would be punished for his crime.

Matt needed to call and check up on Ava. But if he called to get an update on her, she would want one on Kim. A lump grew in his throat as he envisioned having to share this news with her. She would be crushed.

Matt stroked his face, debating on the best plan of action. He wasn't needed here. There wasn't much more he could add that someone else wasn't doing. He would just be in the way. Plus, his procrastination wasn't going to make the blow any less painful for Ava. Making his way outside, he took a few minutes to regroup with the officer that had taken the neighbor's statement. An alert had gone out for the arrest of Ray as a suspect. The search for him was already set in motion.

As he climbed into his car he decided to run to the hospital to get an update on Kim before he faced the dreaded task of telling Ava what horror had befallen her friend.

chapter twenty-two

Matt and Ava walked the halls at the hospital, waiting to hear a report about Kim's surgery. The ER had been unexpectedly busy for the early morning hours and Ava jumped at the chance to get some space and finally move to a private waiting room near the surgical floor.

When Matt had told her about Kim she'd broken down and cried while he held her. In his line of work he often times had to be the bearer of bad news to people, but to give it to someone he loved and cherished was an emotion he had yet to encounter.

When her door swung open he had tried to ignore how vulnerable Ava looked, engulfed in an oversized robe with fuzzy slippers peeking out from underneath. Being the first time he'd seen her without makeup or her hair done, she was still a breath of fresh air.

Over the last couple of hours determination had replaced Ava's earlier sadness. A new strength sprouted from her as she prepared to support her new friend.

They passed a coffee stand just outside the cafeteria. "Can I get you another cup of coffee?" Matt asked while he wrapped his hand around her icy fingers.

"Sure. My first cup is wearing off." He caught her yawning as he filled her cup. The coffee had a burnt aftertaste, but the caffeine would do its job and bring her back to life. The steam whirled from the top as he handed her the Styrofoam cup filled with rejuvenation.

"How are you holding up?" Matt rubbed her arm, fighting the urge to wrap her in his arms, but this was not the place or time.

"I just can't believe this is happening, Matt. Kim was finally getting her life together."

"I know." They stepped to the side to allow two nurses to pass through the hallway. He still wore his uniform and picked up on the looks it created.

"Any news on Ray yet?" With Ray still on the run, yet to be caught, made Matt unsettled with the fact he could be anywhere. Especially since he had already gone after Ava once.

"Not yet. Will you please reconsider getting a restraining order and lying low until he is caught? It would keep a few gray hairs away from me."

She smirked while running her fingers through his hair. "I don't think Ray cares about me. He just wanted to scare me. He is probably more concerned about getting out of town than coming after me."

"Ava, that man is crazy. We can't predict what he will do."

She blew lightly across the top of her coffee and took a small sip. She took a deep breath, taking her time to answer. He couldn't tell if her delay came as a good sign or not. Ava had a stubborn streak in her.

"Okay, I will file the restraining order, keep a low profile, and see if one of my brothers will move in to my apartment with me until Ray is found."

He breathed his first sigh of relief since the moment he heard what Ray had done to her. "Thank you."

"I figure that's the advice I would give Kim, so I should

probably take it myself." Her eyes began to mist at the mention of Kim's name.

"Hey." He lifted her chin with his finger, careful not to touch the bruise staring back at him, reminding him, haunting him, that he hadn't been there to protect her. "Kim is a strong woman and she can still turn this around." He threw all caution to the wind and leaned into her, invading her space. "I happen to know an incredible woman who took the broken pieces of her life and built a stronger one in its place."

He kissed her with a gentle touch and yet long enough for her to get the point. Ava cleared her throat. "This woman must have had an amazing, good looking, and supportive man to help her along the way."

"Ah, he was just along for the ride."

"You're being very modest, Sergeant Thompson." Her eyes sparkled while they flirted. She traced her fingers over the detail in his uniform.

"No, I'm just in love."

"Oh, Matthew." She spoke his name with a tenderness that gripped his heart. He had so much he wanted to share with her, but a sterile hallway with an audience didn't seem very romantic. He put his arm around her shoulder and kissed her head while leading them down toward the elevators. "Come on, let's go check on Kim."

They arrived at the waiting room and met Kim's sister, Stephanie, who had just gotten into town and informed them that she was taking Tessa back with her until Ray was caught. Once things settled down she would bring Tessa back and help out while Kim recuperated.

The doctor walked in briskly after four a.m. and said the surgery went well and that they were able to stop the internal bleeding. Kim would be in pain for a while because of her broken ribs, arm and leg, and until the swelling went down around her right eye, they wouldn't know how much vision she'd lost from the blows. The doctor seemed optimistic about sending her home in the next few days. They had Kim in recovery and a nurse said she'd come and get them when she was awake and ready for visitors.

That time came just before the sun started to rise. They stood outside Kim's door while Stephanie took the first visit so she could get back to Kim's house and clean up the remains of the horrendous night before Tessa got home.

Once Kim was out of surgery and coherent, they had been able to get her statement to confirm what they already knew. Ray had attacked her. An officer took up post guarding the door until Ray was in custody. They would not take any chances of Ray coming back to finish the job. He hoped that Ava understood the precautions they took for Kim and wouldn't give him grief when he encouraged those precautions for her also. She seemed on board...for now.

Ava looked up at Matt through bloodshot eyes. Exhaustion laced her movements. She would need a day to recuperate from being up all night. He didn't weather as rough from sleepless nights like she did. It wasn't uncommon for him to miss a night of sleep. And he wouldn't sleep well until they found Ray and had him locked away.

"Would it be okay if I went in by myself to talk with Kim?" Her determination had returned and he wasn't up for an argument. The sight of Kim would be terrible, but not his decision as to whether Ava could handle the sight alone.

"Sure. I need to make a few calls anyway. I'll be down at the end of the hall if you need me." He brushed his thumb along her cheek and reluctantly left her side.

❧❧❧ ❧❧❧

Ava watched Matt walk away and wondered if she was crazy to do this alone. Stephanie came out of the room and stopped her from calling Matt back. Kim was awake and asking for her. With a final glance at Matt, deep in discussion on his cell phone, she made her way into the room and took the empty chair by the bed.

Kim's right eye was matted shut by the swelling. Her face was also swollen with bruises and cuts, concealing the beauty she once held. A blanket covered her battered body. Ava sighed in relief. It was hard enough to see her face. She couldn't imagine what her body looked like.

"Ava?" Kim mumbled, only able to open her swollen mouth a small amount from the left side. She opened her good eye with effort and fixed her gaze on Ava.

"Right here, Kim."

"I'm sorry Ray came after you. Are you okay?"

"I'm fine. Don't worry about me."

"I do. This is all my fault." Her voice caught.

"I would have done it all over again to help you Kim. Please don't blame yourself."

"I've made a horrible mess of my life. Is God punishing me?"

"Oh Kim, that's not how God works. He loves you and out of that love gives us all the freedom to make our own choices. Sometimes bad consequences come from poor choices and sometimes bad things happen to make us work at becoming a better person."

"I've made so many bad choices in my life and it seems even my good choices turn against me." A monitor went off which sent a nurse rushing in to check her vitals. Ava took the moment to collect her thoughts.

Ava waited until the nurse left to keep their conversation private. "You're a strong woman, Kim, you can turn your life around." Matt's words echoed in her thoughts.

"Where do I go from here?" She coughed and groaned from the pain. Ava fed her ice chips to help with her dry mouth.

"You take time to heal and then face one day at a time. You no longer have to live in fear, and that's a great place to start."

Rebuilding her life would not be easy and many obstacles would be in her way, but Matt told her that once they found Ray he would be locked up for a long time. Without him around, Kim would be able to rest and get back on her feet quickly. She was finally free from a life of bondage.

"Can I still come to the abuse support group at your church?"

"Yes, that would be great. You can continue your counseling that will help you through this transition and they will work with you to find a new job."

The group had a good success rate for helping woman rebuild their lives. It took a lot of work, but watching the women walk away with their heads held high made it all worthwhile.

Ava already expected to spend some time with Tessa, working through these last few months and helping her cope with the fear she experienced.

Kim turned her head away from Ava. Her soft sobs caused her body shake under the blanket. The tortured woman was in pain, physically and emotionally.

"Will I ever find someone that will truly love me for me? My father left me, my husband left me, and now I can add Ray to my pile of pitiful men," Kim cried out miserably.

Ava's heart ached for Kim. On a much lesser scale, she understood her pain of rejection. Thankfully she had her family and friends to help her through the darkest time of her life. She also served a God of comfort who loved her without end. She wished Kim could understand how much the Lord really loved her.

"Kim, you're going to find a great man someday who will

deserve all you have to offer. There is someone, however, that already loves you unconditionally until the end of time, without any strings attached."

Ava wasn't swift on her feet with witnessing. She usually took the path of becoming a friend first and then sharing who God was to her. Someday she would share about her journey with Tim and how God had given her another chance at love with Matt, but that day was not today.

"God?"

"Yes."

"You really think He could love someone like me?"

"Absolutely, and if you allow Him, He will show you how wonderful you are. He made you, Kim, and He's a very proud Father of his children."

God's love was hard to fathom at times and Ava had to work through a lot in the last two years to understand herself how much worth she really held.

"Can you tell me a little more about God?"

Kim's interest in God excited Ava. This was the best path she could take to turn her life around. She set her purse down on the floor and settled back against the chair for the long haul. She'd spend all day here if that's what it took.

chapter twenty-three

The first day of the new school year approached like an express train without brakes. Classes started in less than two weeks and Ava began to feel the pressure to set up her room. Past years she would have been done by now because she had nothing better to do during the summer than spend it in preparation for the new school year. This summer was completely different from her lonely past and she didn't even think about her room until now.

Ava already had the list of students who would be in her class. She and the other kindergarten teachers had decided to wait until school approached to have their kindergarten "meet and greet." They had the date set for the end of this week for all the kids to come and be introduced to their teacher, see their room, and meet all the other children in their class.

This special time for the kids also came as a great opportunity for her to meet each of the parents. She planned to have the parents fill out paperwork about their child so she had a little heads-up about their home life, their likes and dislikes, and where they improved in their learning journey since their first assessment earlier in the year at kindergarten round-up.

She had spent all day yesterday at the hospital keeping

Kim company, not leaving once since Matt had brought her. Ava returned home late last night to see that Jake had set up camp in her spare bedroom. After countless hours of tossing and turning, despite already missing a night of sleep she decided that today was as good as any to begin. She got up before the sun did to get ready for the day. She debated whether or not to wear makeup but then remembered she would have to go to the store to buy supplies and she still sported a pretty ugly bruise. She applied a thick layer of foundation and went a little heavier on her eye makeup to hopefully camouflage her still-darkened cheek. She chose her favorite pair of comfortable jeans, flip-flops, and her new white tank top and headed to the kitchen.

Sitting down at her table while sipping her much-needed coffee, she organized the list of projects she wanted to accomplish today. Ava personally required her room to be uplifting and bright with a lot of color. Decorating was always her favorite part of the preparation, but it also took the most time. During the summer break the teachers had to keep their rooms to a bare minimum that way the janitors could come in and clean. She kept a few things up on the walls, but she had a long road ahead of her to get the room to where it needed to be for the open house. Her plan started with going to the school first to set up what she had and then head to the store to get the finishing touches.

Ava had breakfast ready for Jake by the time he came out of his room, prepared to leave for work. She went all out and made him instant oatmeal from an individual package. Only the best for her guests.

⁂⁂

Walking into her classroom gave Ava the spark of excitement that she needed. She set to work right away pulling charts and signs out of the storage closet. She put the alphabet above the chalkboard and made a handy helper chart to hang next to the door. Each day she would draw a student's name to be her special helper for activities. They would also get to be the leader in the lines to lunch and recess and choose the book for story time. Along with the privileges of being the helper, they also had the responsibilities to feed the class goldfish and turtle. The pet store knew Ava by name last year. A bad turnover of goldfish plagued her classroom for a few months and luckily, goldfish were cheap.

Ava came to a good breaking point around lunchtime. She made a list of items she needed to buy at the store. An idea came to mind and she checked the time to see if it would work.

She hadn't seen Matt since he left the hospital early the previous morning. She had ditched him to spend time with Julia on Friday, Saturday was the attack, and yesterday he stayed busy keeping up with Kim's case. They talked last night after she got home but kept it short so she could spend some quality time with Jake. Matt mentioned he didn't look forward to the paperwork that needed to get done at his desk. Chances seemed good she'd find him easily.

Ava snatched up her purse and headed to the police station to see if she could take her man out for lunch.

⚜⚜⚜⚜

Ava had been to the station a couple of times to see Matt, but it still made her squeamish with unease. She walked in to see Matt's partner Derek right away, relieved to see a recognized face. Ava could easily see why the two friends got along so well. They each had a good sense of humor, were full of spunk, and easily made people comfortable with their outgoing personality. Derek was her favorite of all of Matt's friends. He looked as if he could be a surfer from California with his blond hair, blue eyes and dark tan. Besides being nice and friendly, he had a good heart and an encourager for Matt in their relationship. Ava desperately wanted to set him up with Jules but unfortunately he was casually dating someone at the moment. She would keep her ears open for any talk about him being single again.

"Hey Ava," he strutted up toward her, "you didn't have to go out of your way to come see me. I'm flattered."

"Hi Derek." The man loved to joke around and she couldn't help deliver the response he worked for. She giggled while rolling her eyes at his teasing. "Sorry to disappoint you, but I'm here for your partner."

He snapped his fingers while preforming a fake pout that etched his features. He stepped forward to examine her face. "I heard about your attack. I'm glad you're okay." He squeezed her shoulder to show support. "I think Matt is down in the evidence room. I'll go get him for you."

"Thanks," she said while he turned and walked away down the hallway. Ava waited in the lobby area. To help ease the awkwardness she made herself busy by looking at the new pictures displayed on the wall from the cookout earlier in the summer. She searched the pictures, picking out the officers she had met. Doing her best to try and remember their names. She heard Matt's voice echo down the hallway before she saw him.

He quickened his step when he noticed her. By the look of surprise, Derek must not have told him she was here. She observed the two friends as Derek grinned and skirted out of the reach of Matt's fist approaching his shoulder with force.

"Ava, what a good surprise, is everything okay?"

"Yes." She looked back and forth between the two boys in grown-up clothes. "Did I miss something?"

Matt looked over at Derek and they both started to

laugh. "Well, I was told that someone upstairs was causing problems and I needed to come up and start the paperwork for booking. I expected the drunk I dealt with earlier this morning, not the love of my life." He took her hand and led them away from Derek toward an open desk.

Derek's face exposed his amusement and he started walking back down the hallway, talking over his shoulder. "Goodbye you two love birds, I see my work here is done."

Matt shook his head side to side. "And you think I'm a handful." He leaned against the desk and adjusted his focus back onto her. "So what's going on?"

"I'm working in my classroom today and needed a break."

His eyes widened at her response. "Ava, you shouldn't be out and about by yourself. Where is Jake?"

"He is at work. Where he should be." Ava tried to remind herself that Matt's overprotection was just another way he showed his love for her. "The school is safe. No one can get in without a key. Plus, now I'm at a police station. How much safer can I be?"

He crossed his left arm across his chest, resting his right elbow on top of his arm and rubbed his chin with his hand. Taking a moment to consider what she had said, he replied, "I guess you're right."

"I'd be even safer if you came out to lunch with me. I could use a bodyguard."

"Is it that time already?" He looked down at his watch. "I'd love to. That's a job I would never refuse. Let me go tell Derek and then I'm all yours."

After a few steps away, he stopped and turned around. "Why don't you come with me and before we leave you can file a restraining order against Ray."

The man had an amazing memory and wasn't going to let this go. "Great idea. Any new leads?" she asked while they walked down the hallway.

"A small one. He used his credit card to get gas last night, but we don't know for sure if he is still in the city or if he has left."

Ava hoped for the latter.

✌✌ ✌✌

Ava chose a little cafe across the river. A beautiful day without much humidity needed to be celebrated. They decided on a table in the corner of the outdoor seating.

They ordered right away because Matt didn't have much time. The SWAT team had a training session this afternoon and he wanted to get back with some time to prepare. They both ordered water and club sandwiches to help quicken the process. Their efficient waitress had the food out before either of them needed refills.

Matt took her hand and prayed in his soothing voice. When he finished he didn't let loose her hand. "I missed you yesterday," he admitted as he rubbed her hand with his thumb.

"I missed you, too."

"How's your classroom decorating going?"

"Great. I've finished the walls and now I'm getting ready to arrange my reading area. I have a rug and some pillows, but I thought I'd pick up a few bean bags at the store to add..."

"Matt, is that you?" A woman's voice interrupted.

Matt looked up behind her and smiled. Ava turned around to discover an attractive blonde woman dressed in a short skirt, tight shirt and stilettos standing there. Ava looked down at her baggy jeans and cringed.

She felt homely next to her.

"Hi, Amber."

"Oh my word, I can't believe I ran into you," she laughed as if someone had told a joke. "I was just talking to Liz about you." She placed her hand on his shoulder and took her sweet time removing it.

"Hopefully it was all good," he replied. His smile looked stressed upon his face. At least he looked a little uncomfortable.

"Of course it was. I missed seeing you at church and small group yesterday."

She attended his church and small group? That came as news to Ava.

"I wanted to come but I was working."

"Your job sounds so interesting. I'd love to sit down over coffee sometime and hear all about it." Ava's blood pressure spiked over how painfully obvious this wolf in Prada accessories showed her interest in him.

Matt glanced across the table at Ava. She wanted to shout, *don't mind me*, but kept her mouth wisely shut. "Amber, I don't think you've met my girlfriend Ava yet."

She glanced down at Ava. "Oh hi, Ava, it's nice to meet you." Her smile seemed strained.

"Thanks, nice to meet you, too."

Liar.

Ava's words weren't entirely true and she couldn't tame the jealousy that surged through her.

Amber shifted her attention back on Matt. "Well, sorry to have interrupted your lunch. I'll see you later, Matt." She touched his arm and waved goodbye to Ava as her heels clipped along the cement.

"Bye, Amber," Matt said while she walked away.

An awkward silence suspended their conversation. Despite her best judgment, Ava's insecurities spoke with a hint of bitterness. "Huh...well maybe we *should* start going to church together." They had discussed the idea before. They both had commitments at their own churches, so they attended each other's church and small groups randomly for now. Matt had been pressing the subject more lately, but Ava dragged her feet on the decision. It was silly really. She knew that she continued to make it a bigger deal then what it really was. But the thought of changing churches before their relationship became more concrete scared her.

"Ava." Matt snapped. "I want nothing more than to start attending church together and take this next step with you because I love you, not because you want to keep an eye on me."

Ava didn't back down or try to hide her irritation. "Do you not see how absolutely gorgeous she is? She obviously sees that about you."

"Amber's a nice girl, just overly friendly at times. That's all."

"Do you enjoy her flirting with you?"

"Of course not."

"Then why haven't you mentioned her before?" Jealously seeped through every word.

"Because she wasn't worth mentioning to you. She just started attending my church a couple months ago and joined my small group recently. I hardly ever talk to her, Ava. She's just an acquaintance." He took a deep breath and his face softened. He reached for her hand, "Don't you know I only have eyes for you?"

"Sure, but for how long?" Ava said the words before thinking them through and now there was no turning back. Regret washed over her.

He released her hand with abruptness and sat back against his chair, crossing his arms. "Seriously Ava, we're having *this* conversation? What do I have to do to gain your trust?" He didn't raise his voice, but his words screamed at her.

Did it all boil down to her not trusting him? Is that what caused her to accuse him of something so uncharacteristic? No. She trusted him completely. "Matt, I'm…"

"Is there anything else I can get for you?" The waitress unknowingly interrupted before she could finish her apology.

"Yes, could I have the check, please?"

She handed Matt the bill and he immediately gave her cash. "Keep the change," he said kindly. The waitress's eyes widened. He must have given her quite a large tip.

He stood and pushed his chair in. "Are you ready to go?" His voice was more controlled than before but his face spoke of his displeasure.

"Yes," she responded quietly.

Matt didn't speak a word until they were close to the station. He drove her car and pulled over a block before the entrance. Ava looked over at him, puzzled. "I could use the walk," he explained.

Hot tears poked at the corner of her eyes. She'd messed up, bad. "Matt, I'm so sorry. I had no right to judge you that way."

Matt gazed out the windshield, she assumed not staring at anything, just taking time to collect his thoughts. He sighed and shut off the radio before looking back in her direction. "I know you're sorry, but I can't keep paying for another man's mistakes, Ava."

Her voice cracked, "You're right and you have every reason to be upset with me." She wiped the tears that streamed down her face. "I feel like damaged goods. I've worked through allowing myself to love you, but I guess I haven't had a reason to work on the thought of you being interested in someone else."

Ava expected Matt to console her when her emotions took hold of the situation, but he stayed on his side of the car with a frown upon his face. "Ava, you don't have a reason now." Frustration seeped from his words.

Adrenaline shot through her chest. "So much for patience!"

"What does that mean?"

"It means your words are a double-edged sword. One minute you're saying that you want to walk with me through all my fears and then when I do struggle with something you snap."

"Do not turn this on me, Ava." He checked the time on his watch and released his seat belt. "I don't have time to talk about this right now. I need to get back to work."

He stepped out of the car before she had a chance to respond. She slipped out of her door, not sure what to do or say next. They'd had their disagreements over petty circumstances, but this was new territory. They never fought or left each other upset.

Matt met her on the sidewalk, keeping his distance. "I'll call you later tonight." He turned and left before she could reply. He jogged toward the department building, leaving her stranded on the curb to deal with her past that mocked her.

Ava tersely climbed into the driver's seat and smacked her forehead with the palm of her hand. "You are such a drama queen, Ava," she scolded herself.

She looked over her shoulder to see a man standing on the sidewalk staring at her, clearly enjoying the cuckoo show. Ava threw the car in drive and waved to her admirer.

First things first, she needed to brush off her argument with Matt. It wasn't the best way to end their discussion, but she couldn't do anything about it until they talked tonight. He loved her and she needed to trust that he wouldn't walk away.

chapter twenty-four

Ava couldn't concentrate on her task of making name plates for each child's desk. Between her argument with Matt and the gorgeous weather outside, her afternoon work needed to come to a quick end.

In the last hour she had only gotten three names done and even had to throw one away and start over. Her attention span started out weak and ended pathetic. To continue at this rate would be pointless. Coming in tomorrow would make more sense. She might actually put a dent in her overflowing "to do" pile.

As she doodled over the child's name in front of her, thoughts of this afternoon flashed with regret in her mind. Oh, why couldn't she have just kept her mouth shut or at the very least, put a filter on it? She had accused Matt of having feelings for another woman based on this Amber girl saying hello and flirting with him. She threw everything they had been working on right back at him like a slap in the face. Ava had offended him by her lack of trust and then snapped at him for not being supportive.

To turn it around and accuse him of not being patient was absurd and completely untrue. The text book description of patient should have a side note of Matt's name.

If she was truly honest with herself, it wasn't only Tim

that had made mistakes in their relationship. In the hours she'd sat here pretending to do her work, her thoughts scattered from the past to the present, and the eventual realization she came to about her relationship with Tim became eye-opening.

Yes, the rejection hurt, but better to have been rejected than to have married him. Why did she allow herself to view her worth through Tim's eyes?

Hopefully it wasn't too late to share her new comprehension with Matt. She needed a chance to make it up to him. If that was even what he wanted anymore? A plan came together. She would go to Matt's apartment this evening and wait on his porch and surprise him when he got home. Planning her strategy for later, she put groveling at the top of the list...and ice cream. He wouldn't know what hit him.

Looking down at the flower she had just traced around the "i" in the child's name, she decided it was time to put all these thoughts into action. Matt would be getting off work soon and she wanted to make sure she sat on his front steps waiting for him when he arrived.

Ava left her desk all askew with high hopes of finishing everything tomorrow. Hopefully a new day would give her better motivation. After shutting off the lights and closing the door, she made her way to the entrance. Pushing the heavy door open she squinted at the bright sun that had been disguised behind the school's tinted glass.

Her car sat in the back parking lot. Keeping her promise, she scanned the area. Seeing it vacant, she made her way with a brisk walk to the driver's side door.

As she fumbled with her key to unlock the door in her ancient car that had only manual locks, movement to her right stalled her process. A truck sped out from behind the utility shed, tires squealed as it stopped inches from her door, preventing her from opening it.

Ray jumped out of the truck.

Ava threw down her bags and took off in a sprint across the parking lot. Her flip-flops tore the skin between her toes as she made her way back toward the school, hoping she would have enough time to unlock the door and enter before Ray caught up with her.

Why didn't she listen to Matt? Heed his warning? In an effort to prove she could take care of herself she had made herself a target. And one who had a dart heading right for the bull's-eye.

Her efforts made it twenty steps before strong hands grabbed her arm, yanking her back into his solid chest. With Ray's free hand he grabbed a fistful of her hair and dragged her back to the vehicles, wedging her between the two. Fear ripped through her chest as she screamed for help.

No one else was at the school. Traffic usually stayed sparse on this stretch of road. Ava had never felt so alone.

Ray threw her up against his truck, the back of her head slamming hard against the frame. A headache immediately coursed through her skull, causing her sight to blur from the pain. Nausea washed over her as she tried to focus and stop the spinning.

She could see Ray yelling at her, but the words didn't making sense. His words were muffled as if her ears were plugged. Like the swimmer's ear she would get when spending too much time underwater. He released his grip just enough that she could lift her arm and allow her head to lightly rest in her hand.

Through the fuzziness her survival mode kicked into overdrive. If she was going to walk out of this alive or at least in a hospital bed next to Kim, she needed to start talking, playing into Ray's emotions.

She focused harder as his words became clearer. "You did this! It's all your fault!"

Ray's face became sharper. The strain to focus made her wince as her pulse throb inside her head with each heartbeat. His scent came as a mixture of alcohol and smoke, and the combination made her sick to her stomach. When she had first met him, he seemed polished and business-like. Today he was a mess with his ruffled shirt, unmanaged hair and half-grown beard.

His temper tantrum continued. "She would have taken me back if it wasn't for you!"

Ava cleared her throat, hoping she could muster her voice above a whisper.

"I'm sorry, Ray."

"Oh, you're sorry. Thanks, that fixes everything."

"I was wrong. I should have left you and Kim alone. I'm so sorry." Ava wanted to roll her eyes from the pile of lies she'd just uttered. She wasn't sorry. Not an ounce. But she would say what he wanted to hear to survive.

He began to pace back and forth, his hands shaking as he spoke. "Everything is ruined. Kim is mine. Do you hear me?" He stopped inches from her face, his rapid breathing whipped across her skin. She kept her head down, fearful to look into his eyes.

"Ray, maybe if you got some help, she'd see how much you've changed."

"Kim never had a problem with me until you came into her life."

So much talking. It was hard to keep up with the conversation while attempting to keep a tight lid on her words. Hoping not to upset him, but knowing at this point, it probably didn't matter.

"You were hurting her, Ray. That's a problem, whether she said anything or not."

"I love her. Don't you see that?"

"You love her. The woman who is laying in a hospital bed

191

fighting for her life because of you." The words tumbled out. "You need help, Ray."

"I don't need help. I need Kim. And once you are out of her life, she'll take me back."

She looked up and regretted it immediately. A fire burned in his eyes, like wildfire spreading from a single spark, sweeping across his features, out of control, powerful, unstoppable. She could feel the heat from his anger as if his skin was a smoldering ember.

His hand closed around her throat, stifling the air that needed to escape her lungs. From behind his back he pulled out a gun with his other hand and jammed it in her face. As she looked down the barrel all pride evaporated as she whimpered, "Please don't do this. I promise I'll leave Kim alone. I promise. Please..."

chapter twenty-five

Matt turned on his signal and exited off onto the road that led him straight to Ava's elementary school. His SWAT training had ended early and he needed to right some wrongs with her. When he had some space from her he realized her words held some truth. She had no right to accuse him of being interested in another woman, but he'd let his frustration burst through the seams.

Her accusations about him and Amber had hurt. In all honesty, her battles were getting old and he didn't know how else to help her. But that was the key point. He couldn't rescue her heart or make the difference to help her see clearly, it would have to be God.

Matt assumed she would still be at the school prepping her room. When she worked on projects for school, all time diminished for her. Hours felt like minutes in her time frame. He had decided not to call her and just show up. This conversation needed to happen in person.

As he pulled into the main parking lot he was surprised not to see her car. Pulling out his phone to call her he remembered that she usually liked to park in the back lot, which was closer to her room. Making his way around the building, adrenaline shot through his veins as he spotted what looked like the description of Ray's truck next to her car. Making his way closer he sucked in a jagged breath as he caught sight of Ava up against his truck with a gun pointed at her face.

With the phone still in his hand, he called 911, gave the school name, information about the emergency, and demanded back-up as quickly as he could.

Ray's back was to him and he didn't know if he would be able to get to him before the sound of his car would be heard. Approaching in his cruiser would immediately put Ray on the defense. He was already crazy enough, but if he felt backed into a corner, Matt honestly didn't know what he'd do.

With a last-minute plan, he came to a stop, quick enough to keep up with his adrenaline, but not enough that his tires screeched. Slamming the car into park, he opened his door and took off on foot, hoping to catch Ray off guard.

This couldn't be happening. Especially not after the way they had left each other today. Why did he have to argue with her like that and then just leave? He could have burned a hole through the back of Ray's head from his fierce anger.

As he approached, Ray continued yelling at her, profanities interlaced with his words. Sweat trickled down his back as he advanced on the balls of his feet, his arms up, his gun locked between his hands, finger on the trigger.

Ava cried, begging Ray, and pleading with him not to hurt her. Matt needed to push his feelings for her aside. Push past the fear that would grip him if he allowed himself to look at the circumstances as anything but a routine hostage situation. He could no longer look at Ava as Ava...she had now become just another victim that needed his help. Neither of them had noticed him yet, both were too focused on the other to be aware of the settings around them. As he reached the vehicles he swung around to the left to give himself the ability to seek cover behind Ava's car if he needed it. Back-up would be here soon, but not soon enough. At this point, he had no good shot that he felt confident about that wouldn't risk any harm to Ava. The time had come to make himself known.

"Rockford Police! Put down your weapon!" The words burned like fire out of his throat.

Matt stood on the other side of Ava's car, gun raised and aimed, his eyes locked onto Ray's, trying to anticipate his next move. Matt had startled the crazed man, but not enough. Ray jolted back and without warning took hold of Ava and swung her around, making her into a human shield. Ray lifted the gun again and shoved it against the side of Ava's head.

Dread filled Matt's gut. Ray was a loose cannon and this would not end well.

※※※ ※※※

Ava felt every thumping beat of her heart against the cold barrel pressed firmly on her right temple. Despite her dangerous position, relief flooded through her. Matt was here. His voice, his presence, made her hopeless situation a little brighter.

"Back off or I swear I'll shoot her!" Ray's arm tightened around her neck while he shuffled them further away from Matt.

Matt approached in a slow pace with his gun still drawn, but with his other hand up in attempt to calm Ray down. The shock of Matt being here slowly faded and her fear returned. He was here to save her, but now his safety thickened the destructive situation.

The tears burned her eyes and blurred her vision.

"Hey man, you don't want to do this. I'm sure we can work something out." Matt stopped ten yards away from them but didn't waver from his stance. His eyes smoldered.

"Go away!" Ray's grip tightened. "I'll shoot her and it will be your fault."

"No," Ava pleaded. "Please no." Ava's upper body shook while she cried.

She was going to die.

She had so much she wanted to say to Matt, most importantly to tell him this wasn't his fault. He would find a reason to blame himself if something happened to her. She couldn't bear the thought of him walking away from her lifeless body and putting the blame on himself. "*Oh, God,*" she prayed reverently. *"Help me, save me. Keep Matt safe."*

Matt's voice broke through her prayers. "I know you feel hopeless, but it doesn't have to end this way. Just put the gun down and I'll do all I can to help you." He assured Ray.

"Help me?" Ray laughed as bitterness laced his words. "You don't want to help me. Do you think I'm stupid?" He pushed the gun harder into Ava's skull as she hollered from the mixture of pain and fear.

"I don't think you're stupid at all, quite the opposite, but I can't help you unless you put that gun down." Matt kept his eyes locked on Ray's. "I know deep down you don't want to hurt her. If you shoot her, both of your lives are over, but if you put the gun down I'll do my best to help you. Just let her go and this can be just between the two of us."

Ray tightened his grip on her even more, clearly agitated. The back of her shirt dampened as he pressed her into his sweaty chest. Ray's hands shook as panic rose higher in Ava's chest. Fear of the unknown gripped her.

Ray finally spoke. "Prove you want to help me. Put your gun down first!"

Ava locked eyes with Matt for only a moment, but long enough to see his determination. He would do anything to keep her safe. And that was exactly what she feared from the beginning.

Matt broke his stance. "Okay. If I put my gun down, you have to give me the lady in return."

"You can have her. I just want to leave here alone."

Matt took a step back, crouching down slowly as he placed his gun on the asphalt. Standing up as if he was in no hurry, he kept his palms placed out to show his cooperation. "See, I'm on your side."

"Kick the gun away!" Ray shouted.

Ava's body trembled as the scene played out before her, a nightmare that she just needed to wake up from.

Matt kicked his gun to the side. "Now release her." Matt just became a sitting duck with no protection.

As Ray's grip discharged ever so lightly, the sound of sirens became known and more distinct by the second. Trying to take a step from his hold he kept a firm hand upon her arm.

His hesitation was evident.

The thought crossed her mind just to run. The chance was slim that she would make it to safety before a bullet caught up with her, but being held as a hostage made her think irrationally. She glanced once more toward Matt but reluctantly stayed paralyzed in her spot.

The sirens became louder. The moment she realized those sirens were coming to them...so did Ray.

"You lied to me!" Ray shouted at Matt. His emotions must have caught up with him because he took a step away from her as the gun swept in all directions.

The shot was unexpected.

Ava saw the blast come from Ray's gun while the force pushed them backwards. The sound echoed against the building along with her screams.

"No!" She screamed as their feet became wrapped up in each other's and they tumbled to the ground. Ava landed first. As her head hit the ground she saw Matt twist back and fall before Ray collapsed on top of her, blocking her view.

A domino effect of commotion overwhelmed her senses. Ray jumped up, swearing, cursing the God she served. Matt yelled, moaned and then went limp. Out of the corner of her eye she could see the police cars approaching.

Adrenaline surged through her. "Matt!" Ava called. She crawled over to where he sprawled out on his back on the asphalt. She half expected Ray to finish the job and put a bullet in the back of her head, but instead he jumped into his truck. She glanced back to see him take off across the yard at high speeds, bouncing over each mound and crevice.

Police cars whizzed by on a race to catch up with him. Tuning out everything else around her, she made her way to Matt's side. She froze at the blood seeping out from underneath him. His eyes stayed closed, but his chest moved slightly to prove he was still breathing. "Oh God, please," she begged. "Matt, can you hear me? Matt?"

She cried while leaning over him. Blood pooled under him and she couldn't tell where the bullet had entered. Ava traced her hands over his chest looking for the area he had been shot to put pressure on the hole to help stop the bleeding. Where did the shot enter? Matt winced in pain when he coughed. "Ava,"

His weak voice startled her. "Shhh, don't talk."

Arms took hold of her from behind, pulling her off Matt's body. "No!" she protested. Ava pulled her arm free and placed her hand on the side of Matt's face.

"Ava." It was Derek who spoke calmly in her ear.

"I'm fine, I'm fine. Leave me," she begged.

"Ava," he pulled her off with more force this time. "The EMTs are here. They need room to work on him and I need you to come with me."

"Please don't make me leave him!" She watched as people rushed over. They encircled him and began first aid, talking with vocabulary she couldn't wrap her mind around.

Derek picked her up, ignoring the plea. She buried her head in his shoulder, crying while he carried her. He sat her in the back of the second ambulance and bent down, putting them at eye level.

"Ava," he whispered, gently pushing a strand of matted hair back from her face. "Are you okay? Do you have any injuries?"

Ava took a moment to calm down and suck in a deep breath. "I'm fine. I have a bad headache," she answered while rubbing the back of her head for the first time, noticing how painful the protruding bump was. "I was thrown hard against Ray's truck and hit my head. I just need some Tylenol."

Derek looked at her as if trying to discern the response she gave was indeed the truth. "Okay, but no matter what, we have to take you to the hospital to get checked out. Let me get you inside the ambulance and I'll ride along with you."

"What about Matt? Is he going to be okay?"

"I'm sure he's going to be fine." he paused, reading her face. "Would it make you feel better if I went and got an update before we left?" he offered.

She nodded her head, unable to speak.

"All right, stay here and I'll be right back." He turned and jogged over to the men working on Matt.

Ava tried to compose herself. She wiped the tears off her face and looked down to straighten her shirt. She gasped in horror at the sight of herself covered in Matt's blood. With the combination of her head throbbing like she'd beat it against a wall and the sight of blood, she face began to drain. Everything began to spin and turn black. The last thing she saw was Derek sprinting back toward her.

chapter twenty-six

Ava woke up confused and disoriented, trying to determine whether she had dreamed what happened or if it was reality. She looked over to see Derek watching her with a puckered brow.

She grimaced. It was reality.

Derek leaned forward and rested his elbows on his knees. The tight quarters of the ambulance didn't give him much room to maneuver his tall frame. "Hey, are you trying to get me in trouble with Matt? He will never forgive me for letting you pass out on my watch."

"How about we make this our little secret?"

"I like the way you think."

"How is he?" she asked, her voice thick with concern. "Be honest," she added while lifting her eyebrows so he understood the seriousness of her comment.

Derek didn't look too upset, but his job description revolved around hiding emotion. "I don't know much. He was shot in the shoulder area. He is on his way to the hospital now and will go straight into surgery." He touched her arm to show support.

Ava forced herself not to cry. It would make her headache worse. "Is he in a lot of pain?"

"Probably not. I'm sure he's gotten a huge dose of pain

medication by now."

Derek looked out the front window. "Okay, we're here. Let's get you checked out and then I'll take you to the surgery waiting room. I'm sure you'll want to be there when the doctor comes out of surgery. Oh, and I called your parents. They'll meet you here with some new clothes. I thought you'd like to change into something different."

Not once had he made her out to be a burden. His thoughtfulness didn't go unnoticed and she appreciated the fact that she didn't even need to ask for anything.

⊰꙰⊱ ⊰꙰⊱

The bright light shining in Ava's eyes made her headache more intense. It clicked off and she blinked a few times, trying to erase the white spots that danced across her vision.

The doctor stepped back and started typing in his computer. He looked up over the top of his glasses, "Well, Miss Williams, you have a mild concussion and a small hematoma, um, goose egg, on the back of your head. The examination just showed bumps and bruises, but nothing is broken." The doctor went on to talk about the treatment for the concussion and said that he would send her home with medication for the pain. The headache would probably linger for a few days and could last up to a week. She also needed ice to help decrease the size of the goose egg.

He wrote out a prescription. "Do you have any questions?"

"No."

"Okay, then you are free to go. I'm very sorry this happened to you. If you need someone to talk with, we have a wonderful counselor on staff and our chapel is always open."

"Thank you."

He turned and walked out the door, leaving her alone. Ava sat in her gown, not sure what to do but replay the day in her head. A knock on the door rescued her from the thoughts. A nurse peeked her head in. "You have a couple visitors. Can I send them in?"

"Yes, please."

Her mom bolted into the room once she got the green light and her dad followed behind her. "Mom, Dad," Ava stretched out her arms as her mom wrapped her in a hug while her dad enveloped both of them into his arms. Ava rested in their comfort, finally able to release the emotions she'd held in all day.

Unaware of how long they stayed huddled together, Ava pulled away tired and emotionally exhausted. As much as she needed to be with her parents, she became antsy and longed for an update on Matt. "Thanks for coming."

"Oh Ava, we are so thankful you're okay. What did the doctor say?"

"He said I have a mild concussion and a nice goose egg on the back of my head." She touched the area and jumped from the tenderness. "I have a bad headache, but he gave me some pain medication and said it should improve soon."

"Well, after the day you've had, we should be grateful that it wasn't more serious." Her dad put his arm around her and kissed the top of her head gently. "I'm so sorry you had to experience that, you must have been so scared."

"It was horrible. The worst part was watching Matt get shot." A few tears spilled onto her cheeks and she swiped them away.

"Derek explained everything to us while we waited to see you. Don't worry. I'm sure he'll be okay. Just remember it will take some time to get the image out of your head. We will all be here if you need to talk about it." Her dad always knew what to say to make her feel better.

Ava's mom picked up the bag by the door. "We stopped at your apartment and got you some clothes, your hair brush, and make-up. Why don't you freshen up, it will help you feel better," she said while handing her the bag.

Her mom had chosen the duffle bag she had used since high school basketball. A small rip on one of the side pockets showed its use, but otherwise it stayed in good condition. For Christmas last year Jake had given her a new bag, but it just wasn't the same.

"Okay, but then I want to get up to the waiting area. I don't want to miss Matt's doctor." She slipped off the table and looked in the bag to see what clothes they brought. She pulled out sweatpants, a T-shirt, flip flops and her Chicago Bears pullover sweatshirt.

"Perfect," she smiled over at her mom.

"I figured you wouldn't be going anywhere soon and needed to be comfortable."

Ava went to the bathroom to change. The new clothes warmed her chilled skin. She brushed through her tangled hair, careful not to put pressure on the massive bump protruding from her scalp, and pulled it back in a low ponytail. After washing off the last few traces of blood on her arms she washed her face and applied foundation, eye shadow and lip gloss. There was no need to impress anyone. She just didn't want to look like death warmed over.

Walking back into the room she was surprised to see that Derek had joined her parents. They were deep in discussion until she entered. "Hey, you look better. How are you feeling?" he asked.

"Okay." She walked toward the group, desperate for an update. "Do you have any news on Matt?"

"No. He'll be in surgery for a while longer. I do need you to come with me. The detective on the case needs to ask you a few questions. It won't take long and then I'll personally deliver you to the waiting area to sit around and be bored with the rest of us." He looked over at her parents.

Ava's dad stepped forward, "Your mother and I will go down to the cafeteria and get you some dinner while you're being questioned. Lucy called and said she and the boys are on their way. We'll come and meet you in the waiting room," he looked over at Derek, "if that is okay?"

"Absolutely, there is plenty of room." He opened the door for everyone. "We'll see you there."

Ava followed Derek to the office they had set up for questioning. Detective Trevor Hudson met them in the room and shook her hand when she entered. He seemed younger than Ava expected a detective would be. His handsome appearance had her beginning to wonder if that was a prerequisite for being on the force.

After she answered his questions he praised her for how she handled the situation. "Seeing how you and Sergeant Thompson are in a relationship, you did a great job not to let Mr. Connors know. It could have made the situation much more complicated."

"Did you catch Ray?" Ava asked, trying to keep her anger at bay toward him...and herself. Ray pulled the trigger, but it was her fault for putting Matt in that position. Why didn't she listen to him and just stay home. The "what if's" were choking her.

"Yes. He only made it about a mile away from the school before he reached one of our roadblocks."

Derek turned in his seat and grabbed his water bottle. "Detective Hudson, if you're done now, I believe Ava would like to get to the waiting room. Matt's surgery should be over soon."

The kind detective stood and Ava followed suit. He shook

her hand again, "Thank you Miss Williams, I'll be in contact if there are any further questions."

⚜⚜⚜⚜

The packed waiting room held people who cared about Matt. Matt's parents were there, along with her family, Matt's pastor, and several guys from the department. Ava hugged Matt's parents and talked with them before sitting down with her family. They informed her that his siblings were coming in from Chicago as early as tomorrow to see him. Derek brought her some ice for her head and she leaned against Josh for support.

She had just fallen asleep on Josh's shoulder when he nudged her. "Ava, the doctor is here," he whispered.

Ava straightened and rubbed her eyes. Her headache was not as intense but still a nuisance. The doctor walked over to Matt's parents and his mom waved her over to join them.

Dr. Ross sat down in front of them and Ava immediately became nervous. "Matt's surgery went well. He was shot in his left shoulder." He lifted his arm to show them where the bullet entered. "The reason for his emergency surgery was because of his excess bleeding. We were afraid the bullet nicked his brachial artery." He used his hand to show which regions of the shoulder, back, chest and arm this entailed.

"I know this may sound overwhelming, but Sergeant Thompson was very fortunate." He smiled to prove the words he spoke were true. "It was a clean, through-and-through wound. The bullet not only missed this artery but also his heart by a couple mere inches. It also dodged the median nerve. Injuring this nerve would have created complications for recovery and I'm sure his job. He will have a slow, but complete, recovery."

Questions abounded until everyone felt confident in

Matt's prognosis. "When will we be able to see him?" Matt's mom asked, upset and in need of seeing her son.

"He's in the recovery room now, but in the next hour we should be able to transfer him to his room. I'll have the nurse come and get you when that happens." He shook Matt's dad's hand and then stood. "If you have any further questions, please don't hesitate to page me."

Ava walked back to her family as if a hundred pounds had been lifted off her chest. Matt was going to be okay. Hearing the good news, her family decided to head home and come back tomorrow to see Matt. They offered her a ride home.

"No thanks, I'm going to stay here for the night. But could one of you go get my car at the school and bring it here?" She didn't plan on leaving anytime soon, but she would need her car whenever that happened.

"We'll go get it." Jake looked over at Josh for confirmation.

Lucy came up and wrapped her arms around her. "I'm so glad you're okay. I don't know what I would do without you."

After their extended goodbyes she sat back down on the couch with the floral print that caused her eyes to cross. The tiredness of the day engulfed her as she leaned back cautiously against her head. She had been spending more time at the hospital these days than she liked.

Matt's dad brought over a pillow and blanket. "Why don't you take a nap and we'll wake you up when it's time to go see Matt."

Ava looked up grateful. "Thank you, Peter. I think I'll take you up on your offer." She fell asleep as soon as her head touched the pillow.

chapter twenty-seven

The room was dark except for the overhead light above the sink humming its own tune. Ava sat watching Matt sleeping in his bed. He stirred and rustled, moaning from the pain. His eyes fluttered open and darted over at her.

"What are you doing here?" he asked coldly.

"Oh, um, I was worried about you," she stuttered. His rudeness caught her off guard.

"Thank you for your concern, but it's not needed." He looked up at the ceiling. "Why don't you go home, I'm sure you're tired."

"That's okay. I want to be here." Ava reached for his hand, but he moved it before the touch became final.

"Ava, don't you get it? I don't want you here," he snapped.

"But why, I thought you loved me?"

"I do...I did, but I've just realized you're not

going to change." He pointed to his shoulder. "This situation has opened my eyes." He glared over at her. The coldness from his eyes made her shiver. "I'm tired of having to put so much effort into making this relationship work. Love shouldn't be this hard."

"Matt, you don't mean that. Every relationship takes work. You've just had a lot happen today." Panic rose in her chest.

"Yeah, I've had a lot happen. My girlfriend accused me of wanting to cheat on her just because I said hello to another woman. I'm in a hospital bed shot because you wouldn't listen to me. I'd say that is a long day."

"I am so sorry. Please Matt, please. We can work this out." Ava started begging, holding back no humility.

"Ava, my feelings have changed toward you. There isn't much I want that is left to fight for. Sorry, but we're over." It was as if he poured salt into a wound.

The pain burned.

"Matt, please, no." She cried, desperate to change his mind. She stood, forcing him to look at her. "Please, I love you. Give me another chance to be worthy of your love. Please love me. Please want me!"

He turned his head away from her as his final rejection. Ava put her head in her hands and let the tears flow.

"Ava, wake up." Derek patted her shoulder with ease. His touch came before she could focus on his words. "You're just having a dream."

Her body jerked as her eyes shot open. Derek's concerned face came in to focus as a mirror of her own. Ava sat up and brushed away the tears threatening to expose themselves. She rotated her shoulder and stretched her arms out in front of her to work the stiffness out of her muscles. "It was just a dream?" She sat confused, still not completely sure.

The nightmare seemed so real.

"Matt's in his room now if you'd like to go see him."

He handed her a cup of coffee.

Ava chuckled. "Thanks. Matt told you about my addiction?"

"He has, and I've thought about acquiring stock in the mountain grown because of it." She seized the cup and took a sip. The coffee scorched the tip of her tongue, but there was no need to complain. It didn't touch the throbbing in her head. In fact, the burn came as a good distraction. Her dream didn't help the situation and she became nervous to see Matt.

"I don't need to go right away. You and Matt's parents can go first."

"I'm glad you feel that way, because that's what we did. We didn't want to wake you. We thought you could use the sleep."

Ava looked across the room disappointed to about the empty couch where Peter and Anna had been sitting. She and Matt's mom had been getting close and she wanted to check on how she was handling everything.

Usually she was a light sleeper. How had she missed all the commotion of them leaving? Her apartment faced the street and on many occasions she woke up from a loud car passing by or people walking around outside talking at high volumes.

"Oh, okay, I guess I'll go now." She looked down into the cup, unable to move. She wanted to see him but a part of her still wondered if he would make the horrible dream come true.

Derek caught on to her hesitancy and crouched down, making them at eye level. He was still in his uniform and his slanted eyes exposed his exhaustion. Today couldn't have been easy on him, having his best friend get shot, and yet he made himself a pillar of strength for her in her time of need.

"Ava, there is one thing about Matt that will never change." He waited until he had her full attention. "Matt will always want you."

Ava sat up straighter. "How did you...?"

He snickered at her bewildered expression. "You talk in your sleep."

Ava's cheeks glowed with embarrassment. She changed the subject so as to avert the conversation from herself and this new habit of sleep talking. "How is he?"

"Fine, he's been in and out of sleep, but you can go and sit with him as long as you want." He raked his fingers through his tussled blond hair. "I'll take you up to his room and then I'm going home to get some sleep." He took her arm, pulling her up in slow motion so she wouldn't spill her coffee. "I don't know about you, but I'm ready for this day to be over."

❧❧❧ ❧❧❧

After Derek left, Ava stood outside Matt's door for a moment to collect her thoughts and prepare for the sight of him all bandaged up. The door squeaked as she opened it. The room was dark except for the glow of the full moon that filtered through the window.

Ava walked over to his bed, shoulders heavy from the day. She stood beside him, holding back the tears. He looked peaceful despite the white dressings wrapped around his upper body along with tubes coming out in every direction. She glanced up at his monitors. Everything appeared good.

Not that she knew what good was.

She pulled the bedside chair closer and reached for his hand as she sat down. His warm hand in hers, while watching his chest rise with each breath, comforted her. She stared immobilized, soaking in every detail of his face.

Thoughts of the dream teased her. It hurt just imagining this man not wanting her. Derek's words were reassuring, but she needed to hear them from Matt.

Ava stood and leaned over, tracing his hairline with her fingers. She kissed his flushed cheek. "Please still want me. I can't imagine my life without you. I love you, Matthew," she whispered softly.

"I love you, too." His voice startled her. He opened his eyes a moment later with a smirk that pulled at her heartstrings.

"Matt, you're awake! Are you okay? Do you need me to go get a nurse?" she asked in a rush and turned to go get someone before he could respond to the questions that bombarded him.

He grabbed her hand and pulled her back to his side. "You leaving is not an option right now. Stand there so I can get a good look at you." His voice stayed quiet and his eyes glistened in the moonlight from the tears resting at the brim.

"Honey, are you in pain?" She reached for the button to call the nurse, but he stopped her.

"No, this is just the first time I've seen you since you had a gun to your head." A few tears spilled down the side of his face. He scrunched up his nose and mouth to hold back the emotions. She had never seen him cry before. The rock before her began to crumble. "Ava, I've never been so scared in my entire life. When I drove up and saw Ray with a gun to your head..." His words drifted to a stop.

"I know. But I'm fine...thanks to you." She rubbed her hand along his good arm.

"Are you sure you're okay?

"Yes."

"Did he hurt you?" She wanted to hold the truth from him but he would find out anyway.

"I only have a mild concussion. It's not a big deal. I could have gotten one by tripping over the shoes in my closet," Ava said dryly in an effort to play it down. He didn't need to get upset about her condition when he lay in a hospital bed after being shot because of her. She did, however, look forward to her next dose of pain medication in an hour.

He didn't buy it. She was a lousy liar.

"Not a big deal," he raised his voice a notch. He looked up at the ceiling. "I'm sorry I didn't protect you better. You must think less of me."

Ava took his chin and moved his head to face her. "Hey, look at me." She waited until he did. "I'm only alive because of you. It's hard to protect a woman with a stubborn streak. I have no negative thoughts toward you." She bent over and kissed his lips. "I do, however, have plenty of thoughts about how much I love you. If you haven't noticed, Sergeant Thompson, I'm quite smitten with you."

"I almost lost you today, Ava."

"And I almost lost you, too," she pointed to his injured shoulder.

He grinned. "Oh, this little thing, it's just a scratch."

"I'm sure you'll change your mind once the morphine wears off."

Ava liked how they could still tease despite the day's events. She grabbed the blanket at the end of the bed and covered his legs. A nurse entered the room to check Matt's vitals. Ava unloaded all her questions and the nurse politely answered every one of them in great detail. Ava guessed that Jules mirrored this woman when she was on duty by the concern and care she took over each patient.

By the time the nurse left, Matt and Ava had heard about her grandkids, husband, and how much she enjoyed her job. Ava's spirits heightened upon hearing more confirmation that Matt would recover well. Their conversation calmed her nerves and revived her energy level.

Ava sat back down on the chair she had pulled over earlier, wanting more alone time with him before the nurse came back to do her rounds. She ran her fingers over her dry and cracked lips, in need of moisture. Leaning back, she brought her feet up to rest on the end of the chair while she pulled out her chap stick, thankful that one of the officers had found her purse and brought it to the hospital. It relieved her to have her phone and wallet beside her again. A woman's purse was her identity, a bag of endless treasures that would be worthless to outsiders, but full of wealth for the owner.

Or a great place to put your trash.

Matt eyed her impishly. "As I was waking up I overheard what you said. Baby, why didn't you think I'd still want you?"

Ava had hoped he didn't hear that part or at least forgot about it. "I had a bad dream before I came in here that you didn't want me anymore and that your feelings had changed. I was just shaken up, that's all." She fidgeted with the blanket so she didn't have to look at him. The day had emotionally wiped her out and she wasn't sure if she could handle this conversation tonight. "Derek overheard me talking in my sleep. He helped me feel better about it."

"What did he say?"

"That you will always want me and that will never change." Her voice quivered from nerves as she wondered if he would agree with his partner's assessment. She changed the subject so as to not put him on the spot. "You know you have a great best friend, right? He took care of me from the moment you got shot until he brought me to your door. What did you do, pay him an advance in case of an emergency?"

He smiled. "No." He reached out for her hand and pulled her back up to the side of his bed. "You do know that his words were true? I'll always want you." He kissed her hand.

Their lunch date flashed across her mind as a reminder of how poorly she had acted toward him. She had a list of things that needed clearing up. "I'm really sorry about lunch today. I don't know what was wrong with me. Forgive me?"

"There is nothing to forgive, sweetheart. I was offended at first, but then I put myself in your shoes. I wouldn't have liked a guy flirting with you."

"Yeah, but you wouldn't have accused me of wanting to cheat." Regret consumed her. This man before her was anything but a cheater. He walked in honesty, strong character, and never once wavered on his feelings for her, despite her best efforts to subconsciously change his mind.

"Maybe not, but I don't have the past that you do. Sometimes I need to remember that before I speak or lose my temper. I claim my part of our argument. Sorry I was a jerk." He brushed a strand of hair out of her face.

She gingerly smiled her forgiveness. "Speaking of my past, I had some time on my hands today to think, and I had a little revelation." Ava had been waiting to get this off her chest. Whether tired or not, this needed to be said.

"Oh really? You've piqued my interest, please share."

"You said you were tired of paying for another man's mistakes and -"

He interrupted, "I'm sorry, that wasn't right of me to say."

Ava put her fingers on his lips to quiet him. "You were right, but I realized you were also paying for mine. Tim wasn't the only one at fault. I chose to marry him even though on some level I knew something was wrong. He became distant and I did nothing about it. Honestly, I think I was more in love with the idea of being married than with whom I planned to spend the rest of my life with. As for the fear of being loved again, his rejection doesn't make me worthless or undeserving. I need to find my identity in Christ, not in situations or people."

Ava sat back down on the chair because she couldn't focus while being that close to him. "I would have saved myself a lot of heartache had I trusted my instincts and God. In the end, it was my mistakes that have caused my insecurities now."

"Hmmm, so what are your instincts and God telling you now?"

He was fishing for compliments and she would give them. "That you want me, and without a doubt our feelings are the same."

"Ava, please listen to me. Whether you have another bad dream or see another girl talking with me, I'm in love with you. I've waited a very long time for you to come into my life. You're it, I'm done." He placed her hand on his chest. "This heart will never beat for anyone but you."

His heartbeat pumped beneath her hand. She held no fear over his declaration, only excitement for the life she would someday share with him. Her heart had healed and that realization was liberating.

"And I love you, Matthew Everett."

"Whoa, my middle name. You must mean it."

"More than you know."

Ava yawned, unable to hide her fatigue any longer. Their moment disappeared as Matt looked over at the clock. "No wonder you're tired, it's after midnight. Why don't you go home and get some sleep."

"I'm not going anywhere, you're stuck with me." Ava grabbed the extra blanket from the end of his bed and curled up in the chair. "I'll just sleep here."

Matt glared at her and she glared right back. She wasn't stepping down.

He sighed. "I can see this is a battle I won't win." A victorious smile spread across Ava's lips. "So if you're going to be stubborn and stay, then stay with me." He pulled the covers back and patted the bed.

"Do you realize how many rules we'd be breaking?" His invitation stunned her.

He put his hand up in the air, displaying the Boy Scout's honor. "I promise to be a perfect gentleman. I just need to hold you in my arms...well, arm."

Ava jumped to his side right away before he had the chance to change his mind. She laid her head on his good shoulder and curled up against his body. They laid there quiet, content, until she remembered her idea.

"So is Derek single yet?"

"Why? Are you interested?" Matt laughed alone at his joke. "You spend one day with him and now you're knocking down his door?"

"Quit," with a playful spirit she pretended to punch his chest.

"Hey, I'm a wounded man, remember?"

"I'm sorry," she responded dryly. "I thought it was just a scratch." They began laughing in pure exhaustion. Ava got up on her side, resting on her elbow. "I was asking because I wanted to set him up with Jules. I think they'd make a good couple."

"As far as I know, he's still seeing Chelsea, but I don't think it will last much longer. He's not truly happy. She's a nice girl, but just not right for him. I like your thinking, but

216

we need to hold off. It's not the right timing."

"Sounds good, I've got more than enough to handle right now." She kissed him and lightly touched his bandaged shoulder. "Between starting school and nursing you back to health, I've got a full plate."

"I could get used to having my own personal nurse."

Ava laid her head back down on his chest and listened to him breathe. "Matthew?"

"Yes?" he sounded as tired as she felt.

"Can we start attending church together...and only because I love you?" Ava looked forward to this next step together. They were finally combining an important part of their lives.

"Absolutely," he kissed the top of her head, "I thought you'd never ask.

chapter twenty-eight

<u>One Month Later</u>

Ava froze in the middle of the cvs aisle. she blinked feverishly as the ghost of wedding past stood in front of her, distracted in choosing which item to purchase. She had wondered many times how she would react in a moment like this. Since the day Tim had shown up at her apartment to give his explanation for calling off their marriage, Ava had avoided any updates on his life. They hadn't had many mutual friends, and the few they had drifted away after the disastrous wedding day. Ava didn't blame them. It was uncomfortable for everyone.

Lucy had told her when news had filtered back that Tim and Cara had gotten married, but other than that, Ava knew nothing about them. God had taken away her feelings for Tim, yet it crossed her mind on occasion what it would feel like to run into the pair together. To stand before them alone while they held hands, or maybe even pushed a tiny stroller.

And now here he stood, right in front of her. Despite the shock, Ava was relieved to find she had no old hurt emotions. No little stabs of pain or reminders of the shame that had hovered for months after their breakup.

She was fine, but did she need to be a glutton for punishment. Did she have it in her to open this can of worms and force the past back into the present? The answer came immediately. She could do this. No longer vulnerable or a leper of rejection, she had no reason to turn tail and run, he could no longer hurt her. Debating on how to approach and what to say, her purse clipped a bag of cough drops that landed to the floor with a thud. Her cover was blown as no preparation remained possible when Tim turned toward the noise, his eyes reaching hers. Shock twisted through his features as she approached with caution.

"Ava..." It had been two years since she had heard him speak her name. He looked like a deer caught in headlights as she drew closer.

"Hi Tim. It's...um...good to see you," As the words left her mouth, she couldn't deny the truth in them, "It's been awhile. You look different." Tim did look older, something around his eyes maybe. He had grown out his sandy blond hair and his once smooth face was now covered by a shabby beard. His build was more filled out, his looks less boyish.

Tim rubbed his beard. "Oh yeah, just trying something new. You don't. You look exactly the same as I remember you." His response produced a small smile, replacing his initial look of shock. "Since I moved back, I wondered if we might eventually run into each other. And if we did, if you would turn and walk away or maybe pretend not to see me"

"Why would I do that?" she responded, but realized it would have been true if God hadn't restored her or brought Matt into her life. "Tim, I've forgiven you and moved on. I don't have bad feelings toward you, or Cara for that matter."

A shadow flickered across Tim's face. Like he couldn't quite believe what she said was true. "I mean it, I really do," she said looking him straight in the eyes. "How are you and Cara? I heard you got married and were living in Peoria. But now you're back in Rockford?"

Tim lowered his head as if steadying himself before returning her gaze. "*I'm* back in Rockford. Cara still lives in

Peoria." The impact of his words hung like a heavy silence between them. As if the moment wasn't already awkward enough...

"That's why I thought you would walk away if we ever saw each other again. I figured you knew," he said finally, his voice thick. "And you'd be disgusted with me. I threw away what we had to marry a woman I never should have been with. Six months ago she left me for an old boyfriend and a party life."

There was no hiding the embarrassment Tim felt. She could physically see the guilt that weighed him down as his shoulders slumped forward. Ava began to tell him not to go on—that she didn't need to know any of this, but it spilled out of him quicker than Ava could take in.

"Ava, when I came to your apartment that day, I made it sound like I had it all figured out. I put a lot of spiritual sounding reasons behind the choices I had made. I felt like I owed you answers, but I couldn't bring myself to tell you honestly that I was in a pretty dark place."

Tim didn't bother to stop for a response. He obviously intended to come clean, as if unloading a heavy bag he didn't want to carry anymore.

"When we graduated and I couldn't find a job around here and moved down to Peoria, things were a lot rougher for me than I let on. My walk with God wasn't where it should have been. None of the friends I made were Christians and the more time I spent going out with them, the further I felt myself drift from the life I had before."

Some of the puzzle pieces that had never quite fit suddenly began to make sense to Ava. The distance she had noticed in the months leading up to their wedding. Why Tim never introduced her to some of the teachers he had begun to spend time with. Why he had been so reluctant to find a church. His parting words that day in the apartment rang in her ears; "*You're a better person than I'll ever be.*"

"It got worse and worse to visit you on the weekends—seeing you still doing devotions, serving at church and growing closer to the Lord, while I knew in my own heart I wasn't right with Him. But I was too proud to admit it to anyone! I just played the game while I was here, and then lived the way I wanted in Peoria. Going out to the bar in the evening with my co-teachers, pushing away the feelings of hatred for the person I had become," Tim's rapid fire words didn't hide the emotions.

"Ava, when I broke off our engagement, it was the right thing to do. I knew I was in no spiritual place to lead you as a husband. I was far off track and wasn't sure I could get myself right again."Ava found herself interjecting. "We can never make ourselves right, Tim. That's why we need Christ."

Out of the pain that was evident in Tim, Ava heard the hope in his voice when he replied, "I've been learning that now. I got pretty low, but the Lord has lifted me out of it."

Ava nodded. She never would have imagined all this. As much of a blow Tim had dealt her, she wouldn't have chosen this for him. She had once loved him with everything she had and despite how things ended she would always care for him. It might be wedged down, way back in the corner of her heart, but she did want the best for him.

"I want to tell you about Cara," he continued. "It's no excuse, but she pursued me pretty hard. I'm not sure why—maybe because she grew up in a Christian home and had fallen away, too, and somehow it was like we deserved each other." He paused to suck in a deep breath of air.

"But in the end, we kind of hated each other. I think she finally realized that she couldn't measure up to you. When I look back, I see that I broke your heart and I used Cara's. I'm grateful that you have forgiven me, Ava. I don't know that Cara ever will."

This was the Tim she had begun dating all those years ago in college. Honest and open. Yet as he talked, her thoughts went to Matt, waiting for her at his apartment. She knew Tim was sincere, and that somehow it helped him for her to know what had happened. But outside of feeling pity for the life he and Cara shared, it didn't make a difference to Ava to know the truth. She had been over Tim for a long time. Her relationship with Christ, and Matt's gentle, patient love had healed her wounds of rejection. Words that might have felt satisfying years ago were unnecessary now.

"She may forgive you one day," she told Tim. "Pray for her. If there is anything I have learned over the last few years, it is prayer can heal any heart."

Ava made motions to leave, wanting to get back to Matt. She was here to pick up a refill prescription for him while he went to therapy and didn't want him to have to wait on her for lunch. Tim picked up on her signals.

"You probably need to go, huh?" he said. "I'm sorry I kept you so long. I'm sure anyone who needed Bengay or heating pads decided to go to another store rather than try to bypass us."

Ava laughed, as Tim looked down sheepishly, rubbing the toe of his shoe against the linoleum.

"Ava, could I call you sometime? Maybe we could talk more—I could hear what's been going on in your life, too."

The laughter faded from Ava's voice as she searched her brain for the right response. For an answer that would respect her relationship with Matt while she avoided hurting Tim's feelings. She could stand here all day singing Matt's praises, but she didn't want to throw her happiness back into Tim's face. It would have felt good two years ago, but today it seemed meaningless.

"I'm with someone now, Tim. I'm sorry, but I don't think that would be a good idea." Tim nodded and shrugged his shoulders. "It's okay. I was hopeful, but guessed that might be the case. He's got a good thing. Make sure he knows that."

After Ava said goodbye to Tim and stood in the checkout line, she thought of Matt and his selflessness, patience, and gentleness towards her. It wasn't Matt who had the good thing, she was sure of that. But they certainly had a good thing together.

chapter twenty-nine

"Matt, what do you want on your sandwich?" Ava hollered out to him from his kitchen.

"I'll take the works," he called back.

She bit her lower lip, feeling like an idiot. "Um, what does that entail?"

"Oh, I forgot who I was talking to," his laughter drifted in from the living room. "It means to put all the toppings I have on it."

We'll just see who has the final laugh. A sinister plan took shape. She pulled out all the condiments she could find - ketchup, mustard, jelly, ranch dressing, mayo and barbecue sauce. She tried to keep the giggles to a minimum so he wouldn't catch on to her mischievous act.

Ava took the hoagie bun and filled it with roast beef and hid all the toppings between the cheese and lettuce. She made herself a normal sandwich, grabbed them each a bottle of water, and headed to the living room for the show.

Matt sat on the couch with his arm in a sling, watching the first football game of the season for the University of Illinois. She had a nudge of guilt pulling a prank on a one-winged man, but he had it coming. He had been cranky for the last few weeks and Ava came to the conclusion that nurses were underpaid.

It had been a month since the shooting and Matt was getting a little stir-crazy. He would be getting his sling off soon, but he still couldn't return to work for another week. After returning he had another couple weeks of desk duty until the physical therapist gave him a clean bill of health. After that he would be able to perform the department's mandatory fitness of duty evaluation to prove he could fulfill the duties of his position. He didn't hide his displeasure over the desk duty and his waiting time for the evaluation.

Ava handed him his sandwich and drink and took her spot next to him on the couch. "How's the game going?" She didn't really care, she just needed the distraction.

"Good. Illinois just scored a touchdown to tie up the game." Out of the corner of her eye she saw him take a bite, chew and stop, staying silent. He finally gulped and said, "Wow."

She looked over, pleased. "That good, huh? I hoped it would be memorable." She couldn't contain it any longer and her cackling exploded.

"Ava, what did you do?" The bewildered expression on his face made her laugh even harder. He opened the sandwich and joined her laughter. She was relieved he found the prank funny.

"You said all the toppings, right?" She gave him her innocent face, but he was no fool.

"I guess I deserved this." He set the plate down on the coffee table and put his good arm up around her shoulder. "I've been a bear lately, I'm sorry."

"It's okay, I know you're frustrated. How did your therapy go today?"

He had been pushing physical therapy hard the last few weeks and convinced his therapist to come in and work with him on Saturday mornings. She worried about his determination to recuperate faster than humanly possible but kept her comments to herself.

"Good. Don said I'm making more improvements and that the sling can come off during Monday's appointment. I just have to take it easy so I don't relapse on the progress we've made." He didn't sound like it was good news. Taking it easy didn't exist in Matt's vocabulary. He always moved forward and having to pull back drove him crazy.

"And that is the opposite of what you want to do." She sat her plate and drink down next to his, careful not to mix them up and discover the hideous taste that would make her taste buds scream in disgust. She turned to look at him sitting with her legs crossed Indian style.

"Matthew, I know you're frustrated about being laid up for so long, but you have to take it easy if you want a full recovery." The speech had become like a broken record. The repetition was getting old for both of them.

"It's just so hard that I can't be out there with my team and backing up Derek. Being a cop is in my blood. I feel lost without my job."

"Hey, you'll be back in the field before you know it, chasing the bad guys, keeping the streets safe, saving lives...and hopefully you're done saving mine," she said, referring to the incident with Ray. She rested her head on the back of the couch. "You've actually saved my life twice."

"Twice?" he asked, bewildered.

"The first was when you chose me to love."

He took her hand and intertwined their fingers. "I don't deserve your praise."

Ava didn't like it when he spoke poorly of himself. He had been uncharacteristically negative the last month and most of it had been aimed at himself. "You really want to play this game?" She could win hands down with all the reasons she didn't deserve him. She pumped herself up for the next statement concerning his condition. "I will admit I've been feeling a little guilty."

He scrunched his eyebrows together in confusion. "Why?"

"Matt, if it wasn't for me, you wouldn't have gotten shot and you wouldn't be stuck in this frustrating situation with work." It took weeks to finally get that statement off her chest. She didn't want to add to his stress level, but something needed to be said.

"Ava Williams, you know that's not true."

"Can you honestly tell me you wouldn't have done anything different if the person held at gunpoint wasn't me?" Chills ran along her skin just thinking about the terrifying experience. It had been a month and she still had reoccurring nightmares about that day. Matt hadn't come out and said it, but she could tell by the dark circles under his eyes that he wasn't sleeping well either.

He closed his eyes and shook his head. "I should have known you would blame this on yourself." He shifted his body to look straight at her, his eyes indefinable.

"Ava, my feelings were different, yes. I have never been so angry and terrified in my entire life. Ray was out of control. None of us knew what he was capable of."

He put his fingers behind her neck and rubbed her cheek with his thumb. The tips of his fingers had become softer over the last few weeks and his old calluses were virtually nonexistent. "I'll be haunted for a long time with the image of you at gunpoint, which is also different. But I got shot because a crazy man took a hostage at gunpoint. It would have happened the same way whether you were the hostage or not."

She fixed her eyes on his for a brief moment, letting his answer settle. "Okay," she whispered simply.

"Okay? Just okay? I usually have to come up with a few speeches before you believe me."

"I'm realizing your yes means yes and your no means no." She smirked proudly. "I must say though, you are incredibly hot when you're doing your job, Sergeant Thompson."

She loved flirting with him.

"Oh, really?" He leaned in a little further, placing their faces only a few inches away. "I could go put on my uniform if that would spark your fancy."

"That's okay. I've got a good picture in my head." She closed the distance between them and kissed him tenderly. She sat back and smiled smugly. "Now, is it just so horrible having some time off? God works in mysterious ways. His plans are not always our own. Maybe He has some things to show you in the next month."

"You're right, sorry if I've been a grouch lately. I do appreciate your support and encouragement. I couldn't do this without you. Thank you for putting up with me."

"That's what I'm here for." She grabbed his plate and stood up. "I'm also, and unfortunate for you, here to feed you. Let me go make you another sandwich."

Ava progressed halfway to the kitchen when she remembered her call from Josh earlier this morning. "Oh, by the way, Josh called and wants to hang out with me tonight. I didn't think we had any prominent plans, so I said yes. Is that okay?" She enjoyed her Saturday nights with Matt, but she couldn't pass up spending some time with her brother.

"Actually, that works out great. I thought about going out with some friends tonight." He smiled casually. "What does Josh want to do?"

"He said something about taking me out for dinner." She shrugged her shoulders. "I guess he just wants some quality time with his favorite sister." She put her finger up to her lips. "Shhh, don't tell Lucy."

Ava brought him out a new sandwich and grudgingly returned to the kitchen to clean up and wash the dishes. It looked as if he hadn't touched anything since she was here last. The afternoon sleepiness started to rear its pesky head. If she wanted to fit in a nap before tonight, she needed to work quickly.

School had been back in full swing for the past two weeks and she held the exhaustion again of being around kids all day. It was good to be back and Ava enjoyed her new class, but the last month had been overwhelmingly hectic.

The first week after the confrontation with Ray had been stressful between getting her class ready for the open house, the start of school, and Matt recovering. He had spiked a high fever and the doctors wanted to keep him in the hospital a couple extra days to monitor him.

Ava had been so blessed by her colleagues that week. A few of them came in extra hours to help with the finishing touches on her classroom and the other kindergarten teachers helped prepare some lesson plans. Thanks to them, she was able to spend her evenings at the hospital.

Matt's first week at home went as expected by spending his time either sleeping or at physical therapy. His pain had increased in the first stages of therapy and just wanted to take it easy. A few of his friends from the department would come and go, checking in on him throughout the day. Ava noticed how his mood improved when he spent time with them but after they left it just frustrated him that he was stuck at home.

By last week he'd hit rock bottom. He walked around depressed and quiet, dispositions she had never seen in him before. Matt went down to the station to talk with the chief about when he could return to active duty and didn't get the answer he hoped for. He understood the time frame of returning to work and the mandatory evaluation, but because upset when they told him he would have to do desk duties for a couple weeks.

This week had gone much better for both of them. Matt received a good report on his therapy, which improved his mood. Just knowing each day got him closer to taking the sling off encouraged him. Ava's class finally adjusted to being at school all day and they had worked out some rough edges in matters of obedience. Matt came and surprised her after school one day and kept her company while she prepared the next day's activities.

Last night Matt took her out on their first date since he had been shot - to the restaurant they went to on their official first date. It had been fun talking about that night and how they each had felt. Afterwards he took her to a movie that she had mentioned wanting to see. The last month had been a whirlwind of different emotions and frustrations. She welcomed their lives getting back to normal once again.

And then she ran into Tim today. She needed to tell Matt, and soon so he wouldn't think she was hiding anything. He already sat perched on the edge, would this push him over? She took a deep breath and headed back to Matt. There was only one way to find out...

❦❦ ❦❦

Matt watched as Ava staggered back into the living room exhausted. She was such a trooper and hadn't complained about having to clean up after him. He hadn't been pleasant to be around the last few weeks. Ava had put up with a lot, more than she should. Lately he'd had a temper and she could light his fuse often without even meaning to.

His bad mood started when he got the news that he couldn't return to active duty for another month. That also happened to be the first day of school for Ava. She had a rough day with a little girl who had cried all day and her nerves were shot. She had come over that night to keep him company and had gotten an earful from him, too. He snapped at her a few times, they argued, and then she left crying. He was a jerk and he knew it. He showed up at her door fifteen minutes later, full of remorse. She gave all she could to love and encourage him and he'd acted unappreciative too many times.

That would change tonight.

Ava flopped down on the couch in great exaggeration and threw her arm across her forehead. "I must really love you. I just spent almost an hour in the kitchen. I think I've reached my quota for the month." The sound of her giggling was therapeutic to his soul.

"Poor baby, would you like some cheese with that whine?"

She made a face at him. "No, but I would like a nap."

"I can get you a blanket."

Ava sat up, checking the time. "I should probably go soon. I thought about stopping at Kim's place on the way home. I'll be pressed for time getting ready if I take a break."

"I think you look great."

"Oh, I see, you go for the no shower, greasy hair look."

"I thought I smelled something."

Ava rolled her eyes but let a grin escape. He had missed their playful side over the stressful last month.

He was so in love with this woman.

She made him feel alive. It went deeper than her beauty and kind nature. Ava merged as neurotic and funny all rolled into one. She was the type of person who couldn't enter through a doorway if it had an exit sign on it because it didn't feel right. She could tell if her stapler on her school desk had moved over an inch, but at her home desk you were lucky to find her stapler.

Ava yawned. Matt made another attempt on her behalf, "Ava, why don't you go now. You can see Kim and if you get ready quick, you'll still have time for a short nap."

"Are you trying to get rid of me?"

"No, but I'm sure Josh would appreciate you not falling asleep on him at dinner."

"True. Point taken." She compelled herself to stand up and went to collect her things. Matt didn't want to see her go, but he needed time to get his plan in action. He met her at the door, his free arm outstretched, anticipating her hug.

Something in her demeanor made him hesitate and stop mid motion. "What's wrong?"

She cleared her throat. "I ran into Tim today."

Matt unconsciously stepped back trying to judge this bombshell announcement as a good or bad thing. And of all days, of course the guy would walk back into her life today. "Are you okay?"

She closed the distance between them. "I'm better than okay. It put me one more step further in my healing process. Our conversation was a little uncomfortable, but needed... at least for him. I actually feel bad for Tim. He moved back here when Cara left him. He seems to be really broken."

Tim lived in Rockford again. Running a hand through his hair he battled his inner protectiveness of her. "Did you tell him about us?"

"Yes. When he asked to meet up sometime I told him no because I was with someone."

Why did his blood pressure spike from her response? His red blood quickly turned green. A chill settled over his body at the thought of her returning to Tim. He'd been a mess for the last month, uptight and more often rude than kind. It shouldn't surprise him if Ava would at some point want a chance to talk more with Tim.

"Be honest Ava, did you want to meet back up with him?" He heard the words as they were spoken. Why did he think so speciously? It was silly really, but he had to know.

"Are you jealous?"

"Should I be?"

Her frustration toward him almost came out as a scream. "No!"

"You told him no because of me, not because *you* didn't want too." Why did he have to be so petty and childish? It was as though all rational thinking left when his life with Ava became threatened. It gave him a glimpse at what she must have felt the day at the café with Amber.

She threw her bags down on the floor and shoved her fists onto her hips. Frustration seeped from her words. "Don't you get it? Haven't you heard a thing I've said? I feel bad for the way his life has turned out, but that's it. After all we've been through, you really think I would leave you for him?" Her eyes softened as she placed a hand against the side of his face. "Tim isn't even half the man you are Matt. There is not an ounce of me that wants him. Get it through that thick head of yours, Thompson, you're stuck with me."

Grabbing her hand he pulled her into his chest without any resistance. "Where's the white flag? I surrender." Smoothing her hair down with his free hand he spoke in a soft whisper. "I'm sorry. I just...I just haven't been myself lately. And Tim showing up in your life again just took me by surprise.

"That makes two of us."

"So you are better than okay, huh?" He tipped up her chin, finding the peace he should have had when this conversation very first started.

"Yes, especially since you're not being ridiculous anymore." Her smirk could have brought him to his knees right then and there, but instead he brushed his lips against hers.

chapter thirty

"Wow, Kim, you look great!" Ava hugged her friend and stepped back, admiring the change in Kim's appearance. It had been a month since Ray had attacked her and the only signs from that horrific day were her arm in a hard cast, her leg in a walking cast, and the glasses she now had to wear from the vision she'd lost.

"I feel great!" Kim's smile brightened the room as she ushered Ava into the living room so they could sit and talk. Kim held a new confidence in herself. Once released from the hospital she was able to come home and finally heal without the fear of Ray in her life. The greatest healing came when Kim had accepted the Lord in her heart.

Kim had come back to the support group a week after her attack and there in the meeting she found the love she had always been seeking for, in God. Ava had missed that meeting because she was at the hospital with Matt, but Kim called her that evening to share the good news.

Huge decisions came out of that meeting and Ava shared her happiness with Kim for the positive steps she took for her and Tessa. Kim had decided that it was time for a fresh start. Since she and her sister had made amends, they had agreed it would be best if she and Tessa would move into her place until Kim could find a job. She already had her résumé out to a few businesses in her sister's town. A new home, a new job, a new beginning.

"Have you gotten any interest in your house yet?" One of the members on the leadership team for the support group was a realtor and she had offered to put Kim's house on the market and help sell it for no commission.

"I think so. Wendy called yesterday and said that she had two couples inquire about it and we plan to have the showings sometime early next week before I start packing to move." Kim glanced around the room. "This was a good house, but I'm happy to be leaving the memories it holds behind."

Ava glanced toward the stairs in remembrance of the memories this place held for her too. "I think a fresh start is a great idea, Kim. I am so happy and excited for you."

"Thanks, Ava, I don't think any of this would have been possible without you. Actually, I'm not even sure I would still be alive if you hadn't taken it upon yourself to help me. I will be forever grateful."

The friends hugged again, laughing while they each grabbed a tissue to wipe away their tears. Little feet ran down the stairs. Tessa came into view, running full speed into her lap. "Hi, Miss Ava! Did mommy tell you my special news?" The sweet girl looked back and forth between the women.

"No, I didn't." Kim answered for her. "I thought you'd like to tell her."

Ava scooted Tessa further down on her lap so she was able to look at her without their noses touching. "Last night I asked Jesus into my heart."

Ava wrapped her arms around her, sharing in her joy. "Tessa, that is great!

"Thanks. How is Matt?" Tessa had grown very fond of Matt in the last few months and their sweet bond was proof of what a wonderful father he would make some day.

"He is doing really well. His sling is coming off soon." Ava grinned thinking about the lone autograph proudly displayed on Matt's sling. When Tessa came to visit him the first time since the shooting, he had asked her to sign it. "He told me to tell you thank you for the colored picture you sent him. I saw it today and it is hanging on his refrigerator door."

Tessa's smile beamed. "I think I'll go make him another one. Don't leave until I'm done." Ava didn't have a chance to answer that she would wait. Tessa scurried up the stairs to her room.

The women chuckled at the small child's enthusiasm. "How does Tessa feel about moving?" Ava asked, already missing the child.

Kim looked down at her hands, wringing them. "She is sad to leave her friends, and you and Matt of course, but she says she is excited for us to go live with Aunt Stephanie." Kim sighed. "She is such a tough little girl. I still can't believe the horrible life I created for her when Ray lived with us."

Kim stood and walked toward the window. It was good to see the curtains pulled back, exposing the light that filtered in after months of them living in darkness. Ava gave her a moment to collect her emotions. "Kim, the past is the past. You can't change it, but you can learn from it. You are a new woman in Christ. The old is gone. The new has come. You are a good mom and Tessa loves you."

Kim turned toward her. "You are right. I didn't get this far to fall into the pit of guilt." Kim was a stronger woman than she gave herself credit for.

"So you are moving next weekend?" Ava asked, making sure she had it correct on her calendar.

"Yes. The moving truck gets here Saturday at eight in the morning. I already have a few boxes filled with items and clothes that we don't need for the upcoming week. I think later in the week I'll start packing up my kitchen." If Ava had been the one moving she would have been able to pack the kitchen first. Those were the items she didn't need.

"Give me a call when you start packing and some evening I can come and help," Ava offered.

"Okay, thanks. My arm and leg are better, but still weak. I won't turn away any help."

"Do you have enough help with moving?"

"More than enough. The church made a sign-up list to come help me move and the page is full. They have even offered to drive to my sisters and unload everything for me." Kim grabbed a tissue and blotted her eyes. "I am just so overwhelmed by everyone's kindness."

They walked around the house and pointed out things they could pack first and discussed how to pack as organized as they could. Every box would be labeled by room and what the items were inside. Ava offered to stop at a local business to pick up more moving boxes for her.

Tessa came down shortly after showing off her new masterpiece for Matt. Ava figured that before she moved, Matt's refrigerator would be covered in pictures of flowers, butterflies, and rainbows.

⁂

Ava and Josh had a quiet environment to talk since the Mexican restaurant seemed slow for a Saturday night. It had been too long since just the two of them hung out and it was nice to catch up on each other's lives.

Ava updated him on how the new school year had started and how wonderful it was between her and Matt. She even filled him in on her unexpected run-in with Tim. Josh took on the older brother protective stance, but kept his cool and agreed she handled the situation the best she could. They changed the subject and talked about Ray and how she was coping in the aftermath, along with her concerns about how Matt was handling it.

"How's Kim doing?" Josh asked. Her family had been so good at keeping updated on Kim's situation.

"She's doing well and looking forward to moving next weekend. I hope she is able to sell her house soon and gets her asking price. She could really use the money."

"I signed up to help her move next weekend. Jake wanted to, but he is covering that toxic spill the next county over and thinks it will keep him busy until after next weekend." She was so proud of her brothers and their giving spirits.

"It sounds like a lot of men can help, so getting her moved should go quickly."

The young waitress brought out their food and refilled their drinks. Ava had already reached her food capacity with the chips and salsa, but she was confident she could find some room for the burrito that sat before her. Clapping sounded off behind them and a group of waiters and waitresses gathered around a table in the back, wishing a little boy a happy birthday. His cheeks turned red as they placed a sombrero on top of his head.

"So ... how are you and Valerie doing?" Ava had hoped he would bring up his relationship before she had to, but she grew impatient. A few weeks ago Josh had finally asked out a single mom that attended their church. Ava had met Valerie a few times and she seemed like a good fit for her brother.

Josh laughed at her face that begged for some insight. "It took you longer to ask than I thought it would."

"Quit mocking me and just give me some details."

"It's going well. I really like her."

"That's all I get?"

"For now."

The waitress interrupted and gave them their checks. "Speaking of dating, did you hear about Jake?" Josh asked casually.

"No. What?"

"Remember his high school girlfriend, Erica?" Ava nodded. "She moved back into town earlier in the summer and they ran into each other at our high school reunion last month. Jake said that they have been going out every weekend since."

"The last I heard, Jake had plans to move to Chicago." Jake had a big goal to try and get hired by The Chicago Tribune. When he broke the news to her family, she expressed her genuine excitement, but hid her deep sadness in having him leave.

"I think Erica has stalled those plans for now."

"Why didn't he tell me?" Ava was slightly hurt. If Josh even dropped the bombshell that Lucy was dating, too, without telling her, she'd go nuts.

"You've had a hectic month. I'm sure he planned to tell you soon. I can tell he's excited, but doesn't want to make a big deal about it. I just told you so you'd have more to focus on than my dating life."

"Ha, very funny, I'm not that bad ..." She stopped when he raised his eyebrows and they laughed in unison over the truth.

Josh looked down at his watch. "Whoa, it's getting late, we'd better go."

Ava grabbed her purse that could stop traffic with its bright red color. "I'm sorry, do you have other plans?" She asked, slightly disappointed.

"Err ... no, I just thought we should get going in case someone needs our table."

Ava looked around at the empty tables surrounding them. "Okay," she muttered, confused.

They decided to stop and get some ice cream at their family's favorite spot before they headed back to her apartment to hang out for the rest of the evening.

"Oh man," Josh exclaimed as soon as he turned on the engine. "I forgot my guitar and song list at church. Do you mind if we stop there first? I want to practice some more tonight."

"That's fine, it's only seven o'clock. We've got all night to pack on the calories." Ice cream was her guilty pleasure.

The church was on the way and they reached the parking lot in no time. Josh parked the car in the empty parking lot and shut off the engine.

"My list is on the computer so it might take a while. Why don't you come in with me?"

Ava unbuckled her seat belt, thankful she didn't have to stay by herself. The church sat in the rougher part of town and they'd had a few more attempted break-ins this year since the economy dipped down. "Okay," she agreed with no rebuttal.

Their church had character from the years it had stood. Matt and Ava had decided to start attending her church together. She offered to go with him to his, but he wanted to go with her family. He didn't have the connections at his church that she had developed at hers.

As they headed down the hallway toward the offices Josh came to a halt. "Oh, could you do me a favor? I left my guitar in the sanctuary on the stage. Could you go get it for me while I boot up my computer?"

"Sure. I'll meet you in your office." Ava turned around and headed to the sanctuary.

She opened the door, took a step inside, and froze in place. She gasped in awe at the sight before her.

chapter thirty-one

The entire stage was covered in white candles illuminating the room. The candles illuminated so brightly, lights weren't even necessary. Along both sides of the aisle candles lit a path up to the stage. Soft piano music played and filled the room with its soothing sound.

In the middle of the stage held a vision of Ava's greatest treasure on earth. Matthew. He stood in the center of the stage wearing a black tuxedo.

"Matthew." She could barely speak his name. His smile beamed across the room, right to her heart. She smiled back as the prick of her tears threatening to become visible.

He walked down the steps and stopped at the bottom, waiting for her to join him. She walked toward him, never taking her eyes off his face.

He held out his hand when she approached and she couldn't get to him fast enough. Ava slipped her hand into his and he raised her shaking hand to kiss the top.

"Hi, beautiful." His voice was tender and thick with emotion.

"Hi," she answered back, surprised she was capable of speaking. He led her up the stairs, back to his original spot.

Ava's heart glowed as bright as the candles that surrounded them, while her pulse thumped rapidly.

"Ava, I'm completely and wholeheartedly in love with you. The way you make me feel when I'm with you is indescribable. You bring so much joy into my life. You are beautiful, kind, compassionate, strong, funny, and smart. You are my haven in the craziness of life. Your love for the Lord is proven by the way you walk in His word and how your life shines as a beacon of His truth."

He stopped and brushed off the tears streaming down her cheeks. Ava tried to speak through the way she looked at him, so he could see how much she returned his love.

"You were dealt a shocking heartbreak and for that I am truly sorry. But I'm so thankful the Lord spared you from entering into that life and instead gave you to me. My love for you is much more than a feeling, it reaches beyond the excitement I feel when you enter a room or how my heart beats faster with the softness of your lips."

He leaned in and kissed her with such sweetness. "My love for you is founded on God's love for you. I respect you and desire to do whatever is best for you. I'm committed to you in the good times and the bad."

He took both her hands into his and dropped to one knee.

"I love you, Ava Noel Williams. I have loved you since the moment I first laid eyes on you and I will love you until the day I meet our Maker. You were made for me, and with you by my side I am a complete and content man."

He reached into his pocket and brought out a sparking diamond ring between his thumb and finger.

Ava gasped at his choice. It was perfect, just like he was for her. She bit her lower lip, hoping it would help stop the cry that wanted to escape.

"Marry me, Ava. Become my wife and grow old with me."

As soon as his words were out she dropped to her knees and threw her arms around his neck. "Yes! Yes! Yes! A million times, yes!" She finally allowed the tears to come and her body shook as she cried in his arms.

There was no doubt, no fear, no what ifs…only joy and absolute peace.

Ava pulled back once her emotions were under control. "I love you, Matthew."

"And I love you." He took her shaking left hand, "So let's make this official." He slid the ring on her finger and it fit perfectly in place.

"Do you want to know why I proposed to you here?"

"Yes."

"There are a few reasons." He stood them up, keeping their hands laced together. "First, I wanted to do it in the place where I would eventually make you my bride. Second, because I had a good connection. And third, because I wanted you to see the joy on my face as you walked down the aisle toward me. I wanted to give you the moment that was long ago stolen. You needed to know that this is where I wanted to be."

Ava shook her head in disbelief. "Wow, sometimes I think you know me better than I know myself. I'm not sure if that's scary or really romantic."

He pulled her into his arms and dipped her back before she even had a chance to stop him. He brought his lips to hers, making a point. When he finished he whispered into her ear, "I'd say romantic, but to each their own."

He sat her back up and she took a moment to catch her bearings. Ava touched his shoulder. "Honey, you'd better be careful. That is your bad shoulder. Hey, where is your sling?"

"That old thing, it didn't go well with my outfit."

She frowned.

"I have it with me and I'll put it back on later, Warden."

"All right, but I'm on to you, Thompson." She smiled, looking over his tux. "Speaking of, you look quite handsome.

Compared to you, I look like a sack of potatoes." Ava looked down at her simple jean sundress. At least she had makeup on.

"Well, you're in luck, because I really like potatoes." He winked and she couldn't help but laugh at his corny joke. She would be laughing at them for many years to come.

They moved and sat down on the first step. He wrapped his arm around her waist while she looked down at her ring. "Thanks for not running," he admitted.

"You thought I would say no?"

"No, but the thought did cross my mind. I do know you well, but sometimes you're full of surprises and I'm not sure what to expect."

"Where would the fun be if you knew all my moves? The excitement is in the mystery, right? I can't let you get lazy. I have to keep you on your toes."

He rolled his eyes. "Women."

Ava positioned herself to face him more directly. It was time to put all joking aside. He needed to know the truth. "I'm sorry you had even a second of doubt that I would say no. I want nothing more than to marry you and become your wife. I'm not going anywhere, unless it is with you."

"I'm glad you feel that way because I need you to go with me somewhere now."

Ava sat back in surprise. He was always pulling something out of his hat. "Where?"

"To the engagement party that is waiting for us at your parents' house."

He laughed at her shocked facial expression.

"What! When did you plan this?"

"I've been working on it since I got home from the hospital. If you haven't noticed, I've had some time on my hands. Plus, your mom, Lucy and Jules were more than willing to help." He chuckled. "Actually, I didn't really have a choice."

"Hmmm, a little over-confident, aren't we? What if I had said no?" she provoked.

He caught on to her teasing. "Oh well, I had a backup plan for that. We weren't leaving until you said yes. I can be very convincing when I need to be." His smile made her melt.

Ava took his face in her hands and kissed him. She stopped when the sparkles coming from her left hand became overly distracting. She tilted her palm facing downward so she could take a peek at the ring again. A large princess cut diamond with a small row of tiny diamonds on each side shimmered back at her.

"Matt, this ring is exactly what I would have picked out. Thank you." She wiggled her fingers to see it shine from the light of the candles.

"You are just dying to show that off, aren't you?"

"You didn't show it to anybody?" Ava thought for sure he would have showed it to someone in her family already.

He smiled proudly. "Nope, I knew you would want the honor. I won't say it was easy. Lucy did her best to break me, but I held on strong." He made a fist and flexed his arm.

Ava clapped her hands in delight. "Yay, can we go? I can't wait to go celebrate with everyone."

"Yes, but first we need to blow out all these candles." He looked around the sanctuary. "We should get there in about an hour." She laughed at his joke but wondered how long it really would take. "Plus, I want to change out of this penguin suit for the festivities. A campfire's universal dress code is far from a tux."

Ava saw his face show disbelief that he had slipped her some crucial information. "Ooh, we're having a campfire!" she exclaimed in great enthusiasm. "Who all is going to be there?" Ava thought now would be the best time to press for more information while he was aggravated with himself.

"Listen, I had one slip, but I'm back on top of my game. You're not getting anything more out of me, babe." He crossed his arms and pressed his lips together, affirming his stance on the subject. He tried his best, but he couldn't keep his grin covered.

Ava kissed his cheek and rested her head on his shoulder. She soaked in her last few moments of looking over the room and all the work he'd put into making this her dream come true.

Matt interrupted while she committed the sight to memory. "What do you say we go get this party started? We have a lot to celebrate...and this is just the beginning."

He kissed the top of her head and stood. He turned and took both her hands into his and pulled her up. They stood on different steps which put their heights at eye level. Ava took the opportunity that presented itself and threw her arms around his neck. He let out a huff of breath, not expecting her tight hold, but brought his arms around her waist with the same tightness. Ava clung to him, silently thanking God for rescuing her heart and creating this incredible man that chose her to love.

Natalie Replogle is a busy stay-at-home mom of three young kids and a wife to her heartthrob, Greg. She enjoys escaping the glamorous life of dirty diapers, dishes and laundry to lose herself in writing novels drenched in romance and suspense. She and her family reside in Northern Indiana. You can connect with Natalie on-line at www.nataliereplogle.blogspot.com.

Coming soon
Matt and Ava's story continues in:

A Rescued Life

As Matt and Ava's wedding approaches their relationship is stretched by circumstances that put a wedge between them. In an unforeseen moment, Ava finds herself the target of a dangerous man with a corrupt past that blames her for getting in the way of what he wants. Matt returns back to work, caught between finding the balance of being the attentive man Ava deserves and his need to keep her safe. When Ava turns up missing can he find her in time or will they lose their happily ever after?

Turn the page to read an exciting excerpt!

Excerpt from *A Rescued Life*

The bank closed in a half hour, but the loan officer agreed to fit them in to quickly go over options. Matt looked at Ava as they sat crammed into the tiny office just outside of the lobby. He had been eager to bring up this idea, and her reaction did not disappoint.

It made him happy to be able to give Ava the home she had always wanted. With her by his side, he'd be happy living in a shed, but a home to start their life out together excited him. Except for the large price tag staring back at him, taunting him to panic. Was it getting hot in here or was it just him? His throat tightened as though he had a tie on, choking his airway. He mentally shook off his apprehension. The time had come to strap on his big boy boots and be in debt for what would feel like the rest of his life.

A loud shout interrupted in the lobby as screams followed.

Matt sprang from his cushioned chair, his hand automatically going to the gun strapped to his side. He slid tactically beside the elongated window adjacent to the door that exposed the chaotic lobby. Keeping out of view, he managed to still be able to see two masked gunmen standing in the middle of the tile floor waving their guns around. The muffled sound of them shouting at the people to get down on the floor made its way into the enclosed room.

He watched the shock work its way through Ava's terrified features. Matt wished he could take a moment and comfort Ava, reassure her that everything would be okay, that he would protect her. But time did not stand on their side. One of the gunmen headed toward them already.

Pulling his shirt down further to ensure his gun stayed

hidden, he put his plan into action. "Ava, get under the desk and call 911 after we leave." Ava scrambled around the desk and stuffed herself underneath the dark mahogany as he made eye contact with the loan officer. "Mr. Kline, I need as much information about the layout of this bank as fast as you can give it to me."